MASKED INTENTIONS

MASKED INTENTIONS

A CAMERA CLUB MYSTERY

KARA LACEY

For my family, whose encouragement, love, and support keep me going.

Contents

Praise for the Camera Club Mystery Series

"With Lacey's signature style—transportive prose, fully realized characters, and a fast-moving plot—*Masked Intentions* is another winner in a series that keeps readers guessing and gasping."—**Laurie Buchanan**, The Sean McPherson Crime Thriller Novels

"Filled with quirky characters, danger, as well as a rollercoaster ride of emotions, Bobbie's hunt to prove her innocence and unmask the real killer was a fun and fabulous read. Highly recommended to people who enjoy both cozy and traditional mysteries."—**Trish Esden**, author of the Scandal Mountain Antiques Mysteries

"Kara Lacey gives readers an expertly framed mystery, complete with a high-resolution whodunnit and snappy subplots. Bobbie is a relatable heroine, and her fellow photography club members and friends round out an entertaining cast. The complex and real family dynamics on display upped my enjoyment of the story as a whole."—**Leah Dobrinska**, author of the Larkspur Library Mystery series

"Surrounded by early summer in a charming Vermont village, *Caught on Camera* is a page-turning mystery where the sleuth enlists her sharply focused photography club to help clear her name. Cozy mystery fans will love the quirky characters, well placed doses of humor, and a heroine we can root for."—**Janna Rollins**, author of the Zen Goat Mysteries

Chapter One

The annual harvest festival was in full swing, and the event tent was busting at the seams with partygoers dressed in a dazzling array of vibrant costumes. Paper lanterns in bright red, orange, and yellow to mimic the season's foliage festooned the ceiling. Bluegrass music filled the cool night air, pulsing with the beat of feet stomping to the band's absurdly fitting rendition of "Cuckoo's Nest." Peering through my camera's viewfinder was like looking through a kaleidoscope—bright, loud, chaotic. I clicked, refocused, and clicked again, keeping pace with the frenetic energy.

The festival, starting with the masquerade ball, marked the end of a busy summer season in Stonebridge, Vermont. It was a time to celebrate before gearing up for another long winter, and villagers were letting loose. I was celebrating, too, in my own way. Twenty months after my husband's sudden death, I finally envisioned a future for myself—one that included a thriving photography business as well as a sense of belonging in my new community. It didn't hurt that, costumed as my idol, Annie Leibovitz, I was channeling a renowned photographer's confidence and talent.

"*Bonsoir*, Bobbie," Jackson Gilbert called to me from a line at the bar. Stout and middle-aged, he was dressed in a military uniform, but it was the camera hanging from his neck I was relieved to see.

"Hey, Jackson," I replied before focusing my lens on him and snapping a photo. "Let me guess—Napoleon?" His greeting notwithstanding, it was an easy guess. As one of my camera club members, Jackson's random use of French phrases was nothing new to me. A true Francophile, his love of all things French stemmed from his college days there, as well as regular trips for his antiques business. It only made sense he'd choose a notable military figure like Napoleon Bonaparte.

"*Oui*," he said.

I gestured with my camera, reminding him of our club's commitment to taking pictures. The Stonebridge Keep it Snappy Shutter Club was on the job, and with only six members, including myself, I needed all hands on deck—or rather, all fingers on shutters.

The band transitioned to a new song, one with a softer, more folksy beat. The shift felt like a momentary reprieve. As I looked around for other camera club members, my gaze landed on my sister. Tall like me, Alicia Crowley was easy to spot. Wearing a blue checkered 1950s housedress with a full skirt and a curly red wig, she was convincing as Lucy Ricardo from *I Love Lucy*. I had to hand it to her; no matter where she was or what she wore, Alicia was comfortable in her skin. City girl turned goat farmer and owner of the Stonebridge Country Market, she was as fit at fifty as most people were at thirty. All my life, I'd looked up to her, and four years older than me, she never let me forget her senior status.

Alicia's bright red lips curled into a smile when her eyes met mine. She pointed toward the bar, signaling her plan to join me there, before tapping her husband Nate's shoulder. Looking dapper as Ricky Ricardo, he wore a gray suit and bow tie. His brown hair, which he usually wore tousled, was styled into a slicked-back version of a pompadour. He leaned into Alicia as she spoke before turning to me with a broad grin. Always gregarious, Nate was in his element at social gatherings. I returned his grin, lifted my camera, and fired off a shot, knowing any photo of the Crowleys would be well received in Stonebridge.

I turned in a circle and panned the scene. Something near the bar caught my eye. I stopped to focus my lens. Jackson gesticulated wildly as he spoke to two hooded figures I assumed were women, based solely on their slight stature. The conversation—if it could be called that—looked contentious. I zoomed in as one of the women broke away from the group, leaving me to snap a photo of a red-faced Jackson, lips pursed and arms crossed. *What is that all about?*

Trouble seemed to be brewing, and that was the last thing we needed. I took a step toward the bar but came to a quick halt when my photography assistant, Penny Wright, poked my back. Her annoyed expression, combined with the muffled tapping of her tongue ring behind pursed lips, amplified her frustration.

"We've got a problem, Mrs. B," Penny said—no greeting; no preamble.

"You know you can call me Bobbie, even when we're talking about work." It wasn't that I minded the moniker, short for Mrs. Brooks, but coming from my thirty-year-old employee, it made me feel old.

"Yeah, I know." Penny pushed the mousy-brown bangs of her asymmetrical hairstyle from her face and looked at me through a pair of glasses with round, black frames I knew were costume. "Anyway, like I started to tell you, our consultation appointment never showed up."

"Again? That makes three no-shows in the past week."

"I waited at the studio for more than an hour," Penny said.

"It's not your fault." I let out a slow breath. "Thanks for waiting. Hopefully, we'll get to the bottom of this soon."

"I'll dig around our website tomorrow morning to see if I can figure it out, but I think our booking system is wonky." Penny peered at me from beneath her fringe of hair. "We should have that new guy—what's his name—take a look at our website.

"Ciarán Donovan." That was the *new guy's* name. He'd recently relocated his web design business from Boston to Vermont, and local establishments were singing his praises. I doubted I could afford him. "Yeah, maybe I'll give him a call." I probably wouldn't. Cost wasn't the only reason, but I didn't have to explain myself.

"Just saying," Penny muttered.

She wasn't wrong. I knew our website needed professional oversight. It had only been four months since I'd excitedly hung my carved wooden sign—In The Moment Photography—outside my studio. In my rush to get my business running, I'd set up the website myself, using a template I found online. All in all, I thought it looked professional. But no-show appointments were becoming an ongoing nuisance.

I had more immediate concerns, namely the festival. "Did you get the club's schedule for the festival posted?"

"Yep, and I posted our photo prompts, too." Penny pulled her phone from a pocket and tapped the screen. "Music, motion, sparkling, landscape, tradition, and silhouette."

"Thanks for doing that," I said. Providing prompts for the festival not only challenged our members, but they were also fun—a scavenger hunt, of sorts. I purposely chose open-ended cues, hoping to encourage a wide range of interpretations.

I may have made a mistake with my website, but hiring Penny as my assistant was one of my smarter moves. When she joined the club, she'd been both shy and sullen—a tough nut to crack. But she had a certain something I'd wanted to nurture. We'd come a long way, and there was still plenty to work on, but I found myself relying on her in ways I never expected. I took in her unusual eyewear, her striped necktie, and hooded cape. "Harry Potter?"

One of her rare smiles lit her face. "Mackenzie is Hermione Granger." She stood on tiptoe. "Have you seen her?"

"Not yet." Normally, Mackenzie Miller's bright pink hair would stand out, but in this masked, wigged, and hooded crowd, she could be anywhere.

"You're looking for Mackenzie?" Alicia said, appearing at my side. "I just saw her a minute ago. She was talking to Jackson near the bar."

"It's fine," Penny said. "I'll go look for her and take photos on my way."

"Perfect." I turned to my sister. "Where's your camera?" As a member of the club, she was on duty, too.

"Relax." Alicia pulled a tiny camera from a pocket in her dress. "I'm using my point-and-shoot tonight. It's less cumbersome." She lifted it to her eye and clicked the shutter before putting it back into her purse.

Note to self: Be sure the cute little close-up of my perturbed expression gets deleted.

Alicia plucked a bit of yellow dog fur off my sleeve. "You never wear black."

"Darcy is pretty much the reason for that." Although my yellow Labrador retriever was adorable, his fur was not.

"Remind me who you are, again?"

I suppressed an eye roll, but I was less successful at taking the snark out of my voice. "Annie Leibovitz. Photographer extraordinaire. Maybe you've heard of her?" With Arts and Entertainment as the party's theme, I thought my costume was a no-brainer. But I was sure my all-black ensemble—slacks, blouse, shoes, and costume glasses—would be met with many blank stares.

"Why not just dress as yourself?" she asked. "Bobbie Brooks, talented photographer and leader of a scrappy camera club."

I chuckled. Alicia meant well. But this was a costume party, and I wasn't even in the same stratosphere as Annie Leibovitz. Still, I appreciated the vote of confidence. Alicia was my biggest cheerleader. If it hadn't been for her prodding, I'd still be living in Boston, mourning for a life that died with my husband.

Last winter, in the way only big sisters could get away with, she'd declared I needed a change. When she showed me the little farmhouse cottage with a cute barn and Main Street location—right across from the village green—the only thing holding me back was my fear. Alicia had a point; it was time for me to move forward.

"Did you see the schedule and photo prompts Penny posted to our group page?" I asked.

"Sure did," Alicia answered while pointing toward the bar. "Let's go get a drink. Tonight's signature cocktail is hot apple cider with or without a splash of spiced rum."

"Yes, please." The tempo of the party had picked back up with another lively song. The beat of the music made the ground throb beneath my feet. Getting into the spirit, I dance-walked toward the bar.

"I saw Emma earlier," Alicia said, smirking at my dance moves.

A grin spread across my face. My twenty-three-year-old daughter had surprised me with an impromptu visit, and I was beyond happy about it. Since she graduated from college last June and began her career as an oncology nurse at one of Boston's top hospitals, she'd been understandably busy. I wasn't the reason she made the trip, of that I was certain. No matter, I'd take what I could get.

"She and Connor are wearing coordinating costumes," Alicia continued. "Hunger Games, if I'm not mistaken."

"Totally sounds like they're *not* dating," I snorted. Connor Crowley was one of Nate's many distant cousins once removed, and a man Emma insisted was Only. A. Friend.

Alicia replied with a raised eyebrow, warning me to *Stay. Out. Of. It.*

"Yeah, yeah." I waved her gesture away. I tried not to pry into Emma's life, truly I did. I liked Connor. A lot. I only worried that Emma was moving too fast after a recent breakup. The mama bear in me didn't want to see her get hurt again. I was about to say as much when a shrill noise caught my attention. I froze, straining to hear through the music and chatter. It sounded like a… woman's scream?

"Did you hear that?" I asked Alicia.

She held a finger to her lips and nodded.

There it was again. Yes, definitely a scream, reverberating from somewhere on the village green.

To see the shocked expression in Alicia's brown eyes felt like gazing in a mirror. Then, in one swift movement, she grabbed my wrist, and we pushed our way through the crowd, outside the tent, and onto the village green.

Chapter Two

"Which way?" I stopped to get my bearings. The sun had already set, and an October chill was setting in. Lamps on tall posts added a dim glow to the gray sky.

"Over here," a panicked voice called.

I recognized the voice and exchanged a worried glance with Alicia. Typically, Harmony Santos, another member of our camera club, was the voice of calm and serenity. If she was alarmed, something was wrong.

We broke into a jog, rushing along a walkway that led to the fountain at the center of the green. Tall and round with three tiers and a bald eagle gracing the top, it was one of Stonebridge's most prominent features. After the festival, it would be drained for the winter, but for now, the water continued to flow over the tiers to the base.

Time slowed as I stopped to observe the scene, as if viewing it through my camera's lens. Beneath the lamplight, Harmony's sleek black hair created a stark contrast with her shimmering white gown. A camera hung from her neck, nearly touching her waist. Tarot wasn't my thing, but I recognized her as the High Priestess. A fitting costume for our village yogi. But it was the urgent expression in her dark eyes that concerned me. They told me the situation was bad.

Adjusting my imaginary lens, I zoomed in on the fountain, where Emma sat on its broad base. From what I could see, Emma was cradling someone's head in her lap. The person, who was wearing a long, black, hooded cape, appeared to be lying facedown. The dim lamplight made it hard to see, but I thought their hood looked darker, or a bit shinier. Probably wet. I wondered if they had stumbled and fallen face-first into the fountain.

"Thank you, universe." Harmony rushed forward to meet us. "The party is so loud, I was afraid no one would hear me."

"What happened?" Alicia asked. "Has anyone called 9-1-1?"

Harmony took a long, deep yoga breath and exhaled, just as she'd taught us in class. "I did," she said, sounding a little less frantic.

I moved toward Emma, but still couldn't see who was lying in her lap. A woman, I thought, based on her smallish size and black ballet flats. I crouched down. "How is she doing?"

"I'm not getting a pulse." Emma's voice was calm and matter-of-fact, the voice of the nurse she'd become. "It could be faint. Let's lie her down so I can see if she needs CPR."

"I'll take her feet." Grasping incredibly dainty ankles, I helped move the woman away from the fountain. Her body seemed warm, but she wasn't moving. As we lowered her to the ground, gently rotating her to lie on her back, her hood fell away, revealing pointed elf ears that poked through a pale-blond pixie haircut.

"Iris," I gasped. I stood and moved back to give Emma the room she needed. Iris Svensen. I'd just seen her that afternoon. It didn't seem possible.

No sooner had Emma started pumping Iris's chest than a wall of partygoers appeared like a massive wave gushing through an open flood gate. Jackson led the pack.

"*Ma jolie fleur,*" he wailed, nearly knocking Emma over as he knelt beside her. He set his camera on the ground and grabbed Iris's limp hand, bringing it to his cheek. There was a possessive air in his actions that baffled me.

"My happy flower?" I wondered. My college French was rusty at best. But now wasn't the time to puzzle over translations. I leaned to peer at Emma and Iris. The sound of Emma's counting gave me hope. Surely Iris would be okay.

"I think it translates to pretty flower," Alicia whispered.

"What?" I didn't realize I'd asked the question out loud.

"*Ma jolie fleur.* My pretty flower," Alicia said, turning her attention to my daughter and her patient. "It's a good thing Emma is here."

Emma's calm efficiency as she cared for Iris filled me with motherly pride. I doubted she'd expected to use her nursing skills at the party.

"What's going on?" Nate's voice preceded his appearance as he strode toward us, with Connor by his side. A man followed behind them, wearing the fluorescent yellow vest of Stonebridge's volunteer fire department over a white sweatshirt with a smattering of black spots. A red baseball cap with spotted dog ears hanging from the sides topped a thick mop of silver hair. A dalmatian—how perfect. I smiled despite myself.

The man introduced himself. "Greg Lacey, Stonebridge Fire and Rescue."

Emma looked up. "I'm Emma Brooks, a registered nurse from Boston." Her expression was grave, but she said nothing about Iris's condition.

"An ambulance is on the way," Greg said. "In the meantime, I'll secure the scene." He raised his hand and called out to the growing mob, instructing us to return to the event tent to await further instructions.

At first, the mumbling seemed to grow louder. But with Nate beside him, whistling shrilly, Greg repeated himself, and the crowd slowly dispersed, trudging back toward the tent.

Connor pressed his way toward Emma and crouched at her side. I couldn't help my urge to ignore the directions, if only to make sure my daughter was okay.

"Bobbie," Nate said as I approached. "You should head back to the party. Mr. Lacey has given me the okay to stay with Emma. The EMTs will have questions for her." His voice was gentle, but his message was clear.

"Is Iris going to be okay?" I asked.

"I don't know," Nate said. As a lawyer, he rarely gave things away.

Alicia motioned for me to walk back to the tent with her, but I peeked over Nate's shoulder first. Emma had stopped the chest compressions to call Greg over. He kneeled close to Iris before looking at Emma and nodding. They seemed to reach an agreement and rolled Iris to her side.

I turned to Alicia. "That's a good sign, isn't it?"

"Possibly," Alicia said. "Come on. Getting out of the way is our best way to help."

"I know, but isn't rolling a patient on their side a recovery position? I'm pretty sure I learned that in a CPR class."

"Mmm." Alicia's non-committal response irked me. I couldn't understand how she could be so calm.

Inside the tent, the music selection was more subdued, no longer the foot-stomping, toe-tapping tunes from earlier in the evening. We found an empty table, and I collapsed onto a chair. The evening had started so well—perfect, really. It was one of those autumn nights I was sure only happened in Vermont. The air was crisp, cool, and clean, and the mountain's foliage, in bright oranges and reds, had sparkled in the last rays of the setting sun. It had been nothing short of spectacular.

"Does it seem weird that Iris would fall into the fountain?" I asked.

"We don't know what happened yet." Typical Alicia, always pragmatic.

"I guess it could happen. Even with the lamps, it's kind of dark. Maybe she wasn't paying attention." It was the only scenario that made sense to me. "I just hope she's okay."

"Let's hope so." Alicia leaned forward to adjust the straps on her shoes.

"I ran into Iris this afternoon. She and Saskia were making deliveries." The way Iris's young daughter had danced around Darcy, butterfly wings flapping, had been beyond adorable. It looked like a game of duck, duck, goose, and Darcy loved it. If dogs could smile, he'd been grinning ear to ear.

"I saw you." Alicia's gaze drifted across the village green toward my house on the other side of Main Street. "I was here, working with the festival committee. We were putting the finishing touches on the tent." She sounded tired, reminding me of how much work she'd put into organizing the festival.

I admired the decorations. Glass lanterns filled with fairy lights adorned each table. Together with the lit paper lanterns, they gave off a magical glow against the backdrop of the deepening darkness outside.

"You did an awesome job," I said before letting my mind drift back to Iris. "Iris told me she was preparing for a trip. I hope she'll still be able to go."

Alicia stood, peering at me with a concerned expression. "I need to gather the festival committee," she said. "I don't see how Iris's accident would change things, but it's best to be proactive. You seem a little shaken. Do you want to come with me?"

"I'm fine," I said. I wasn't, but I would be—and so would Iris.

Chapter Three

The tent filled as partygoers returned. The band was taking a break, and everyone seemed confused about whether the party should continue. I folded my arms on the table and rested my forehead on my hands, remembering my earlier conversation with Iris.

"I'm going to be away for a while," she'd said while pulling a bag of herbal tea from a basket on her arm. She didn't mention where she was going, but Saskia had seemed excited about seeing *lav'der fields*. Lavender fields, I assumed. But it seemed like the wrong time of year for that.

I'd watched them walk away while holding the bag of tea to my nose—chamomile with a blend of nutmeg, cinnamon, cardamom, and ginger. Aptly named Sereni-Tea, it was my favorite for a cold winter night—and there would be plenty of those ahead.

After letting the memory go, I lifted my head and caught sight of my friend Rose Lavoie on the arm of her new beau. I stood, raising my camera to snap a quick shot of the happy couple as they entered.

"Hey, girl." Rose stopped in front of me, lifting her foot behind her in a playful pose while planting a kiss on William Johnson's brown cheek. She made an adorable flapper in a knee-length lace dress, which did little to conceal her very un-flapper-like curves. Daisy Buchanan and Jay Gatsby, I assumed—William's influence, no doubt. As the owner of Long Trail Booksellers, the village's popular bookstore, his quiet, bookish demeanor complemented Rose's more jovial party-girl nature. Four months ago, I introduced the two, and they hit it off from the start.

"You look fantastic." I gave her a quick hug.

"You look nice, too." A furrowed brow accompanied William's compliment.

He was being polite, I knew, questioning my costume—or apparent lack of one. But really, I didn't usually dress this way. I was more of a jeans-and-sweater sort of gal. I brushed another strand of Darcy's fur from my sleeve.

"So sexy," Rose teased.

"Oh, hush." I laughed. "Annie Leibovitz is known for her photography skills, not her sexy wardrobe. Besides, you have no idea how hard it was for me to forgo wearing a scarf in my hair." I pushed my long chestnut waves behind my shoulders.

"You do look kind of naked." Rose giggled. "Well, I mean, your hair does."

William's glance slid over my costume. "A famous photographer. I should have guessed. The glasses are a nice touch."

"I thought the camera a rather fitting prop, too," I teased, while adjusting the plastic frames of my costume eyeglasses.

"I feel like we missed something," Rose said. "When we first got here, the place was a madhouse. Now, I'm getting an uber weird vibe."

"We were here earlier," William explained. "But we had to run back to Rose's apartment. She'd forgotten her camera." He gestured to Rose's camera bag, which was slung over the shoulder of his tuxedo.

Catching William's glance, Rose giggled. "Guilty. It's not every day I get to dress as a character from *The Great Gatsby*. I was having so much fun getting dressed, I totally forgot about it. Besides, my camera is going to look terrible with my costume." She touched the jeweled headband that adorned her red corkscrew curls.

I ignored her camera comment and filled Rose in on the events of the evening. As I spoke, her expression morphed from joyful to concerned to horrified.

"You didn't see a bunch of people near the fountain when you came back?" I asked.

"That's where it happened? There were a few people out there. I figured they were wandering around, enjoying the evening air." She placed a hand on my arm. "Poor Emma. How's she holding up?"

"Nate and Connor are with her," I said. "I think she automatically jumped into her nursing mindset."

"She would," Rose said. "And Iris? Is she okay?"

"I think so." A hush fell over the party when the ambulance drove away, lights and siren off.

"Is Iris in there? They don't seem to be in a hurry," Rose said. "Shouldn't they be?"

"Maybe the EMTs got her stabilized?"

"We need a drink." Rose grasped my arm and added, "Desperately."

"I'll save the table." William sat in my vacated seat and set Rose's camera bag in an empty chair.

"Good plan." Rose winked as we headed to the bar.

"It would seem we aren't the only ones with a desperate need to imbibe." I tilted my head toward the growing crowd milling around the bar.

Rose's ex-husband, Travis Lavoie, manned the cocktails, hustling like the seasoned bartender he was. He paused briefly as we approached, his eyes grazing Rose. The drop of his jaw would have been easy to miss, lasting only a second before he lifted the corner of his mouth into his usual smirk. Flashing another glance at Rose, he smoothed stray strands of hair toward his man-bun and lingered for a moment to flirt with a young witch who may have already had one cider too many.

"He's jealous," I whispered.

"He's totally not jealous." She waved my words away, but couldn't hide the rosy flush of her freckled cheeks.

Alicia sidled up next to us. "Oh yeah, he's green with envy." She flashed Rose with a knowing look before changing the subject. "I wanted to let you know Nate is staying with Emma. The state police will arrive soon. They'll need to ask her questions."

"The state police? But why?" I blanched, remembering their last investigation in Stonebridge. The dreaded Detective Cram. There was no love lost between us, which was completely justified on my part. The man had accused me of murder. And while he was busy focusing on my supposed guilt, I'd solved the crime—not that the tunnel-visioned detective would ever admit it.

"Nate didn't say." Alicia held up her phone, showing his text. "But you know how it works. Since Stonebridge doesn't have a police force, the state police are called in for anything big."

"And Iris falling into the fountain is considered big?" It still didn't make sense to me, but I was finding I had a lot to learn when it came to all things Vermont.

Alicia ignored my question. "I'd better get back to the festival committee. I wanted to pass along the message that Emma is in good hands."

"Thank goodness for Nate." Thinking about Detective Cram grilling my daughter made me shudder. I knew from experience how wily he could be. But Emma was smart. Besides, she had nothing to do with Iris's accident.

"Let's get the camera club together, too," Rose said. "You know, give Harmony and Jackson some moral support. They must be beside themselves."

Harmony was Iris's roommate and close friend, making Rose's worry about her understandable. An image of Jackson patting Iris's hand came to mind.

"What's up with Jackson, anyway? He acted so strangely earlier, calling Iris his *jolie fleur*." It wasn't the phrase so much as his behavior toward Iris that puzzled me. "He seemed oddly possessive." I paused while Rose pinned me with a quizzical stare. "Wait, are Iris and Jackson... a thing?"

"You seriously didn't know? They've been dating almost as long as William and I."

I raised my palms. This was news to me.

"You weren't expecting him to wait forever, were you?" Rose teased.

"For me, you mean?" I sniggered. "That was never going to happen." Sure, Jackson had been solicitous toward me when I first moved to Stonebridge. I'd deflected his attention, making it abundantly clear I wasn't interested.

Undeterred, Rose squeezed my hand. "When you never mentioned Jackson and Iris, I just figured you didn't want to talk about it."

"Even if I'd noticed, what would we talk about?"

The last few months had passed by in a blur. After renovating my barn to turn it into a photography studio, I'd used every ounce of energy I could muster to launch my business. It had felt good, too, focusing on my future. In my self-centeredness, Jackson's love life—not to mention his lack of attentiveness—hadn't been on my radar.

I pushed my bangs back and looked at Rose. "I guess I've been busy."

"Kudos to you, girl," Rose said. "I'm amazed you didn't notice before now."

With a shake of my head, I let the subject go. I had more pressing matters on my mind. "Let's get our drinks. Gathering our club is a good idea. With Iris in the hospital, we might need to adjust the schedule to allow more breaks for Harmony. Jackson, too."

Thinking about our club gave me a warm feeling. Last spring, when I thought about starting a camera club, I'd envisioned a group of photography enthusiasts connecting through monthly photo shoots, critique sessions, and shared challenges. After a rocky start, we'd developed a bond that turned into so much more, one I never would've predicted.

"I wonder how Iris is doing," Rose said as she took a cup from Travis.

So did I. But something else was bothering me. Lost in thought, I thanked Travis while clasping the steaming cup of cider. Then, despite the cup's warmth, a shiver ran up my spine. I lowered my voice and leaned into Rose. "I still don't get why the state police are investigating an accidental fall."

Chapter Four

Ciders in hand, Rose and I jostled back toward our table. We'd almost reached our destination when I spotted Penny. To get her attention, I raised my hand and signaled for her to join us.

"I seem to have lost Mackenzie," Penny said when she caught up to us.

"I saw her near the bar earlier," Rose said.

"It's a bit nuts right now," I said. "I'm sure she'll come find you once things have settled down."

"Yeah, you're probably right." Penny peered over my shoulder anyway, looking for her partner.

"Can you join us? After all that's happened, we might need to rethink our plan for this weekend."

"Sure thing. But first, I want to grab one of those." She eyed my hot drink.

As I took the last few steps to our table, Connor appeared. "I tried to stay with Emma, but I got booted from the scene." He pulled out a chair and offered it to me. "She's fine. Nate is with her while the state police are asking her questions." He stood with his hand on the back of the chair next to me. "Mind if I join you?"

"Please do."

Connor sat, smiling in a way that made me think of Nate. Tall and broad, with mussed light-brown hair and hazel eyes, it would be easy to mistake Connor for Nate's son rather than a distant cousin.

"What was Emma doing out on the green, anyway?" My fingers reached for the comforting silk of my scarf before I remembered I was in costume. I dropped my hand to my lap, wishing I could go back to a time when the presence of the police didn't make my heart race. Emma was an adult, I reminded myself. She would be fine.

"I'm not sure," Connor said. "We were hanging out with a few of my friends, and she told me she'd be right back. Now I wish I'd gone with her."

"That sounds like Emma. You couldn't have known what would happen." In social situations, Emma was a lot like her dad, needing breaks from the commotion. If Connor had offered to go with her, she probably would have waved him off.

"Speak of the devil." Rose looked up. "Have a seat."

I breathed a sigh of relief as Emma sat next to Connor. I was especially relieved to see she didn't appear as rattled as I'd been after meeting Detective Cram for the first time.

"OMG." Emma's voice was soft.

"You poor sweetie," Rose said. "I'm sure this wasn't the party you drove up here for."

William stood. "I think we need a few more ciders."

"I'll help you." Connor placed his hand on Emma's shoulder while leaning in to whisper in her ear. Although they'd known each other since childhood, the friendship that seemed to be developing between them was new. I had to admit, they looked cute together, wearing nearly identical costumes—Katniss Everdeen and Peeta Something-or-Other.

Emma gave Connor a weak smile and watched him walk away before turning to me. "So, your police detective, Wyatt Cram—"

"Is a tool," Rose finished Emma's unspoken thought.

"I was going to say he's intense," Emma said. "When I found the lady, Iris, I hoped she was alive."

"She wasn't? But…" My voice caught in my throat. I'd convinced myself Iris was okay. "But you stopped CPR and put her on her side." I blinked as tears stung my eyes, cursing the way they always came so easily—too easily.

Emma shook her head. "We thought she'd rallied for a few seconds. But no, I'm sorry. Were you friends?"

"We weren't close," I said. "But this is a small community. She'll be missed."

"The detective made me feel like I did something wrong for pulling her from the fountain. *Disturbing the scene.*" Emma swiped the corner of her eye. "I'd never leave someone like that—as if it isn't against everything I believe in as a nurse."

Leave it to Detective Cram to make Emma feel bad about helping. Just thinking about him made my neck prickle.

"The French guy... Jackson?" Emma asked. "I take it he was Iris's boyfriend?"

"Something like that," Penny said as she set her cup on the table and joined us.

"I felt kind of bad for him," Emma said. "He was holding Iris's hand, and the detective made him leave. Jackson seemed kind of sweet, but also a bit odd. I don't know how to describe him."

"Unlucky in love." Rose's voice was soft. "First your mom, now Iris."

I glared at Rose. She was only trying to lighten the mood. But still.

Emma jerked to look at me. "You and Jackson?" Her voice squeaked. "No. Just no. That's so cringe."

"Rose is kidding." I gave my head a vehement shake while wondering which part my daughter found so cringey—me and Jackson, or me and anyone. Not that it mattered. Not really. I loved Dan as much as ever. Dating another man was not in my plans. Even so, I liked to think of myself as dateable. My eyes met Emma's. That was a discussion for another day. Maybe.

"You can't blame Jackson for being sweet on your mom," Rose said.

Emma's nose scrunched. "I can't even."

To my relief, Connor and William rejoined us, saving me from further comment. Steam rose from the cups they set on the table, carrying the scent of apple, cinnamon, and spiced rum—Vermont autumn. Connor slid a cup toward me, and I pushed my unfinished drink aside, preferring the warmth of the new one. As I lifted it to take a sip, I spied Jackson making his way through the confusion.

"*Mon Dieu,*" Jackson said, dropping into a chair next to Penny. He slumped forward, placing his head in his hands.

"I'm so sorry for your loss," I said to him. I may not have been aware of his relationship with Iris, but I knew what an unexpected loss felt like.

Jackson lifted his face. "How could this have happened?" He ran his hand along the side of his bald head. "Do you think she tripped and hit her head? Her cape was too long. Such a bad idea."

Tripping was the only explanation I could think of. I caught a movement from Emma, one she seemed to think better of. When I turned to face her, her expression was a blank mask. I knew my daughter; there was something she wasn't telling us. I pinned her with my best mother's stare, the one that said, *fess up*. She answered my stare by pinning me with one that looked a lot like, *I'm not a kid anymore, so back off*.

Lately, this had been the crux of our relationship. Ever since I'd *interfered* by giving her ex-boyfriend a scathing, but much-deserved reprimand, she'd put me on notice. I was not to get involved. Of course, I knew Emma was old enough to handle her problems. That didn't mean I regretted my actions.

I exhaled slowly, conceding the battle. Emma had her reasons for not giving anything away. My mind shifted to Harmony. I hadn't seen her since the chaos near the fountain.

"Has anyone seen Harmony?" I asked. "She must be devastated."

"Harmony and Iris were so close," Rose said.

"Roommates, too," Penny added. "They've lived together ever since Harmony moved back to Stonebridge."

"The police let her go home." Jackson crossed his arms over his chest and scowled. "Something about Saskia."

"I can't believe I forgot about her." My heart sank, thinking of Iris's young daughter fluttering about. How would Harmony tell her that her mom wasn't coming home?

"They should let me leave, too. *C'est relou*." Jackson slouched back in his chair.

Once again, the exact translation of Jackson's words eluded me. I deduced he was lamenting life's annoyances. To be fair, he had a nothing-feels-real look about him. Most likely a result of shock.

"As if life is fair," Penny muttered, her French apparently better than mine.

"A cider might help." William pushed a cup across the table. "It's very relaxing."

"Sure. Thanks," Jackson said.

We sat in silence for a few minutes, each of us lost in our thoughts. I wondered whether the festival would continue as planned. I was about to broach the subject of adjusting our photo-taking duties when Penny's partner, Mackenzie Miller, appeared at our table, unsteady on her feet.

Penny sprang from her chair and steadied Mackenzie with an arm around her shoulders. "I was wondering where you were." There was a gentleness in her voice that contrasted with the sullenness I'd grown used to.

Mackenzie slumped into Penny's deserted chair, nearly toppling to the floor. Her words slurred when she spoke. "I wan' go home." Framed by her bright pink hair, Mackenzie's face was a deathly shade of gray, made even more ghastly by the flickering lantern light.

Penny knelt on the ground. "Were you drinking the cider?" she asked. "This isn't like you."

Mackenzie moaned, her head rolling to the side before resting on Penny's shoulder.

"I'd better get her home." Penny rose, struggling to lift Mackenzie.

"I'll help you." Connor jumped up.

Penny secured her arm around Mackenzie's shoulders. "If Detective Cram wonders where we went, tell him it was an emergency."

"We'll explain the situation." I was almost certain Detective Cram wouldn't be interested in excuses. I eyed my cup of cider, the effects of the rum making me slightly woozy. Travis might have been a bit heavy-handed with it, but it would take one or two more drinks before I had trouble standing. I watched Connor and Penny help Mackenzie to her feet.

Looking somewhat more aware, Mackenzie shook free of their grasp. "I feel awful." She clawed at the neck of her cloak.

"Keep it on." Penny adjusted the hood. "Once we step outside and we're no longer next to a heat lamp, you'll get cold."

"Do you think she had too much to drink?" Rose asked as she watched them walk away.

Emma's eyebrows drew together as she stood, watching Penny and Connor lead Mackenzie from the tent. "It's not like her to get hammered?" she asked.

"Mackenzie? Not that I've ever seen," Rose said. "She's our village librarian—always so put together."

"I can't think of anything bad to say about her," I said.

"Not that you ever would, anyway." Rose turned back to Emma. "Your mom is right. Mackenzie is super sweet."

"This doesn't sound right. And I'm not convinced she's drunk. Her pupils were small, even in the dim light." Emma pushed her chair in. "I should be all set with the detective, but if he comes looking for me, tell him I went to help Mackenzie."

"We'll let him know," Rose said.

It only took me a moment before I decided to risk Detective Cram's wrath, too. I got up to follow.

I raced behind Emma to the edge of the village green, where a streetlight illuminated the area near the sidewalk. Connor was standing over Mackenzie, who was lying in the grass with Penny kneeling by her side.

"What happened?" Emma asked, dropping to crouch near Penny. She pressed a finger to the spot on Mackenzie's neck, right below her ear.

"She said she couldn't walk anymore." Penny raked her fingers through her hair, pushing it from her face. "What's wrong with her?"

"I wish I knew if she'd been drinking," Emma said. "Her pulse is irregular. Has anyone called for an ambulance?"

When no one answered, I dug my phone from my pocket. "On it."

"I'll go get the police." Connor took off running. The police barracks were right down the road, but with Detective Cram and his officer gathering contact information at the party, Connor wouldn't have to go that far.

In the glaring light, Mackenzie looked small and childlike. She was curled into a fetal position, moaning while clutching her stomach.

"No, no, no, no, no." Penny rocked back on her heels. "Mackenzie, I need you to be okay. Please, please, please be okay."

Greg Lacey appeared beneath the streetlight. "What can I do to help?"

"Mr. Lacey," Emma said. "Any chance you can get an ETA on the ambulance?"

Mr. Lacey pulled a device from his pocket and took a few steps away from us.

Connor returned, running alongside Detective Cram.

The detective's beady eyes peered down over his beak-like nose, and his thin lips curled into a sneer that felt more familiar than I liked. Neither of us spoke as our eyes met for no more than a moment before he transferred his attention to Emma. His lanky body folded to the ground when he kneeled.

"Did she take any drugs?" he asked.

"N-no," Penny said. "She's not like that."

"Any prescriptions? Antidepressants, maybe?"

Penny shook her head, raking her hair back. "I don't think—"

Mr. Lacey returned. "The ambulance is almost here."

Moaning, Mackenzie lifted her lids briefly, causing Emma and the detective to exchange a glance. "Small pupils," Emma said in a soft voice. "I don't think alcohol is the problem."

Detective Cram shook his head and looked directly at Penny. "It won't help your friend to keep secrets. If she's taking any drugs, you need to tell us now."

Penny's eyes widened. "She's not. I swear."

Sirens blared, and flashing lights flooded the sky as the rescue vehicles came to a stop. The EMTs wasted no time assessing the situation. I held Penny, my arm around her slim, quivering shoulders. It was more than she'd allow under normal circumstances. She seemed so small and helpless, never looking away as her partner was loaded onto the stretcher. Mackenzie lifted her head briefly before closing her eyes again.

As the EMTs prepared to close up the back of the ambulance, Penny jerked forward. "I'm going with her." It wasn't a question. She turned to me. "I need one more thing. Could you call Mackenzie's aunt? She's babysitting Hope, and I need her to stay the night."

"Will do," I said to Penny as she climbed into the ambulance, assuring her that her infant daughter would be cared for. I didn't relish the task. Mackenzie's aunt was part of a group Rose and I referred to as the Righteous Sisters. They'd been generous with their scathing judgment when my scarf was discovered at a crime scene. Even after proving my innocence, our relationship was little improved.

Chapter Five

When Vickie Sue Miller answered her phone, the surprise in her voice was obvious. I was probably the last person she expected to receive a call from. As I explained what had happened, her concern for her niece took over, and she agreed to stay with Hope for the night. Mission accomplished, I wandered back to the party and found Alicia chatting with Rose and William. Emma and Connor were nowhere in sight, and it appeared Jackson had also left. Snuggled against William, Rose was the image of contentment, making my breath catch. I was happy for my friend, but I couldn't help feeling wistful.

"It's been quite the evening," Alicia said when I sat down. She started to push her hair from her face, but seemed surprised when her fingers touched the red wig that covered her usually straight, blonde hair. Her hand fell to her side.

"Poor Iris, and now poor Mackenzie," I said. "Everything started wonderfully, and then…" I couldn't finish my sentence.

"It did, didn't it? I'm impressed with the way everyone went all out on their costumes." Alicia gave me the once-over as if she considered me the exception.

Whatever.

"Anyway, the festival committee has events planned for the entire weekend. There was a lot of debate, but we decided, as tragic as it is, it's too late to cancel everything. This is Vermont's biggest tourist weekend of the year. Local businesses rely on this festival. Besides, the weekenders and leaf-peepers are already here."

"That makes sense," I said. "I'll need to do some shuffling to make sure the camera club can keep up. It would be unfair to expect Jackson and Harmony to make the festival their priority. And now, with Mackenzie in the hospital, Penny probably needs a break, too. It'll be you, me, and Rose." I paused to gather my thoughts. "What do you think happened to Mackenzie?"

"Travis might have been a little too generous with the rum," Alicia said.

Rose lifted her head from William's shoulder, about to say something. Despite the contentious nature of her relationship with her ex-husband, her default reaction was always to defend him. With a soft sigh, she leaned back against William without saying a word.

"Emma didn't think Mackenzie was drunk," I said.

With a shrug, Alicia continued, "It's going to be a busy few days. Having Detective Cram skulking about the festival isn't going to help."

Before I could answer, Nate appeared, loosening his tie. Tall and rugged, he was a Vermont farm boy at heart, but he looked as natural in a suit as he did in a pair of jeans and a flannel shirt. Our urbane parents had thought Nate an odd choice for their city-savvy daughter. But Alicia, with her usual aplomb, had defied their wishes, married her college sweetheart, and moved to Vermont without a backward glance. I'd never doubted her choice. There wasn't another man on earth who'd be able to hang onto her.

Nate pulled a chair close to mine, his hazel eyes full of concern. "Is Emma planning to stay the whole weekend?"

"I believe so."

"Okay, good. Unfortunately, Detective Cram is going to have more questions."

I stiffened. "He can't possibly think Emma had anything to do with Iris's death."

"No, nothing like that. But I suspect the autopsy will raise more questions, and Emma's insight about the minutes after Iris's death will help."

I nodded. Just because I understood didn't mean I liked it. Trusting Detective Cram didn't come easily for me.

As if reading my mind, Nate said, "I can understand how your early interactions with him might color your perception, but Cram is a decent detective."

"If you say so." I wasn't convinced, but I also recognized my bias.

"Emma's a trooper." Nate placed his hand on my arm. "It's going to be okay."

How many times during the previous murder investigation had Nate assured me everything would be okay? In the end, he'd been right, even if I hadn't believed him. I let out a calming breath and scanned the thinning crowd. "Where is she?"

"Emma and Connor headed to The Crow," Alicia said, referring to Stonebridge's most popular watering hole, The Mad Crow Tavern.

"I thought we had to stay here."

"The police are all set for now," Nate said. "The detective spoke with both of them after the ambulance drove off. I believe you were making a call for Penny."

"The good news is we're all free to go," Rose said. "We were waiting for you."

I had so many questions. "But what about Iris?"

Nate tilted his head and looked at me. "The police will look into what happened."

"I don't get it." Rose sat up to join the conversation. "She slipped and fell, right?"

"When I saw Iris at the bar earlier, I thought she might have had too much to drink," Alicia said. "If she fell, that could be why."

Nate shook his head. "It's probably best if we don't repeat that. The autopsy will show more."

"On a more positive note," Alicia said, changing the subject, "Nate and I are also heading to The Crow for a nightcap. You're all welcome to join us."

Rose and William exchanged a glance, and I caught an unspoken message between them. I knew they'd grown close over the last few months, but I couldn't help being just a little surprised they'd already become *that* couple—the kind who communicated without speaking.

"Rose and I plan to go to the Mill House Inn," William said.

A broad grin spread across Nate's face. "Excellent choice. A romantic way to end the evening." He turned to me. "Care to join us at The Crow? You remember the new web designer I mentioned—Ciarán Donovan? He couldn't make the masquerade party, so I promised we'd meet up at The Crow afterward. He's finally moved in, and I get the impression he's looking forward to meeting you."

I'd almost spoken up, ready to accept Alicia's invitation, but my words caught in my throat. An image of Nate's friend filled my head. It had been four months, but I would never forget the way our eyes met across a busy restaurant. Tall, dark, and handsome was an understatement, and the last thing I needed—or wanted—in my life.

"Another time, maybe. I'm super tired and was thinking of calling it a night." I swallowed my fib.

Alicia studied me before leaning in to whisper, "Bobbie... I get that you're not over Dan, but I think you know deep down that's not what's holding you back."

My jaw clenched. How could she possibly get it? "Is that so?" I was unable to hide my annoyance.

Alicia's expression softened. "You think of yourself as a widow—and you are—but that's not *who* you are." She gave my arm a gentle squeeze. "You think I don't understand. What I do know is you don't close yourself off from meeting people. Ciarán's a nice guy. I think you'll like him."

That was the problem, but I wasn't about to admit it to Alicia. I stifled a groan and said, "You're probably right. You always are. It's just..." Just what, exactly? Without Dan by my side, I didn't know who I was supposed to be. And meeting someone new, especially a man I might like, meant pushing his memory aside. Didn't it? I wasn't ready.

"No worries." Nate's voice was as affable as always, but I suspected he understood more than he let on. "It's been a difficult night."

Tears threatened as we parted ways, and loneliness settled over me. It was a feeling I was getting used to. For a brief moment, I considered changing my mind. But as their shadowy forms disappeared into the darkness, I pushed myself up from my chair to head in the opposite direction, toward home. I'd had enough emotional turmoil for one evening.

* * *

When I opened my front door, Darcy greeted me, his tail beating the floor, the wall, and my legs.

"Hey, boy." I bent to scratch between his ears while nudging the loafers from my feet. "I hope you had a better night than I did." I didn't expect him to answer, but when he looked up at me with his big brown eyes, he seemed to commiserate all the same.

My house was dark and quiet. Although I'd grown used to living alone, the silence was something I was still learning to get comfortable with. I flipped a light switch and ambled toward my entertainment center, where I turned on my Bluetooth speaker and chose a folksy playlist. Remembering a bottle of sauvignon blanc I'd left chilling in the refrigerator, I headed to my kitchen. A quick peek at the clock on my fireplace mantel as I walked by told me it was a few minutes after eleven. On a typical night, I'd be in bed, letting my eyelids grow heavy while reading. This wasn't a typical night, and I was much too restless to think about sleeping.

After letting Darcy out the back door to do his business, I poured myself a glass of wine and took a sip, enjoying its cold, crisp flavor. The leaves rustled in the breeze, carrying the sounds of the rushing river from behind my barn. My scattered thoughts refused to quiet, and they drifted back to the party. This was my first Harvest Festival Masquerade, and it sure hadn't gone as I'd expected. Iris's death was unthinkable, and I still felt a knot of worry in my stomach over whatever was wrong with Mackenzie. Detective Cram had hinted—none too subtly—about drugs.

Back in my living room, I set my glass on the coffee table, lit the candles in my favorite glass hurricanes, and hummed off-key to the music. Letting the melody and lyrics of Brandi Carlile's "This Time Tomorrow" wash over me, I settled on the end of the couch. The song was like a lullaby, meant to comfort children after their parents' death. I viewed it as something more, finding comfort in the idea that loved ones were always together.

Candlelight illuminated the wine in my glass, a pale iridescent gold, reminding me of our club's photography prompts. I got up to grab my camera, and after a few adjustments for the low lighting, I snapped several photos.

Not fully satisfied, I recomposed the shot so that the flickering flame in the background created the soft, out-of-focus balls of light photographers called bokeh. I twisted the dial to let more light into my lens and clicked. When I'd created the prompt—*sparkling*—I had the lanterns and string lights at the masquerade party in mind. No matter. It wasn't the cue that was important, but the photographer's interpretation.

I set my camera on the coffee table and settled back on the couch. Darcy jumped up next to me and yawned, curling into a big, furry, yellow ball. Stroking his velvety ear, images of the evening swam in my mind. The costumes had dazzled me. The villagers had let their creativity shine. Now, an unexplained death would cast a pall over the festivities. My heart went out to Iris and her family.

Although I'd hoped the wine would help me relax, it seemed to be making me morose. Even with the music playing, my home was too quiet. A part of me regretted not accepting Alicia and Nate's invitation. I could picture everyone gathered at the horseshoe-shaped bar, a fire crackling in the open fireplace, casting its glow on the polished wood-paneled walls. Everything that had happened earlier in the evening would do little to dampen the tavern's warm and friendly ambience.

As annoyed as I'd been with Alicia, she was right. Avoidance was completely unlike me. Normally outgoing, I enjoyed meeting new people and going to parties and social gatherings. At least, that had been the old me. The newer version of myself was someone I didn't recognize.

Once again, my mind flashed back to that evening last June when Harmony entered The Crow with a man I'd never seen in Stonebridge before. I'd been going through a dark period in my life. But on that particular night, I was feeling hopeful. While chatting with William at the bar, I looked up and met the startling green gaze of a handsome stranger. I could still feel the way the quick encounter made my heart race. Embarrassed to be caught gawking, I'd spun on my barstool, nearly tumbling to the floor.

None of that mattered now. I settled back, allowing myself to relax. Soft light from the hurricanes created a halo on my fresh, creamy-white walls and simple wooden blinds. It had taken several months of renovations to make my small cottage feel like home. Gone were the heavy brocade draperies and drab golden wallpaper of the previous owner. Now, my living room was light and simple—minimalistic, but for the piles of books and scattered photographs.

I pulled a throw blanket off the back of the couch and snuggled it close, remembering my old home. Dan and I had lived there for more than twenty years. It was the home where we raised Emma. We'd always planned to move to Vermont someday, leaving the city behind. I still missed it, though.

After Dan's death, I felt unsure whether I could follow our dreams on my own. But I made the leap, and I couldn't help feeling a little proud of myself. On days when the pang of missing Boston felt overwhelming, I reminded myself how far I'd come. I was starting to feel like I belonged here.

As I sipped my wine, my mind shifted to Iris's accident, and I stifled a shudder.

Chapter Six

Darcy's ears perked to the sound of footsteps on my front porch, and I realized I'd lost track of time. It was after midnight. I'd been completely lost in my thoughts, humming along with the music. Outside, Emma's giggle was followed by the deep murmur of a male voice—presumably Connor's. As their chatting continued, muffled from behind the closed door, Darcy jumped from the couch, his whole body wagging as he stood in the hallway waiting for one of his favorite humans to materialize. When Emma finally burst inside, her face glowed in the dim light.

"Hey, Darce. Were you waiting up?" She bent to scratch Darcy's head before raising her gaze to look in my direction. "Oh, hi, Mom." Her cheeks were the rosy pink of happiness and cool autumn air.

"Hi yourself."

"Why are you still up?"

Lifting my wineglass, I said, "I wasn't ready to go to bed."

"Oh, totally," she said. "Mind if I join you?"

"Please do. Did you have a good time at The Crow?"

"Mom…" She kicked off her shoes and headed to the kitchen, Darcy on her heels. "Please tell me you're not asking about Connor and me." Her voice was a warning. Right. No more interference. In all honesty, despite worrying that she was setting herself up for more heartache, I admired how Emma had bounced back after a tough breakup.

"I'm sure we can find other things to talk about."

Emma returned and poured herself a glass of wine before plunking the bottle on the coffee table. Settling onto the couch with Darcy between us, she tucked her legs beneath her. Even with the warnings to back off, I loved having an adult daughter. It was like a reward for making it through the turbulent teen years.

"Just so you know," I said. "I like Connor. I always have." I'd known him since he was a young boy. After losing his father to lung cancer, he'd spent countless hours at the Crowley farm, with Nate taking on the role of surrogate dad. Several years younger than Connor, Emma, along with Nate and Alicia's twin sons, had followed him around like puppies. With an abundance of patience, Connor had played endless games of checkers and Go Fish with them. It wasn't until last summer, when Emma had come to visit, that he seemed to notice my daughter was no longer a little girl.

"Mom…" Emma said again. This time, a smile accompanied her much-expected eye roll. "You just promised. Besides, I've told you repeatedly, we're only friends. I live in Boston, he lives in Vermont… Remember?"

I pantomimed zipping my lips. She was fooling herself. Long distance or not, there was a chemistry between them that hinted at something deeper than friendship. Still, I was more than a little relieved to note her playful expression.

Emma toyed with a curl while peering at me over her glass. She was skeptical, no doubt, about my ability to keep my mouth closed. *Fair.*

I let out a sigh. "I only want to know how you're doing after everything that happened tonight."

"I'm fine. I automatically went into nurse mode."

I sipped my wine, remembering the scene. "Can you run me through what happened?"

Emma set her glass on the coffee table. "Connor and I had been dancing…" she paused, lost in thought. "I remember seeing the lady with the pink hair—Mackenzie—arguing with the bartender."

"Mackenzie was arguing with Travis?" The thought surprised me. But then, arguing was Travis's modus operandi. "Could you hear what they were saying?"

"No, and I didn't think anything of it."

I stashed the tidbit in the back of my mind. "Then what happened?"

"The song finished, and I told Connor I'd be right back. I just needed some air." Emma blushed. "That's when I heard Jackson call out to Connor."

"Really? Jackson?"

"The guy in the military uniform, right?" Emma asked. "Anyway, when Connor stopped to talk to him, I walked to the fountain. And then I saw Iris."

"I'm so sorry this happened to you," I said.

"I was so surprised to find someone lying there." Emma paused. "I lifted her face from the water, but I knew I couldn't move her myself. She seemed small, about my size, I'd guess, but it's amazing how heavy an unconscious person is. That's when Harmony appeared."

"I wonder what Iris was doing there. Or Harmony, for that matter." I took a sip of wine, not expecting an answer.

"Same as me, probably. You have to admit, the party was a bit rowdy." Emma paused. "After that, everything happened so fast. Someone said she was an herbalist?"

"That's right," I said. "And she occasionally taught yoga classes at Harmony's studio, Heart and Harmony."

"I saw her earlier, dancing with some friends." A blonde curl escaped Emma's ponytail, and she pushed it aside.

"Any idea why Jackson wanted to talk to Connor?"

"Oh yeah, no. I forgot all about it and didn't think to ask." Emma reached for her wineglass. "I can ask him tomorrow if you want me to."

"It's probably not important. I was just trying to picture the scene."

Another Brandi Carlile song played, and I hummed along while pondering Emma's story.

Emma set her glass on the coffee table and unfolded her legs before turning to me. "I met Uncle Nate's new friend tonight. You know, the tall Irish guy. Ciarán, I think his name is."

"Oh." The change of topic caught me by surprise. It was bewildering the way the mere mention of someone I'd never met could make my breath catch. When Emma didn't continue, I tried to maintain nonchalance and asked, "What was he like?"

Emma's eyes searched mine before she spoke. "Nice. Yeah, he seemed super nice." She shrugged. "When Uncle Nate said you weren't up for coming to The Crow, I got a little worried. That's so not like you."

"No need to worry," I said. "I'm starting to learn the value of alone time."

The tilt of Emma's head told me she wasn't buying it. I couldn't blame her. Unlike my shy, introspective daughter, I wasn't someone who normally sought alone time.

"You haven't met him?" Emma asked. "That's odd. He seemed disappointed you didn't come."

"Who? Nate's friend?" My voice sounded casual, I thought. Not nearly as shaky as it felt, so I continued. "No, we've never met."

"Right, well." Emma let the subject drop. "I'm so excited about Gran coming tomorrow."

"I'm looking forward to seeing her, too." It was the truth, mostly. My relationship with my mother had always been a little complicated. Fiona—I always thought of her by her first name—was like Alicia, driven, pragmatic, and fierce when needed. At the other end of the spectrum was me. Outwardly emotional with ever-ready tears, I wore my heart on my sleeve. After my father passed about five years ago, my mother sold off the Beacon Hill townhouse where I grew up and moved to Florida. With her so far away, I didn't see her often. I was thankful that she and Emma kept in close touch.

Emma stood. "Anyway, I worked the night shift last night, and I'm pretty cooked. I think I'm going to head upstairs, maybe read in bed. Are you planning to go to yoga tomorrow morning?"

"Maybe." I'd completely forgotten what day of the week it was. "It depends on whether Rose comes to get me. She's out with William right now."

"Isn't she the one who always drags you there?" Emma asked.

"She's my Saturday morning alarm clock. I guess I'd better plan on going."

"Cool. I'll have coffee ready when you get back."

"Just so you know, I've learned to make it myself." To be sure, my coffee-making prowess was rather hit-or-miss. Nonetheless, I thought I deserved a big pat on the back for learning to use the gleaming state-of-the-art coffee maker my kitchen designer had talked me into. But with Rose's café right next door, I rarely bothered.

Emma traipsed up the stairs, her nose glued to her phone. I poured another splash of wine into my glass and settled back into the warmth of my couch. I couldn't shake the image of Iris's lifeless body from my mind. Another death in Stonebridge, and Detective Cram was on the case. I sipped my wine and pushed my thoughts aside. Since Iris's death was an accident, it might not be quite so terrible having him around.

Chapter Seven

"Namaste." Harmony bowed to the class. True to form, Rose had arrived at my door wearing a broad smile that made me groan. No one should be that cheerful so early in the morning. It had taken her months of cajoling before I'd agreed to join her on Saturday mornings for an hour of twisting, stretching, and contorting. I had to admit—if only to myself—I was glad she'd persisted. As I rolled my yoga mat, I squinted at my friend's bright fuchsia leggings and neon floral top. I could always count on her to brighten the day.

Considering the previous night's tragedy, I thought Harmony might cancel class. But when we arrived, she announced she was holding the class in honor of Iris. Yoga, she told us, helped her feel closer to her friend and more at peace.

With the confidence and grace only a yogi could master, Harmony glided across the room and lifted the heavy shades from the oversized windows. Bright morning sunlight streamed into the studio, promising another beautiful day for the Harvest Festival. If all the out-of-state cars flowing down Main Street were any indication, the turnout would be huge.

"So, last night…" I whispered to Rose as we lifted our rolled mats. "You and William were adorable as the Great Gatsby."

"Dressing up was so much fun." Rose let out a dramatic sigh.

"Did Daisy and Jay enjoy their nightcap at the Mill House Inn?" I teased.

"It was so romantic." Rose's cheeks flushed. "Let's get smoothies."

I would've preferred a shot of caffeine, but taking our smoothies to a park bench for some chit-chat had become our Saturday morning ritual. Rose's teenage son, Ethan, was old enough to prep the coffee shop before opening.

"Romantic…" I echoed belatedly as we got into line. "I'm beyond happy for you."

Rose let out another sigh. "I had such a wonderful time. The Great Gatsby is so dreamy—not that I've read it—but of course I've seen the movie." She paused, an unfocused gleam in her eyes as she sighed yet again. "It was like being a princess. I just feel so bad about Iris and Mackenzie. What do you think happened?"

"Iris must have tripped," I said. "Hopefully, we'll find out more about Mackenzie today, too."

"Having the police creeping about gives me the heebie jeebies. I'm glad we won't need to investigate this time." She paused, crinkling her nose. "Remember the atrocious bar we went to looking for clues?"

"As I recall, you had fun at that atrocious bar." I laughed, remembering how my vivacious friend had charmed all the bikers while I'd been completely out of place. But we'd made a dynamic duo, uncovering vital information.

"Oh, yeah. I did, didn't I?" Rose giggled. "Well, remember when you said if you ever dated again, we'd go on a double date—somewhere classier?"

"Mm-hmm." I was uncomfortable with the shift in the conversation.

"The Mill House Inn definitely qualifies." She turned to me with an impish smile. "You'll find out tonight at the wine and cheese party. I'm beyond excited. Parties two nights in a row. It's unheard of around here!"

"I've been to the Mill House before. Although not for a romantic nightcap," I said. "Anyway, my party-girl friend, try to remember we're working tonight."

"Killjoy," Rose deadpanned. "I don't care what you say, there will be plenty of time for dancing *and* taking photos."

We reached the counter and placed our usual order for green smoothies. "I'm glad you had a wonderful night," I said, picking up where we'd left off.

"I really did. I had a glass of sparkling wine, and we were home before midnight."

I grinned, unable to miss the twinkle in her eye. *Lucky, lucky girl.* I was about to say so when Harmony grasped my arm and pulled me back. I spun on my heels, nearly knocking into her.

"Bobbie," she said. "I need to talk to you."

"Umm, okay." I resisted the urge to shake off her hand. Her frenzied manner wasn't like her. So much for new age tranquility.

"Not now." Her eyes darted around the room. "Can you come by my house later this afternoon? I'm doing mini-meditation sessions for the festival all morning. But I should be home in the afternoon. You know the one, right? I live in the white farmhouse on West Hill Road."

"What's the address?" I asked. There could be any number of white farmhouses on that road. Making a note of it on my phone, I ran through the festival events in my mind. The club was shorthanded, but with Alicia spending the day at the festival and Rose running back and forth from her café, I thought we had most of the events covered.

Harmony relaxed her grip, and her serene expression returned. She moved behind the counter to help with the smoothies.

"What was that all about?" Rose asked, handing me a cup full of the greenish sludge I'd learned to enjoy despite its reputation for being healthy.

"I wish I knew. She wants to talk." We stepped outside and faced the village green. The sky was a bright, clear blue. In the winter, skiers would declare it a bluebird day, perfect for hitting the slopes. It was perfect for a festival, too.

"Do you think she wants to talk about Iris or what happened to her?" Rose lifted her cup and slurped from the straw.

"I can't think why."

"Still, Harmony seemed odd, don't you think?"

"Definitely," I said. "When she sheds her whole peace and love persona, it's more than a little unnerving."

"Be sure to fill me in at the party tonight." Looking across the green toward her coffee shop, Rose rolled her shoulders. "I'd better skedaddle. The café is going to be hopping today. Fortunately, I managed to finagle enough help so I can be at the festival during the pie-eating contest. No way I'm going to miss watching William. Can you believe he's doing that?"

"Ha, no." Picturing Rose's trim and gentlemanly boyfriend with blueberries dribbling down his chin seemed all wrong. "I may need to see it for myself."

"I know, right? Gotta go get changed and relieve poor Ethan. I'll see you at the party tonight, if not before. Be sure to wear your dancing shoes." With a giggle, she twirled and walked away.

"Sounds good," I said to Rose's back while watching her scamper across the village green toward her apartment above the coffee shop.

I started walking, too, though at a more leisurely pace, and without the twirls. My thoughts were scattered. Paying little attention to where my feet led me, I found myself standing near the fountain. Everything, it seemed, was back to normal.

Dropping onto a nearby bench, my gaze wandered from the fountain to the huge pavilion where the masquerade party had taken place. In a flurry of activity, vendors were already preparing for the day's events. With my eyes closed, I tilted my face to let the sun warm my cheeks while the previous night's scene came back to me. I could almost hear the music floating from under the tent and the sounds of dancing on the wooden platform. When Alicia and I had arrived at the fountain, Emma was holding Iris's lifeless body. I willed my mind to recall the rest of the scene.

"How did I know I'd find you here?"

When my lids blinked open, Alicia shadowed me. Dressed in her usual jeans and T-shirt, and her straight blonde hair clasped in a large barrette at her nape, Lucy Ricardo had all but vanished. My sister was once again a middle-aged farmer and award-winning cheese maker.

"I can't stop wondering what happened," I said.

Alicia sat on the bench. "I'm trying to forget about it, and I advise you to do the same. There's nothing for you to solve."

She was right—so like our mother, always certain. It was immensely irritating. I considered telling her about Harmony's request to meet. She'd have ideas about what our friend wanted. Instead, I asked, "Why was Iris here at the fountain, rather than dancing in the tent?"

"Taking a breather, I imagine."

"You don't think Detective Cram will treat Emma the way he treated me, do you? She was only trying to help." He'd treated me like a murderer—rather unjustly, I might add. I wouldn't be able to stand aside if he copped that attitude with my daughter.

"I can't imagine why. The situations are completely different." Alicia's stare was telling me to chill.

I opened my mouth to protest, but closed it again. "Sometimes your self-assuredness is annoying," I said.

"You hate it when I'm right."

"True."

"We missed you at The Crow last night," Alicia said.

I shrugged in a way I hoped signaled my desire to close the topic. I could tell Alicia wanted to say more, but thankfully, she didn't. Instead, she tipped her head, greeting a woman in the crowd. I didn't know her, but I was pretty sure I'd seen her at the coffee shop with the Righteous Sisters. I smiled when our eyes met. Either she didn't notice or she ignored me while reaching for the hand of a young child and leading her away from us.

"Who is that woman?" I asked my sister.

"I guess I'm not surprised you haven't been introduced. She's the newest member of the Women's Guild. Muffy McCain. Recently widowed and definitely on the prowl."

My heart lurched. "But she seems so young to be a widow." People generally thought of me as a young widow, but I easily had ten years on her.

"She's young; her husband wasn't. They've been second homeowners for years. I used to see them when they stopped at the market on their way into town for the weekend. He always seemed nice enough. A little distracted and stressed out, the way weekenders tend to be on Friday nights." Alicia let out a wry chuckle. "They moved here full-time a few months ago, right after he retired from some hot-shot hedge fund in Manhattan."

"What happened?" I asked.

"He died in his sleep," Alicia said. "They say it was a heart attack, but the doctors seemed baffled. Evidently, he'd had a physical not long before, with no signs of heart trouble."

"That's terrible," I said. "I can't even imagine what she's going through.

And with such a young child. I guess I shouldn't begrudge her finding a home with the Righteous Sisters."

"You and Rose need to stop calling them that," Alicia said. "The Women's Guild does good work for the church."

I waved her off. "We're not talking about the Women's Guild—only Lorraine Adams and her snooty entourage. Honestly, I think they live to make me feel excluded. I have to admit, with everything that's going on, I'm relieved they're away on a church retreat."

"They weren't happy about it coinciding with the festival," Alicia said. "Apparently, the retreat won out."

"Works for me. I'm glad that Lorraine, in particular, is out of town."

"I take it you didn't notice Muffy at the party last night?"

"She was there?" I asked. "It was all so chaotic. What was her costume?"

"Some Audrey Hepburn character, I think," Alicia said. "Princess Ann, maybe? Like you said, it was chaotic. But I remember her being there."

Beyond a party of tourists, I glimpsed Muffy standing in line at one of the food concessions. Slim and stylish, with short brown hair cut to accentuate her round doe eyes, she was easily Audrey Hepburn's doppelgänger. "She's pretty, isn't she?"

"If you say so," Alicia said. "If you're curious about her, you should talk to Mackenzie. There's some buzz about Muffy giving Mackenzie a hard time about the book selection at our library."

I stifled a snort. Our village was fortunate to have a creative, energetic librarian. But when it came to acquiring books, her enthusiasm was no match for the library's tiny budget. "It's not Mackenzie's fault the library doesn't have the funds to buy all the hottest sellers."

"I'm under the impression Muffy cares more about the library lending out the wrong type of books than she does about their newness." Alicia stood. "Anyway, I'd better get moving. The festival is going to be busy today. Thank goodness Mom insisted on getting herself a limo from the airport. She even decided to stay at the inn rather than at the farm."

Stunned by the idea of book banning, it took me a moment to register the second part of what Alicia had said. "Wait, Mother's staying at The Mill

House?"

"She insisted. Something about not being a bother on a busy weekend. And, since Emma is in your spare room, she decided to give the inn a try. She says it got a good write-up in some travel article." Alicia shrugged. "You know Mom. Besides, she can afford it."

"For sure," I said.

"I'd better get to it. Cheese doesn't sell itself."

I laughed. "Yours pretty much does."

Alicia lifted the corner of her mouth into a half-smile. She knew it was true, but she wasn't one to boast. "The parade will be starting soon," she said. "Lucky you, you get to watch it from your very own front porch. It beats hanging around here reliving last night. And don't forget, Mom will be at the wine and cheese party tonight."

Chapter Eight

Emma and Darcy were lounging on the front porch when I returned home. Darcy was in his usual spot at the top of the stairs, keeping his eye on the pre-parade activity on the sidewalk, while Emma sat on the porch swing, hugging one knee to her chest. As I climbed the steps, I spied my curmudgeonly next-door neighbor, Lester Miller, relaxing on his porch recliner. His face and unruly gray beard were shaded by the brim of his baseball cap. In his usual faded flannel shirt and worn overalls, he looked completely at ease.

With a wave, I called out, "Hey, Mr. Miller."

"Humph," he said without looking my way.

Undeterred, I added, "Enjoy the parade." I knew not to expect a second response, and didn't receive one. Not so long ago, his lack of outward friendliness bothered me. Since then, I'd learned how deceiving his grouchiness was.

Chuckling to myself, I bent to scratch Darcy's head before stepping around him and joining Emma on the swing.

"I made coffee." Emma lifted her stoneware mug, and the coffee's warm fragrance wafted its way to my nose. "How was yoga?"

"I'm starting to get into it," I said. "If I keep working at it, I might even get my old dancer's body back. Or rather, the forty-six-year-old version of it."

Darcy ambled over to sit beside me, plopping down on the floor with a groan. It seemed he'd decided that head scratches were more desirable than monitoring the goings-on. I stroked his soft ears while watching the growing crowd. From the other end of the village came the faint clatter of drums. Parade watchers lined the sidewalk in front of my house, some setting folding chairs along the street. Next door, customers flowed in and out of the Rosebud Café, to-go cups in hand. On my other side, my harrumphing neighbor sat on his throne, so to speak, and observed the activity of his kingdom. A descendant of one of Stonebridge's founding families, Mr. Miller was village royalty, whereas I would always be an outsider from one of the less mountainous states. A *flatlander*.

Emma's attention was trained on her phone, her thumbs flying over the keypad. I itched to catch a glimpse of what she was typing, but held myself back, reminding myself that interference was a no-no.

"Connor?" I asked. Okay, so I might not have learned my lesson quite yet.

With a sigh, Emma gave me a distracted glance from over her phone. "Yes, Mom." A smile played at the corner of her lips to lighten her reprimand. "He's marching in the parade with the Little League team he coaches. He says he finally managed to round up his rambunctious little crew." Her smile vanished. "He's also telling me not to look at the Stonebridge Scandal."

The mere mention of The Scandal raised my hackles. The owner of that particular Facebook page was unknown. Whoever it was, they seemed to have their finger on the pulse of all things Stonebridge and had no trouble publicizing everything they'd heard, true or not.

I gave Emma a pointed look as she opened her Facebook app. "Sounds like good advice. Even though I've reactivated my account, I refuse to follow that page." Then, because she seemed to be ignoring me, I added, "For good reason."

Without acknowledging me, she let out a slow groan. "They're making it sound like you and I are some kind of mother-daughter murder duo."

"Surprise, surprise," I said, unable to tone down my sarcasm. Emma's reaction reminded me of how much I'd enjoyed my year-plus hiatus from online socializing. After Dan's death, the contrast between my friends' happy lives and my grief-filled one was more than I could handle. Just a month ago, I'd given in and reopened my profile, but only so I could participate in the camera club's group challenges. Watching Emma made me wonder how much I'd regret it.

Emma stomped to the porch railing while stuffing her phone into her pocket. She leaned over to watch the commotion out front. "How do you live here? It seems so cliquey."

"I know how you feel, honey." City life came with a fair amount of anonymity built in. Not so in a small village like Stonebridge. Culture shock aside, I loved my adopted village most of the time. Behind the old-time rivalries and more rumors than I could keep track of, there was a powerful community full of good people.

I walked over to her and placed my hand on her back. "Believe me, I'm aware it's easier said than done, but I learned the hard way that it's best to ignore the gossip."

"Connor says the same thing," Emma said. "It's not myself I'm worried about. But making stuff up about Iris's death is just so wrong."

I knew how she felt. I also knew most villagers didn't take the Stonebridge Scandal seriously. As I watched the crowd gather on the street, I let my frustration go.

"I used to love watching you twirl your baton in the parades back home." Not so long ago, Dan and I, along with countless proud parents, had staked our spots along our city's parade routes so we could get the best view of our daughter.

"That used to be so much fun," Emma said. "I can't wait to see Connor with his baseball team. He's so good with little kids."

"Mm." I pretended not to notice the hint of pride I detected in her words. "I think I'll go inside and get myself a cup of coffee before the parade comes by." The smoothie had been filling, but it was past time for my caffeine fix.

The sound of beating drums grew louder, but there was no sign of the parade. Before heading back into my house, I raised my phone for a quick shot of the activity. I'd call it *Parade Watchers*. As I snapped, I spied Mackenzie's aunt and Muffy with a small group of women standing on the sidewalk amid the growing flock. Clinging to Muffy's leg was a toddler whose gold cable-knit sweater and leggings matched her mom's. According to Alicia, she'd moved to our village about three months ago, and I couldn't help marveling at how quickly she'd entrenched herself in a group that seemed to enjoy shunning me.

Vickie Sue's soft voice drifted through the noise, surprisingly clear. "Mackenzie was admitted to the hospital last night," she said to her friends. "They're keeping her for observation.

I leaned over my porch railing, hoping to catch their conversation.

"I heard she drank too much?" Muffy asked.

"She didn't. That's the mystery. The doctors think she's reacting to something poisonous." Vickie Sue pivoted and caught my eye.

I wasn't sure which startled me more—Vickie Sue's revelation or being caught eavesdropping. To regain my composure, I fixed my expression into something more neutral, something more friendly than nosy. After being the one to call Vickie Sue the night before, it was only natural that I'd be curious about how Mackenzie was doing. She ignored my smile and mumbled something to her friends, who turned to stare at me.

One of the women led the group farther down the sidewalk toward Mr. Miller's house. Sheesh—there was no winning the group over. I turned away. Their rejection was nothing new.

Still.

Time for a mug of coffee. Thinking about Mackenzie, I walked into my house. Poison? I was overcome with unease. Two accidents in one night felt more than a little strange, but what else could it be?

Mug in hand, I rejoined Emma on the porch with my camera hanging from my neck. I sipped the sweet, creamy brew and picked up my phone. I'd already decided a visit to the hospital was in order; I just needed to find space in my full agenda. As my phone lit up, I noticed a text from Penny I hadn't seen earlier. In it, she mentioned her plan to spend the afternoon with Mackenzie. Even better. Since Mackenzie and I weren't close, visiting her might have seemed strange. Checking in on Penny gave me the perfect excuse.

I placed my coffee on the porch railing and raised my camera, focusing on the line of drummers. As their drumsticks kept the beat, I zoomed in and snapped a close-up of a drummer's hand. It was a tricky shot, requiring quick choices on aperture and shutter speed. I aimed for just enough blur to evoke a sense of motion. If I got it right, the viewer would almost be able to "hear" the rat-a-tat of the drums.

Motion. Satisfied I'd captured another shot for our group's scavenger hunt, I lowered my camera and took in my daughter's beaming face. Connor and his baseball team followed directly behind the band, and I didn't dare say it, but Emma looked every bit the proud girlfriend. I couldn't blame her. His young ball players waved as they passed by. The camaraderie among the team was palpable. Again, I focused my lens, this time for a shot of Connor with his cheerful group.

"They seem to be having fun," I said after clicking a photo of a boy tossing a ball in the air—another potential motion shot. I'd decide which one to post for the club's challenge later.

"Yeah." Emma seemed miles away.

"What are your plans for today?" I asked. "I'm going to be running around all afternoon."

"I'll probably hang out at the festival for most of the day. Connor is planning to gorge himself at the pie-eating contest." Emma shook her head with a closed-mouth smile. "The things guys do."

"I'm hoping to get back in time for it. William is participating, too."

"William? I can't picture it. Where else are you planning to be?" Emma asked.

"Here and there," I said. "I need to get changed. Then, my first stop will be across the street at the festival. I want to check on Jackson—see how he's holding up." I wasn't certain Jackson would be there, but I thought he'd mentioned setting up a tent for his antique shop.

As the parade ended, the normal flow of traffic resumed on Main Street, and the village green filled with festivalgoers. Within minutes, the festival was underway. Last night's huge event tent served as the central gathering spot. Smaller vendor tents surrounded it, forming a marketplace with paths that wended throughout the green.

"I feel so bad for him," Emma said. "You mentioned running around. Where else will you be?"

I told Emma about Harmony pulling me aside after yoga.

"Is that normal?"

"We're friends, but no, not normal," I said. "I told her I'd stop by her house. Then, on my way home, I'll stop by the hospital to check on Mackenzie."

"The hospital is so not on your way home." Emma's eyes narrowed. "I overheard that lady say Mackenzie reacted to something poisonous."

"Do you have any idea what it could have been?" I asked. We'd all thought Mackenzie might be drunk, but Emma had known better.

"It could have been anything," Emma said. "Most things are poisonous if taken incorrectly or taken with the wrong thing. Even water. Are you thinking there's something suspicious going on?"

"No. It just seems strange," I said. "Like you said, Mackenzie could've had an adverse reaction to any number of things." I kept my voice light, not wanting Emma to see how unsettled I felt. I'd try to keep my cool until I learned more, but two accidents on the same night seemed like a big coincidence.

Chapter Nine

After a quick shower, I threw on a pair of faded straight-leg blue jeans, my favorite tan ankle boots, and an ivory fisherman sweater. A silk scarf in muted shades of burgundy and green served as a headband to hold my heavy, damp waves from my face. I gave my hair a quick scrunch and checked myself in the mirror. Satisfied with my sweater-weather outfit, I headed down the stairs to the front hallway.

The click of Darcy's toenails sounded on the wooden floor as I reached for the doorknob. His hopeful brown eyes begged me to take him to the festival. I preferred to go alone, but when he did his tilty-headed thing, I knew I'd lost the battle. I clicked a leash to his collar with a stern warning that we weren't going on a hike in the forest, and he was *not* to get too excited. He only wagged his tail harder. For him, every outing was an adventure. With all the food tents I'd spied earlier, scavenging scraps off the ground should provide all the excitement my garbage scow of a pooch needed.

The house was otherwise quiet, and I assumed Emma had already joined the melee on the village green. On a normal day, ten fingers would be enough to count the number of people wandering about the village. But this was no normal day. The activity brought a liveliness to my quiet little town that was more Boston Common than southern Vermont. I felt right at home.

Darcy and I wove our way through group after group of people, searching for Jackson's tent while music played over speakers, adding to the din of chatter. As expected, Darcy seemed content to amble along beside me, his snout to the ground as he gobbled crumbs.

"You'd better not have a bellyache tonight," I said.

No doubt, proud of his efforts to keep the festival grounds clean, he looked up at me with bright eyes. I had to admit, scarfing up crumbs was his forte. My kitchen floor rarely needed sweeping.

We approached the far side of the village green, and I stopped to look around. Maybe I'd been wrong, and Jackson's grief had kept him at home. I wouldn't blame him if he'd decided to wallow a bit.

I was about to give up on finding him when the familiar carved wooden sign for his antique shop came into view. *Maison des Souvenirs*, the sign read in golden script, catching glimmers of sunlight—House of Memories.

"Hey, Jackson." I entered his tent, keeping Darcy close. The last thing I needed was a broken French country knickknack. A group of elderly women was examining a set of dishes, passing pieces to one another under Jackson's watchful eye.

Darcy nudged Jackson's hand, sniffing for a treat. With his attention focused on the women, Jackson ignored my dog, and Darcy sat with a loud groan.

"*Bonjour*," Jackson greeted me, holding up a finger before shifting his attention back to the group of women.

"*Madame*," he said, addressing a portly woman with wiry gray hair. "This set, I found in the most charming chateau overlooking the Mediterranean."

The women shared smiles and approving nods, seemingly impressed. Jackson turned to me. "Busy morning," he said. "I thought about staying home, but what good would that do? I'm at my best surrounded by my antiques." Gone was the suave faux-Frenchman. His expression was haggard, and I wondered if he'd gotten any sleep.

"How are you doing?" I asked.

He shifted his weight, leaning against a table piled with rusted cooking utensils, which looked a lot like old junk to me. But what did I know?

Running his palm over his bald pate, he said, "I can't believe Iris is gone."

I'd never forget the shock of finding out Dan had died suddenly while at work. It wasn't the same as what had happened to Iris, but deep down, I felt Jackson's numbness and disbelief.

"It just doesn't seem real," I said. "Have you heard anything new?"

"*Non.*" The word sounded sharp, in proper French form. "The police don't share information. Just questions and more questions."

"I thought the whole thing was an accident."

"It was. But that didn't stop them from interrogating me. I don't get it."

I reached for my scarf and rubbed its silky tail. "What sort of questions did they ask?"

"Nothing alarming. But why would they care about my movements? I was nowhere near Iris when she fell. I told them so."

Emma had told me about Jackson calling to Connor from the edge of the tent. Before I could ask him about it, Jackson continued.

"It's almost like they thought I caused her accident. Like I'd ever do something like that. Iris and I were planning to leave for France next month. We were going to live there for the better part of a year."

I was stunned. Jackson hadn't so much as mentioned going on a trip, let alone being away for so long. But Iris had alluded to it. "What about Saskia?"

"She was coming with us," he said.

Fields of lavender. Wasn't that what Saskia had said? It had meant nothing to me at the time, and Iris had brushed it off. Before I had a chance to get my thoughts together, the wiry-haired woman approached, carrying a piece of the dishware. Her friends had already wandered to other displays. It seemed likely she would be taking a souvenir home from her leaf-peeping weekend in Vermont, and I didn't want to interfere with the sale.

"You'd better get back to your customer," I said. "Besides, I've got to run. I promised Harmony I'd stop by her house, then I want to check in on Penny and Mackenzie at the hospital."

Jackson blinked. "Hospital? Why are they at the hospital?"

I paused, regarding his puzzled expression. Hadn't he been sitting with us when Mackenzie was whisked away in an ambulance? I dismissed the thought, remembering how he'd been in his own world—inconsolable. "That's what I hope to find out. I overheard someone say Mackenzie was reacting to some kind of poison."

"Poison? Do they know what kind of poison?" His normally pasty face became an even whiter shade of pale.

I answered with a shake of my head. Jackson's potential customer was setting the dish down. I shot her an apologetic smile and turned to leave.

"I need to know what you find out," Jackson called to my retreating back.

I left his tent and led Darcy toward the looming marquee. He seemed happy to be moving again, his tail wagging as strangers patted his broad head.

The main tent was overflowing with festival-goers. Alicia stood near a display of pies by the entrance, ready for a baking contest. I was trying to guess which one my more domestically-abled sister had baked when Darcy's ears perked. At the sight of his favorite aunt, he gave his leash an excited tug and barked.

"Quiet," I said, using my sternest tone of voice.

When Darcy looked up at me with the bright-eyed expression of a mischievous child whose obedience would come at a cost, I knew I'd made a mistake. He stopped barking and jerked his leash with a force that nearly pulled my arm from its socket as he took off running. No match for his strength, I ran behind him, struggling to maintain my balance. I was relieved when we arrived without hitting anyone.

While I caught my breath, Darcy greeted Alicia—who appeared to be stifling a grin—with his full body wag.

"Don't," I huffed. "Don't say a word."

"I never knew you to be a runner," Alicia smirked. "That was impressive."

"What part of *don't* did you *not* understand?" By that time, Alicia was feeding my naughty dog a treat from the seemingly endless supply she kept in the pocket of her sweatshirt. Thankfully, my breathing returned to normal, and I found myself laughing. "We must have looked comical."

"To say the least," Alicia said. "Are you here for the contest?"

I checked my watch. "Doubtful. Which pie is yours, anyway?"

"The maple walnut one." She gestured toward a deep-dish pie topped with chopped walnuts. "It was a good year for syrup, and we have a lot left over." Alicia surveyed the crowd. "Weird, isn't it?"

"Maple walnut? No. It sounds delicious." My mouth watered.

"Not the pie. The pie is fine," Alicia said. "I mean, it feels weird that everything is so normal. It shouldn't be."

Like any other holiday weekend, I only recognized a handful of the people milling around us. "Tourists. They wouldn't know about Iris. What's the scuttlebutt?"

Before Alicia could answer, Harmony glided by—ethereal, as always. "I'm heading home soon," she said. "Are you still planning to come?"

I nodded as she disappeared into the throng, her long skirt flowing behind her.

"Should I ask where you and Harmony are going?" Alicia asked.

Probably not. Although I didn't know why Harmony wanted me to visit, I knew Alicia would read something into it. Darcy, presumably exasperated to be standing still, plopped to the ground with an extremely rude grunt.

"Harmony wants me to stop by her house." I'd never been able to keep secrets from my sister.

"She wants you to go to her house? I take it you don't know where she lives."

"Sure I do. On West Hill Road."

Alicia chuckled. "It's the big farmhouse with the trailers in the backyard and lots of cars parked out front. You know, the one you and Dan always joked about being a commune."

I could picture the rambling house with all the beater cars and trucks in the yard. "Oh… Really?"

"Yes, really," Alicia said. "Why does she want you to drop by?"

"Your guess is as good as mine."

"Okay, my guess says you shouldn't go." Alicia's eyes narrowed.

"I can't imagine why not. Harmony is my friend."

"I bet she wants to talk about Iris's death. I heard the police were at her house this morning."

"What would that have to do with me?" Something wasn't sitting right. My voice squeaked when I said, "Iris tripped and fell. Why would she need to talk to me about that?" Between the gossip flowing through my sister's market and Nate's more official sources, Alicia always had the latest scoop.

"I don't know anything for sure," Alicia said. "But think about it. Why all the police involvement? It makes me wonder if Iris's death wasn't an accident. For that matter, we don't know what happened to Mackenzie."

I drew in a quick breath. Alicia always had a way of cutting to the core. Still, I wasn't ready to jump to conclusions. "None of that explains why I shouldn't go to Harmony's house."

"Harmony is fine, but have you ever met Iris's ex-partner? River Pelletier. He's Saskia's father, and he lives there, too." Alicia pushed a strand of hair from her face. "You're not going to take my advice, are you?"

"I guess I don't get your trepidation."

"All right then. Go see for yourself, but text me when you leave Harmony's. I want to know you're safe."

Her request seemed excessively cautious, but I agreed.

"Okay," Alicia said. "I need to make the rounds before the pie contest starts."

I looked down at my disgruntled dog. "Ready boy?" His tail thumped the ground as he pushed himself up, and I turned back to my sister. "Good luck with the contest. Your pie looks wonderful."

"Pfft," Alicia said. "Pie baking isn't my thing. I only entered the contest to uphold the Crowley Farm tradition. You should stick around. It's amusing to watch the old biddies duke it out. The competition is brutal." She gave Darcy a sober look while scratching his head. "Remind your mom to text me."

After Alicia left, I took one last gander at the pies, and my stomach grumbled. All the delicious aromas coming from the food stands reminded me of the green concoction I'd slurped down earlier. A smoothie hardly counted as real food, so I followed my nose toward the sweet, greasy aroma of fried dough. When I caught sight of Travis behind the counter, I hesitated, but only for a moment. Another sparring match with Rose's ex-husband was a small price to pay for the treat.

"If it isn't Nancy Drew," Travis said as soon as I reached the counter. "What can I get you? Or did you see the police here earlier, and now you've come to question me about it?" He awarded me with the glower I swore he reserved just for me.

"It's lovely to see you, too," I murmured. If the police were asking questions, it made sense they'd talk to Travis. He'd been behind the bar all evening, placing him in the position to observe everyone. I returned his scowl with a sugary-sweet but fake smile—the one I reserved just for him—and ordered fried dough with cinnamon-sugar. It wasn't that I disliked him. As far as ex-husbands of best friends went, he was more of a major nuisance than a major jerk.

Travis reached for a pair of tongs, and I remembered Emma's comment about his argument with Mackenzie. Before I thought better of it, I said, "I heard Mackenzie was hanging out at the bar last night."

Travis scoffed. "And there it is. Miss Marple returns." He eyed me as he pulled a piece of dough from the fryer. "Sure, her and everyone else."

The English major in me winced. "Did you squabble with everyone else, too?"

"What can I say? My library book is overdue." He chuckled. "You know how testy librarians get about overdue books."

I suppressed an eye roll at his joke. He was enjoying himself way too much. "I'm shocked you even know where the library is," I said. "I'm asking because she wound up in the hospital. I'm planning to visit her there later."

Travis seemed to consider this as he shoved the fried dough across the counter. "Hospital, huh?"

"Poison, apparently," I said. I wanted to continue, but the person behind me shifted their weight with an audible sigh. Probably a tourist who had yet to get their Vermont on.

Travis looked exasperated. "I don't know anything about that." He held out his hand for payment, ending our discussion.

I carried my sugary dough to an empty picnic table and sat. Nothing said festival like empty calories. Darcy lifted his snout toward the table and sniffed. When I pulled the plate away, making it obvious I had no intention of sharing, his ears sagged, making him look incredibly crestfallen. It was almost enough to make me cave, but I was determined. Finally, he gave up and rolled on the ground.

Tearing off a bite of dough, my thoughts turned to Travis. As usual, he'd evaded my question, leaving me none the wiser about his argument with Mackenzie. I was trying to decide whether it mattered when I heard the heavy footsteps of someone approaching.

"Hey, Baby Doll." Gino Morelli, the head chef at the recently reopened Mill House Inn, landed on the bench opposite me with a thud. "You shouldn't eat that stuff."

I grinned as he pulled a piece from my doughy blob and popped it into his mouth. I wasn't sure where my nickname came from—I was no baby, and at five feet nine, I was hardly a doll—but I didn't hate it. Gino's brash style was unapologetically New York, Brooklyn born and bred. He had a boisterous voice and an even more boisterous laugh. He was the Mets to my Red Sox and the Jets to my Patriots. Rivaling sports loyalties aside, I knew the minute I met him we were destined to be bosom buddies. It had only been a couple of months, but we'd formed a fast friendship.

His heavy black eyebrows furrowed. "What's eating at my best girl? Do I need to have a word with Travis?"

It wasn't worth going into, and I shrugged. "Travis is Travis."

"I heard all about what happened last spring. Your penchant for asking questions is known throughout the village. While I'm not terribly fond of the guy, Travis is a good worker. He never left the bar last night. I hope that helps answer any questions you have rattling around that pretty little head of yours."

"No questions from me." First, Travis, then Gino. The way they seemed to think I was looking into Iris's accident was starting to feel more than a little off-kilter. "Shouldn't you be in the kitchen whipping up delectable appetizers for tonight's wine and cheese soiree?"

"You don't know the half of it." He pushed his salt and pepper hair back with his forearm, revealing sparkling brown eyes and a wide grin that didn't look in the least bit harried. "I trust I'll be seeing you tonight."

"I'll be there. The camera club is taking photos." It had been a couple of weeks since I'd last hung out at the inn's bar. Gino had been tied up taking care of customers, and his partner, Jason, had kept me entertained.

"I hope Jason is coming to the party," I said. "I've got him pegged as my dance partner."

"Oh, Baby Doll, where have you been?" Gino laughed. "Jason is so yesterday. After this madness we're calling a festival is over, swing by the bar. We need to catch up."

"I'd enjoy that more than you could possibly understand," I said with a long sigh. I leaned my chin on my hand and glimpsed Muffy sauntering by our picnic table. Wiggling her fingers at Gino, her lips curled into a laughably flirtatious simper.

He waved back, grinning as he watched her pass by. When she was no longer in view, he turned back to me and seemed surprised by my raised brow.

"What?" he said. "It's not my fault if women can't resist my charm."

"Oh yeah, you exude oodles of charm," I said.

Seemingly unbothered by my sarcasm, he stood and pinched one more bite of dough. "I'll see you tonight," he said. "And throw that mess on your plate out, or you'll wind up looking like me." He popped the dough into his mouth and patted his round stomach with another grin before lumbering off.

I eyed the last sugary clump and decided to take Gino's advice. Gathering my trash, I leaned to pat Darcy's head. "Let's head out. We have time for a short walk before I head to Harmony's."

Chapter Ten

It was late afternoon by the time I parked my Subaru on the side of the road in front of Harmony's farmhouse. A newer model sedan and a pickup truck were parked on the lawn next to Harmony's faded blue compact, which I guessed was circa 1990. At the edge of the woods behind the house, two abandoned RVs were nearly hidden by overgrown weeds and shrubs. I looked through my windshield, taking it in. Alicia had called it. Harmony lived in the rambling, ramshackle farmhouse on West Hill Road that Dan and I had always joked about—not that communes were unheard of in southern Vermont.

The house looked welcoming, and I scolded myself for my snobby Bostonian attitude. Sure, the siding needed a paint job, but colorful, painted pots lined the porch railing from which a rainbow flag hung. On one side of the yard, a meadow was dotted with wildflowers. And chickens, a whole flock of them, pecked along the front walkway.

I caught a movement across the yard, and Saskia appeared, carrying a chicken in her arms. She stopped abruptly when I smiled at her, then twirled around and ran back to where she'd come from. My heart clenched at the sight of Iris's daughter.

As I opened my car door, a man stepped onto the front porch and stood unnervingly still while staring at me. For whatever reason, the first thing I noticed was his bare feet beneath a pair of worn-out Carhartt cargo pants. I dragged my gaze higher, taking in his plaid work shirt and long, scruffy beard. He was about average in height and thin in a way that made him look sinewy and tough, rather than scrawny.

"Hi," I called as I stepped from my car. I couldn't help but compare the man with Jackson, whose style was considerably less… mountain man. Surely he wasn't Iris's ex-partner.

The man tipped his chin, his beard bobbing with the movement. His eyes looked wary.

"I'm Bobbie." I stepped away from my car. "Harmony invited me to come by."

"Huh," he said in a gravelly voice. "She didn't mention that."

We seemed to have reached an impasse, and I wasn't sure what my next move should be when Saskia appeared from around the corner of the house, this time holding Harmony's hand.

"River, this is Bobbie," Harmony said to the man on the porch. "I invited her for tea."

"Huh," River said again, giving me a once-over before stepping back into the house and closing the door.

"He doesn't bite, I promise." Harmony's voice held a hint of affection. "I'll admit, he's like a mean old bulldog until you get to know him."

"I'll take your word for it." Alicia's warning echoed in my mind, but River didn't strike me as dangerous. He gave off more of a hermit vibe than a misanthrope one.

Saskia had been silent during the exchange. Harmony bent down and enveloped her in a loose hug. "Why don't you run out back and play. I'm going to take Mrs. Brooks into the kitchen for a grown-up talk."

Saskia looked up at me with wide-eyed innocence, and I felt an overwhelming sadness for her. As soon as Harmony released her, she swooped to pick up another chicken and skipped around the side of the house, her blonde pigtails bouncing as she went. Harmony signaled for me to follow. "Let's go in through the back."

Like the front yard, the ground behind the house was overgrown. The only notable difference was an area enclosed by wooden pickets. The garden inside was lush with a variety of plants.

"May I?" I asked, walking toward the flimsy gate.

"Besides the meadow, this is my favorite part of the yard. Iris's herb garden." Harmony opened the gate.

"I've never been much of a gardener," I said. "It looks like Iris's thumb must have been Kelly green."

"It truly was."

The garden was brimming with a mixture of leafy plants, all neatly labeled.

"Herbs?" I asked. "What did she do with them?"

"Tea blends mostly. Some tinctures, some supplements." Harmony's voice turned flat. "Wild Meadow Herbs. I wonder what will become of her business now."

"I love her Sereni-tea blend," I said. "Tinctures and supplements? That sounds interesting." I sniffed the air and turned to follow the distinctive scent. Outside the fence, nearer the woods that bordered the property, I spotted the source. "Pot?" I asked.

"Hemp," Harmony said. "But Iris was licensed to grow cannabis as well. She was experimenting with CBD products."

"Body creams and that sort of thing?" I asked.

Harmony nodded. "Among other things. Over the years, she built up a considerable clientele for a variety of ailments."

"People came to her instead of a doctor?" *Interesting.* I couldn't imagine what ailment would have me buying supplements from an herbalist.

"It wasn't quite like that. She was extremely knowledgeable, and everyone trusted her." Harmony pointed toward the house. "Let's go inside. I'll make a pot of her hibiscus blend tea, and we can have a chat."

We entered a roomy kitchen through a rusted screen door. River stood at the stove, stirring a pot of something that gave off a warm, earthy scent. He turned briefly and lifted his chin in greeting. That's when I noticed his apron, which read, *Your opinion isn't in my recipe.*

My kind of cook. I stifled a chuckle. "Smells good."

"Wild rice and mushroom soup," Harmony said. "River is very creative with all things culinary."

A large woman, wearing a faded floral print skirt and a baggy T-shirt, entered the room with Saskia. I couldn't quite get a read on her age, but I guessed her to be in her late twenties. She gave me a timid glance as she opened a cookie jar and handed a cookie to Saskia. "You run along now," she said in a soft, girlish voice that seemed incongruous with her size.

"Bobbie, this Tallulah," Harmony said, "one of our housemates."

As I greeted her, she mumbled a greeting while pulling a strand of lank brown hair back toward her low ponytail.

Harmony touched Tallulah's arm. "Lula, would you mind putting the kettle on? We all need to have a chat."

The woman murmured agreement before lifting a kettle and carrying it to the sink.

"Have a seat," Harmony said to me while gesturing toward a large wooden table, scarred from years of use. I sat in one of the mismatched chairs and observed the bustle of activity. As Harmony pulled stoneware mugs in a variety of shapes and sizes from an open shelf, River set a lid on his pot, and Tallulah filled the kettle before handing it to River with a shy smile. The way they moved together looked comfortable and homey.

"I'm sure you're wondering why I asked you to come here." Harmony pushed her thick black braid behind her shoulder and placed the mugs on the table. She sat down and waved for Tallulah and River to do the same. Tallulah joined us, but River leaned his backside against the counter and folded his arms across his chest.

Harmony drew in a slow breath, her eyes clouding. "As you can imagine," she said, "Iris's death is a devastating shock to all of us."

"I'm so sorry," I said.

"You can help."

I remained silent, waiting for her to continue.

"You remember Detective Cram, of course," Harmony said. "You must remember how convinced he was that you were the murderer."

How could I forget? I nodded, sensing the direction this conversation was taking. I didn't like it.

Harmony pinned me with a steady stare. "He's doing the same thing to us." She circled her finger to indicate her housemates.

"But…" I stopped myself from repeating my worn-out line about Iris's death being an accident. Detective Cram was asking questions, almost as if he were gathering suspects. I shook off the thought. No, not suspects. Details. Iris's accident was unusual, and it was the detective's job to determine what happened to her.

"Obviously, there is a lot we don't understand," Harmony reached for the teapot and poured tea into the mugs. "When the detective came to our house this morning, the way he interrogated us gave the impression that he thinks we're guilty of something. We'd never harm Iris. But that's the way he made it sound. If this keeps up, we'll be all over the Stonebridge Scandal page."

I blew across my mug. "I never took you for someone who cared about village gossip."

"Not normally," she said. "But a scandal muddies Iris's memory. And if my customers believe it, Heart and Harmony could lose business. People come to my yoga studio seeking serenity." Her eyes fixed on mine, pleading. "I only want to find the truth."

"I'm not qualified to investigate." I was surprised Harmony was overlooking my reluctance. "Besides, Iris's death was an accident. We need to give the police time to sort it out."

She reached across the table and grasped my hand. "Please. I need to know why the police are questioning us."

"You heard the lady," River said to Harmony in a gruff voice. "We don't need anyone nosing around our business." He turned to leave.

Something in his gruff dismissal raised my hackles. Wondering how he felt about Iris's impending trip, I said, "Jackson mentioned that Iris and Saskia were going with him to France." I hadn't meant to bring it up, but my curiosity got the better of me.

Harmony's eyes lit up. "I knew it. You're already looking into it." She turned to River, who seemed far less pleased.

"No way Iris was going to France," he muttered.

Tallulah spoke in a voice barely above a whisper. "She wouldn't do that to River."

"I'm not looking into it," I said. "When I ran into Jackson earlier, he told me about it."

With a long sigh, Harmony said, "Tallulah and River are right. Iris changed her mind about going to France. She was planning to tell Jackson at the party last night."

"I'm guessing she never got around to it," I said.

Harmony bit her lip. "She promised she would. Maybe she didn't get the chance."

"I'm done here," River grumbled before disappearing through the doorway. Tallulah stood and cast me an apologetic smile before rushing after him.

As I watched them leave, I couldn't help wondering when Iris and River had split up, and how Tallulah fit into the picture. I was probably too traditional, but the dynamics seemed odd.

My curiosity kicked in again. "Tell me more about Iris's supplements."

"I'm not sure what to tell you," Harmony said. "Everyone in the village came to her for alternative therapies. She had an extensive clientele."

"Did her therapies ever make anyone sick?" I asked.

"Not that I'm aware of." Harmony's brow furrowed. "It was usually the other way around. Why are you asking?"

"I'm not sure," I admitted. "I heard this morning that Mackenzie is recovering from being poisoned. The idea of herbal supplements popped into my head just now."

"Poison?" Harmony's eyes widened. "Iris was a certified herbalist and cared deeply for her clients."

"I didn't mean to suggest..." I left my thought unfinished and sat back, taking in the room. From the floral wallpaper to the faded gingham curtains and stacks of stoneware dishes, the room looked nothing like my newly remodeled kitchen with its shiny appliances that I rarely used. And yet, it was comfortable in a way no designer could ever replicate.

"I suppose our arrangement seems strange to you." Harmony studied me. "Some people refer to us as a commune."

Heat crept up my neck, and I held my mug in front of my face, hoping she wouldn't notice.

She noticed. "It's okay. If anything, we're more of a dying commune—not that we were ever a commune per se. In actuality, we're just a group of adults who prefer communal living."

Harmony shifted in her seat. "This was my grandma's home. When she passed a few years ago, she left it to me. I was living in New Mexico at the time. That's where I started practicing yoga." Placing her hands in her lap, she continued. "A bunch of my friends and roommates, including River and Iris, hopped into a van and drove here to live. Those RVs out back? They used to be occupied.

"We all contribute. I run my yoga studio, Iris had her herb business, and River cares for the chickens, handles the household accounts, cooks, and acts as our handyman. We all mind Saskia. It takes a village, as they say."

"And Tallulah?"

"Tallulah hasn't been with us long. She came shortly before Mackenzie moved out, but she fit right in. She helps out around the house and was starting to help Iris dry herbs. She's getting her feet beneath her, so to speak."

I struggled to imagine how it all worked, but I admired Harmony for sharing her home.

"It turns out Tallulah and Mackenzie grew up in the same neighborhood in Brattleboro." Harmony laughed. "They didn't even realize it at first. But then, Mackenzie is several years older than Tallulah."

"And they both wound up here? It seems like an odd coincidence."

"Not really," Harmony said. "I volunteer at a community center in Brattleboro, and that's where I met each of them. Before moving here, Mackenzie ran an adult literacy program at the center in the evenings. Tallulah ran a morning program for children. They're only two of several women who've come to live here. My home provides a soft place to land."

"Your home seems very calm," I said.

"We try to keep it mellow," Harmony said. "One night after the discovery of Mackenzie and Tallulah's shared neighborhood, Mackenzie and I sat here talking. It seems they both had difficult childhoods. Their situations were different, but both of their mothers were troubled." Harmony's gaze grew distant. "I suppose we all have our hang-ups from the past."

I sipped my tea and thought of my mother, Fiona. My childhood had been privileged, to say the least. Wealthy parents, a stable home, the best schools... But all these years later, my relationship with my mother was complicated. I always blamed her for being too busy, too uninvolved in my little dramas. If we all had hang-ups, that would be mine.

My mind went back to Harmony's request. "I'm sorry," I said. "I don't think I can help you. I'm not a detective, and I'm not convinced you need one."

"Please think about it." Harmony placed her hand on mine. "You seem to have a way of figuring things out."

I chuckled. Most people just called me nosy. This was different from the last time. To race into an investigation would be jumping the gun. But there was something about Iris's herbal supplements that niggled my mind.

"I'm assuming Iris kept sales records," I said.

"Of course. She had a ledger. Do you think it will help?"

I wasn't sure it would. I remained silent while mulling it over. Harmony perked up, and I felt bad if my interest gave her hope.

"We won't get into anything dangerous." Harmony stood. "I'll ask Tallulah if she knows where Iris kept it."

"I'm not promising anything," I said. I wasn't even sure what I hoped to find. It seemed unlikely the key to Iris's accident would be in her sales records.

Harmony returned, notebook in hand. She placed it on the table. "Let me know if you find anything. Maybe we can get the club to help, too."

I felt a tingle of excitement as I picked up the notebook and stood. It wouldn't hurt to learn more. "I'm not convinced that will be necessary," I said. "I need to run. It's getting late, and I want to get to the hospital to visit Mackenzie."

As I pushed my chair back and thanked Harmony for the tea, I stifled a yelp. Leaning against the doorframe, River watched with his arms crossed. Behind him, Tallulah wore a curious expression I couldn't quite figure out.

Chapter Eleven

I'd always hated hospitals—even our local one, which was laid out more like an overgrown cottage. Despite its homelike appearance, the halls still smelled of antiseptic, and like every hospital I'd ever visited, the atmosphere was charged with the anxiety of nurses, patients, and family members. I hurried down a long, grayish-white corridor to the room whose number matched the one given to me at reception.

"Bobbie." Penny stood to greet me as I entered. "What are you doing here?"

"I was worried," I said. "I wanted to find out how Mackenzie is doing. You, too."

Penny motioned for me to enter. "She's doing great. Come see for yourself."

"Hey, Mackenzie." I held a bouquet of wildflowers Harmony had insisted on picking before I left her house. "These are from Harmony."

Mackenzie smiled. "That's so sweet of her, and you too, for bringing them."

While Penny took the flowers to the bathroom to fill a glass with water, I sat next to Mackenzie. "You look great," I said, which was true. Gone was the gray pallor from the night before. "Have they figured out what caused it?"

"Nah. Toxicology will take days if not weeks." She waved a dismissive hand. "It doesn't matter. I already know what made me sick."

Penny reentered the room and set the glass of flowers on the windowsill. "You can't know that for sure," she said.

"I do," Mackenzie insisted. "It was the mushrooms."

I gaped at Penny's partner. "As in magic mushrooms?"

Mackenzie laughed. "No, sorry to disappoint you. Just the plain ones. I was out foraging for butt'nuts the other day, and wound up picking mushrooms, too.

Penny seemed to read my confusion and said, "Butternuts. They're like walnuts, but better." She turned to Mackenzie. "You should have asked me to check your mushrooms."

"I didn't even think of it," Mackenzie said, before looking back at me. "The mushrooms were the only out-of-the-ordinary thing I ate all week."

So—not related to Iris's death. Relief washed over me, easing my worries. It was good to understand what had happened, and even better to see Mackenzie on the path to recovery. I didn't stay long after that. Since Mackenzie would be in the hospital for one more night, I assured Penny she needn't worry about the wine and cheese party. Between caring for her partner and her daughter, she seemed frazzled.

By the time I'd pulled out of the parking lot, the sun was low in the sky, painting it with streaks of pink and orange. I adjusted my visor and turned my car onto the road leading back to Stonebridge.

Lost in my thoughts, I wasn't sure how long it took me to notice the bright beam of light reflecting off my rearview mirror. A glance over my shoulder showed headlights rushing toward me. Checking my speedometer, I realized I was driving like a slowpoke, and I sped up. "Sorry," I mumbled—a reflexive response I knew the person behind me couldn't hear.

Unable to keep my thoughts from returning to Harmony's concern over Detective Cram's questions, an unsettled feeling came over me. My mother would say I was borrowing trouble. Maybe I was, but the thought didn't calm my nerves.

Headlights glared in my mirror. Driving faster hadn't helped. I'd hoped to put some distance between me and the car behind me, but they were still dangerously close.

"Sheesh, what's the rush?" I muttered.

Traffic in Vermont was usually laid back, nearly nonexistent most of the time. But this was a holiday weekend, and tourists often brought their stress with them, along with their aggressive driving habits. There was nowhere to pass on this stretch of the road, and no shoulder for pulling off. I sped up again, trying to appease the driver. As they pulled even closer, I heard a loud clanging sound and chanced another quick backward glance. From the size and height of the headlights, I guessed the vehicle to be a pickup truck—an old one, if the rattling was a sign.

My hands shook on the steering wheel as I navigated the winding road. When I rounded a corner, a street sign came into view. I was going too fast to make the turn, but I cut my wheel anyway, praying all four wheels of my all-wheel drive remained on the ground. My heart jumped to my throat as I took my foot off the gas and braced for the impact of hitting the rutted dirt road at high speed.

My car bounced, but stayed upright. I pumped the brakes, my heart pounding furiously. I couldn't seem to catch my breath. Gulping air, my mind raced. I needed to stop my car to regain some semblance of composure. Then, I could turn around and head back to the main road, where I'd be able to drive home at a more comfortable speed. It felt good to have a plan.

My moment of calm was just that—one quick moment. The rattling grew louder. Headlights glared in my mirror once again.

"What the...?" I choked with the realization. The reckless driver wasn't some leaf peeper rushing to the festival to satisfy a fried-dough craving.

I was being followed.

I stepped on the gas, not daring another glance. My heart jumped as my car lurched forward. Afraid of what might happen if I slowed down, I took every bump and rut like I was on an off-road adventure. Somehow, my car remained in control, unlike my jaw, which slammed shut. My teeth gnashed together on a hard bounce. If not for my seatbelt, my head would hit the roof. I couldn't outpace the truck. The headlights grew bigger and brighter in my mirror.

The road was unfamiliar. I feared it would dead-end, leaving me lost in the dense forest. As trusty as my SUV was on the mountainous roads of Vermont, I knew it couldn't go into the woods. No time to think about it.

The road curved sharply. I spun the wheel, narrowly missing a tree, but something jolted me forward. The truck was on my tail, striking me from behind. I swerved, hitting another rut. My chest slammed against the steering wheel. To drive at this speed on a deserted road was a recipe for disaster. I offered a quick prayer that if the worst happened, my body wouldn't remain lost in these dark woods forever.

Then, up ahead, I spied an opening. Across my line of vision, a car sped by on what looked like a paved road. A familiar house came into view. I knew where I was. I'd made a loop around the village and was approaching Main Street from the opposite end of town.

After slowing just enough to check for oncoming traffic, I peeled out onto the state highway toward the center of Stonebridge. The truck pulled onto the road behind me, still tailing me, but I knew the village was only a short distance ahead. I sucked in air and exhaled slowly. The police barracks came into view. I signaled my turn and pulled into the parking lot. Not surprisingly, the truck kept to the road. I twisted to catch a glimpse as it drove past. Although shadows hid the driver, a beam of light from the police station illuminated an old gray pickup truck. Hardly a smoking gun. In Stonebridge, Vermont, pickup trucks of all ages and colors were about as plentiful as people.

I sat in my car, gripping the steering wheel as my mind spun. Had the truck driver been trying to kill me, or were they just sending a message? If it was a warning, it was a dangerous one. My heartbeat slowed, and my fear bred anger. I'd only meant to sit in the parking lot long enough to regain my composure before driving the rest of the way home. But one thing was clear: I was involved in something I had never planned. I flung my car door open and marched across the parking lot. It was time for answers.

With steadfast purpose, I strode into the police barracks. Behind a wall with an open window, the young woman at the reception desk glanced up from her computer. She twirled her ponytail and looked past me.

I turned back toward the door, but there was no one there. "Hi Olivia," I said as I walked to her desk.

"Oh, hi, Mrs. Brooks. Is Mr. Crowley with you?" She glanced over my shoulder again.

I hesitated. Was she asking about Nate? "No. Should he be?"

Olivia's cheeks flushed. "Well, no. But whenever you come here, he's with you."

"Not this time," I said. Thank goodness this visit didn't require an attorney.

Olivia started typing on her keyboard, presumably losing interest since my tall, handsome, married, and much-older-than-her brother-in-law hadn't accompanied me.

I leaned toward the window and cleared my throat.

Olivia looked up and blinked. "Is there something you need?"

"Is Detective Cram in?" I swallowed my nervousness. Never had I expected to seek him out.

"Oh, right." Olivia twirled her ponytail. "Do you want me to page him?"

Before she picked up her phone, I heard an all too familiar voice. "Did someone say my name?" Strutting toward Olivia's desk from a side hallway came the lanky figure of the state police detective. A condescending smirk replaced his casual expression. "Mrs. Brooks."

"Detective Cram." I craned my neck to hold his gaze, ridiculously annoyed that he was one of the few men tall enough to require it. We seemed to be playing chicken.

In a tight voice, he asked, "Is there something I can do for you?"

Uncertain whether to tell him about being chased, I opened my mouth and closed it again. Old pickup trucks were abundant in Stonebridge. I thought better of it. "I hear you've been asking questions about Iris's death."

The detective wagged his head from side to side, making his gelled spikes sway as he assessed me. "I hope you're not here to interfere with our murder investigation. As you may recall, your meddling put you and another innocent person into a threatening situation."

Heat rose to my cheeks, and several scathing retorts came to mind. As I held my tongue, understanding hit me. He'd told me all I needed to know.

"It's true, then. Iris's death was no accident." My knees felt weak with the gravity of his admission. There was a murderer in Stonebridge.

Chapter Twelve

I left the police station to the sound of Detective Cram's sputters. Reeling from his revelation about Iris's murder, I hadn't waited for his response. I didn't need one. After trudging back to my car, I sat in the driver's seat to gather my thoughts. Nothing felt real. Being chased by a truck was already like a bad dream. And Iris's death…it wasn't an accident. I couldn't believe anyone would want her dead.

I started my engine and turned onto Main Street, my mind in a tumult. In less than an hour, the wine and cheese party would begin, but I needed to talk to someone right away. I drove toward my house and noticed a lamp shining from Rose's second-floor apartment above the Rosebud Café. She was probably dressing for the party—something I also needed to do—but her light was like a beacon. I parked my car in my driveway, cut through a break in the hedge separating our yards, and rushed up the back staircase to her apartment.

"Hey, Mrs. Brooks." Ethan opened the door as soon as I knocked. "I thought you were Jeremy."

"If Jeremy is a friend of yours, I saw a car with a teenage boy pull up as I arrived," I said. "A mop of dark hair?"

"Cool, that's him." Ethan turned to shout over his shoulder. "Mom, I'm taking off." He lifted a duffel bag from the floor.

As I stepped aside to let Ethan pass, I panned the room and felt calmer. Rose's place was like home. The clutter of pillows, magazines, candles, and stray shoes, along with the lingering scent of Rose's floral perfume, comforted me. We'd spent many evenings in this room, sharing bottles of wine. *Wine and whine*, we called it.

"Hang on a minute," Rose called as she appeared in her bedroom doorway. Her eyes lit with surprise when they landed on me. She strode toward Ethan, who had almost made it out the door.

"Have fun," Rose said, standing on tiptoe to ruffle Ethan's strawberry-blond hair. "And don't forget what I told you about the proper way to treat girls."

"Mo-om." Ethan ducked from her reach and ran his fingers through his hair, playing with it until he seemed satisfied it was as he'd styled it. He was nearly a head taller than Rose and wore a lopsided grin not unlike his father's. But on Ethan, it looked lighthearted and elfish. "It's just a bunch of friends. I gotta go."

"Off with you, then." Rose gave him a playful push. "And be back early tomorrow to help in the café. It's going to be totally nuts."

Ethan's footsteps clomped as he bounded down the stairs behind the coffee shop. Rose's eyes raked over me. "You're not dressed," she said. "Surely you're not going to the wine and cheese party looking like that."

Ignoring her barb, I said, "He's such a good kid. I can only imagine all the girls in Stonebridge swarming around him."

"He'll be the death of me," Rose said. "Judging from all the texts and closed-door phone conversations, I'd say there's only one girl he's interested in. That's what worries me. Fifteen-year-old hormones." Rose stopped. "That's not why you're here. You're acting like you've seen a ghost." She gestured toward her bedroom.

"Or was chased by one," I said, following her.

If her living room was cluttered, her bedroom was a jumbled disarray of girlishness. Discarded clothes, an open cosmetics bag, and fluffy pillows—including a bright fuchsia velvet, heart-shaped one—strewn the puffy mint green comforter on her bed. On her closet door hung a dress in a rich shade of maroon.

"Is this what you're wearing to the party?" My fingers ran along the lace hem.

"Too over the top?" Rose crinkled her nose. "It's too fancy. I knew it."

"It's beautiful," I answered. "And you'll look gorgeous wearing it. I might need to step up my game a little. I was planning to wear a sweater dress with my black suede boots."

"There's hardly ever any reason to get dressed up around here." Rose sat at a white vanity with a three-sided mirror. "And now, two nights in a row! I need to take advantage of it."

I laughed. "This is Vermont. You know the dress code. Anything goes."

"That's the problem." Rose sighed. "Anything goes means wearing our best dungarees with a clean flannel shirt." She wasn't wrong.

"I'm sure there will be plenty of that, but you shouldn't let it stop you from wearing the dress." I stood behind Rose and caught her eyes in the mirror. "What are you doing with your hair?" I lifted Rose's curls, pulling them back from her face.

"You play with my hair while I finish my makeup. I'm waiting for you to tell me why you're here rather than at home getting dressed for the party."

Hesitant to break the mood, I grabbed a hairpin and secured a lock to the back of Rose's head. In a subdued voice, I said, "Someone followed me home from the hospital."

"What do you mean?" Rose turned to look up at me.

"An old rattle-trap of a truck. Someone followed me." The memory of it made my fingers tremble. I tried to calm them by fussing with Rose's hair. "They were right on my tail, and we were speeding down a dirt road—"

"Wait. What dirt road?" Rose's brow furrowed. "The hospital is right down Main Street. Granted, it's more than ten miles away, but the road is fully paved the whole way."

"Right. I thought they wanted to pass me, so I pulled off."

"But they followed you?"

"That's what I'm saying." I twisted Rose's head so I could resume working on her hair. "Followed would be putting it nicely. It was more like they chased me."

Rose's eyes widened. "But why?"

"That's what I want to know. Guess what else I found out."

Rose brushed powder over her nose and cheeks while I pulled more hair from her face and pinned it in sections so her curls cascaded over her shoulders.

"Iris's death wasn't an accident," I said.

Rose dropped her powder brush and spun around. Her open lips formed a perfect circle.

"On a positive note," I continued. "Mackenzie knows what made her sick." I filled Rose in on my conversations with Harmony, Mackenzie, Penny, and Detective Cram. "Harmony thinks the detective is focused on her and her housemates."

"Is that why she wanted to talk to you?" Rose asked. "We need to do something. We both know Harmony would never hurt a fly."

"She wants the club to help out. Do you think we should get together at the party tonight to talk about it?"

"Definitely. Are you thinking whoever chased you had something to do with Iris?" Rose leaned forward to peer in the mirror as she swept mascara over her pale eyelashes.

I paused. Did I? "What else could it be?"

Rose capped her mascara. "But who knew you were going to be at the hospital?"

"Well, Alicia and Emma for starters," I said.

"I think we can rule them out. Who else?"

I thought back to everyone I'd talked to. "Jackson knew. I told Harmony, and I'm pretty sure River and Tallulah heard."

"Tallulah?" Rose asked.

"New housemate," I said. "Oh yeah, and I think I mentioned it to Gino and Travis."

Rose blew out a puff of air. "Plus, anyone at the festival who might have overheard you. Did you see who was chasing you?"

"I could only see that they were driving an older gray pickup truck."

Rose's shoulders slumped. "Travis drives one of those."

"Yeah," I said. "There are lots of them in Stonebridge. Besides, Gino says Travis never left the bar last night."

"If being Ethan's mom doesn't kill me, being Travis's ex-wife will." Rose tilted her head and checked out my handiwork in the mirror. "Hey, that looks awesome. And William loves it when I leave most of my curls loose." She batted her eyes in the mirror.

"He'll enjoy taking all these pins out, too," I teased.

"Go you!" Rose flapped her hand at me. "You need to get changed. And I happen to know you have a closet full of cocktail dresses. Sweater dresses are for The Crow. I'm treating tonight like a gala, and you should too."

Rose's use of the word gala made me think of my mother, whom I'd almost forgotten would be at the party. I groaned. "You're right. My mother will be there. I'll need to be properly attired."

"Fiona?" Rose was the only person who knew I thought of my mother by her first name. She pressed her palms together. "I get to meet your mom? I'm so excited."

It had been several months since I'd seen my mother, and it surprised me a little to realize I was looking forward to seeing her, too.

"Go," Rose shooed me from her room. "You need to get dressed."

Just a few minutes earlier, I hadn't felt like going to a party. With Rose's excitement over dressing up, my semi-eagerness to see my mother, and the promise of a club pow-wow, my enthusiasm hitched up a notch. I left Rose's apartment and crossed our yards, back to my house, debating which dress to wear. In my anticipation, I almost forgot about my harrowing car chase.

* * *

The light in my bedroom was dim as I surveyed the contents of my closet, contemplating what to wear to the party. A closet full of cocktail dresses was an exaggeration, but not by much. Several hung in the back corner— reminders of my former life. They were remnants of the years I'd spent attending fundraisers, first with my parents at their various charity events, then with Dan to support his research foundation. It felt like a lifetime ago.

After choosing a forest green silk dress with a bateau neckline and three-quarter length lace sleeves, I held it to myself, examining my reflection in the mirror. I liked how the dress fit through the bodice before flaring at the waist to skim my knees. Better yet, Fiona would approve. I gathered my hair behind one ear into a low side ponytail and freshened my makeup with a dusting of blush and some smudgy eyeliner. It would have to do. I was expected at the party…ten minutes before.

While getting dressed, I'd thought about what I knew and what I needed to find out. A chart formed in my mind. Suspects, motives, and opportunities. The problem was, I couldn't think of any suspects yet. Travis drove an old pickup truck, but he had an alibi. If I were to follow Detective Cram's lead, I'd add Harmony. That wasn't happening. Like Rose, I was certain she wasn't involved. I didn't share Harmony's confidence about her housemates, though. River seemed sketchy, and although Tallulah seemed nice enough, the way she looked at River made me wonder if she had a crush.

Love or money, wasn't that the saying? A crush could be a motive. But what would River's motive be? He didn't want Iris to go to France, especially if she was taking Saskia with her. Whether Iris had changed her mind about leaving Stonebridge was a question that niggled. Harmony said one thing, Jackson another. Saskia had been excited about lavender fields. That didn't sound like cancelled plans.

Darcy sat on my bed watching as I strode to my closet to dig around for a pair of shoes. I chose a pair of nude patent leather slingbacks with a low heel and sat next to him to buckle the straps.

"Sorry, boy." I scratched behind his ears as soon as I'd fastened my buckles. "Tomorrow I'll take you to play with Harry and Sally." He tilted his head at the mention of Nate's black labs. Sundays at the Crowley farm were the highlight of Darcy's existence. I gave his back one last scratch and started down the stairs. I'd almost reached the bottom when my doorbell rang, and Darcy bounded past me.

Chapter Thirteen

I opened my front door and nudged Darcy to the side. He seemed to lose interest, retreating to the living room when a rather dapper-looking Jackson greeted me. Instead of his usual jeans with a collared shirt, Jackson wore a crisp pair of gray chinos and a black sport coat over a black polo shirt. He ran his hand along the side of his head while his eyes skimmed me from head to toe and back up again. I'd gotten used to Jackson's once-overs. Still, I winced.

"Jackson?"

"*Bonsoir, mon ami.*" He stepped into my foyer.

"We're supposed to be at the Mill House," I said.

"I'll escort you there. It will give us time to chat."

"What about?" It was a warm evening for October in Vermont, so I left my coat on the hook and grabbed a cashmere wrap instead. I hoisted my backpack from the floor. Not quite the elegant clutch my dress called for, but my camera equipment was a must.

"Can't two friends walk to a party together?" Jackson stepped out the door. "You promised to tell me what you learned."

I'd made no such promise, but I couldn't blame him for wanting to know more about his girlfriend's death. Even so, his insinuation that I was investigating irritated me. When I visited both Harmony and Mackenzie, that hadn't been the case. The truck chase, along with Detective Cram's revelation, had changed that. I wondered if Jackson had heard about Iris being murdered.

I jiggled the doorknob after pulling it shut and said, "Let's head to the party. We'll talk on the way."

We walked in silence until we reached the village green. I stopped and placed my hand on Jackson's arm. "Did you know they're investigating Iris's death as suspicious?"

"I knew something was up. When I spoke with the detective this afternoon, he was none too friendly. I want to help you investigate. We need to find out what happened to my sweet Iris."

We resumed walking, and I filled Jackson in on my visit to Harmony's. "She thinks the police are concentrating their efforts on her and her housemates."

"That makes sense," Jackson said.

"What makes you think that?"

Jackson shrugged. "Nothing specific. What else did you learn?"

I told him about going to the hospital. "Mackenzie ate a poisonous mushroom. Thankfully, that rules out a connection with Iris's death."

"Is that what the doctors said?"

"Mackenzie is adamant, and it fits," I said. "They're running a toxicology, but that takes time. Possibly weeks." I drew in a long breath and told him about being chased home.

Jackson's eyebrows flew up to what should have been his hairline. "Did you see who it was?"

"No. Only an old gray pickup truck."

We'd arrived at the Mill House Inn's front porch, but Jackson appeared to be processing everything I'd told him. I touched his arm again, not wanting to rush him.

He let out a gust of air. "I hope this is resolved before I leave for France."

My hand dropped as my sympathy evaporated into the night air. "You don't plan to stick around?" I couldn't imagine leaving without an answer.

"Nothing is set in stone," he said. "But what good would it do to stay here?"

Even if I disagreed, he had a point. Then, I remembered the discrepancy about Iris's plans. "Harmony and her housemates are under the impression that Iris changed her mind about going to France with you. She was supposed to tell you last night."

"No way. She told me no such thing." Jackson's ears reddened. "In fact, she mentioned how hard it was to talk to River about it."

Music poured from inside the inn. On the porch, Jackson and I hesitated, needing to finish our conversation before joining our friends.

"Harmony is asking for our help," I said. "I think the club should get together and talk about it."

"Count me in." Jackson opened the door and offered his forearm. "Time to join the party."

When I ignored his gesture, he changed tactics and circled his arm around my waist to guide me inside. Though I tried, I couldn't slip from his grasp before meeting Rose's wide-eyed stare. Next to her, Alicia wore a similar look of surprise.

Great, just great. Iris had been dead for less than a day, and anyone who didn't know better might think I was making a move on her boyfriend.

"Thanks for walking with me," I said to Jackson with as much graciousness as I could muster before wriggling from his grasp. I made a beeline for the high-top cocktail table where Alicia and Rose stood. They seemed to be enjoying my discomfort. With a shake of my head, I whispered, "No, no, no. Wipe those grins off your faces. You know there's nothing between us."

"Nothing between who, darling?"

I spun toward the unmistakable, throaty voice of my mother. Stunning, as always, her erect posture gave her an air of someone who was both confident and genteel. Her close-cropped, silver-streaked blonde hair complemented her high cheekbones, while softening her sharp jawline. In a shimmering midnight-blue tunic with a deep V-neck flowing over satin pants in a matching hue, she emanated an elegance I could only aspire to.

"Mother," I dropped my backpack on the floor beneath the table before walking around it to give her a tentative hug. After receiving an air kiss aimed at each of my cheeks, she held me at arm's length. The moment of examination. Mirroring my mother's confidence, I asked, "How was your trip?"

"Blissfully uneventful." She let go of me. "You look well. Green has always been becoming on you."

Relieved to have passed her inspection, I let my shoulders relax. That was when I noticed the man standing next to her—a man I almost didn't recognize without his overalls, baseball cap, and overgrown beard. His beard sported a neat trim, and he wore a blue dress shirt. My harrumphing next-door neighbor, Lester Miller, cleaned up surprisingly well.

"I see you've met Mr. Miller." I nodded to my neighbor, who nodded back, thankfully without his usual *humph*.

"Indeed, I have." My mother let out a deep chuckle. "I'm finding his stories quite charming."

Charming? Of all the adjectives I might use to describe him, that one wouldn't top my list. But then, I'd never heard his stories. Leave it to my mother to find a gate in fences I could only peek over. Even so, I liked to think that my neighbor and I had become allies of sorts over the past several months.

My mother—Fiona—lifted a sequined clutch from the cocktail table. "We were about to go to the bar for a glass of wine."

"Can we bring you something?" Mr. Miller asked.

My jaw dropped, and I snapped it shut lest my mother admonish me over my lacking manners. She and Lester seemed to have formed a quick and otherwise unlikely friendship. Gathering myself, I smiled. "Chardonnay would be lovely. Thank you."

Out from under my mother's scrutiny, I surveyed the inn. This was the first year for the newly reopened Mill House Inn's wine and cheese gathering. It was a ticketed event with an open bar and hors d'oeuvres. It looked like all of Stonebridge had turned out for the occasion.

From where I stood, an oversized parlor, decorated with plush velvets in rich jewel tones, was visible through an arched opening. Normally, I'd find the heavy fabrics and dark colors suffocating, but within the walls of the mid-nineteenth-century stone abode, they combined to create a warm ambience.

Through another arched doorway, opposite the parlor, Gino and Travis scurried around behind a wooden bar that was polished to a gleaming shine. Flickering votives and pots of colorful mums decorated wooden tables. In the restaurant beyond the tavern, an area had been cleared to create a dance floor. I could barely make out the DJ through all the guests.

"Rose told me someone chased you home from the hospital?" Alicia asked, pulling my attention back to our gathering.

I held my finger to my lips, shushing her. The last thing I wanted was for Emma, or anyone else, to hear about my latest adventure. "It was nothing," I said. Where was Emma, anyway? I craned to get a better view.

"Bobbie, seriously? It's totally not nothing," Rose chimed in. "You were as white as a ghost when you stopped by my place."

"I was, but I'm over it now." I averted my eyes at the lie, pinching my lips tight. This wasn't the place to discuss it. I smoothed my ponytail before adding, "We need to focus on what happened to Iris."

"I take it we're not leaving this for the police to sort out?" Alicia asked before lowering her voice. "I want to hear about the truck that followed you."

"I didn't see much. It looked gray—probably old."

"Well, that narrows it down," Alicia said with a wry smile.

"Travis." Rose pressed her fingertips to her temple.

William joined us, placing an appetizer-sized plate loaded with various cheeses and hors d'oeuvres on the table before greeting me with a hug. "Is something going on with Travis?"

I smiled, greeting William with a quick hug before answering him. "He has a gray truck."

With a questioning glance at Rose, William took a slice of cheese from the plate.

"I'll tell you later," Rose said.

"Jackson has a gray truck, too," William said. "He uses it when he's out scouting for antiques."

Wait, what? When I told him about seeing the truck, he failed to mention that he drove one. I reined in my surprise. *Very interesting.*

"Hey, Mom." Emma swished past on Connor's arm. With a giggle, she added, "Time to hit the dance floor." They wove their way past the bar and disappeared.

"Good turnout," Alicia said before taking a sip of her wine. "I'm a little surprised. But then, maybe we're all feeling the need to stick together."

"Speaking of which," I said to Rose and Alicia, "I want to gather the club. We need to strategize on ways to help Harmony. Have you seen her?"

"Not yet," Rose said. "I wouldn't blame her if she didn't come."

I looked around the room. The music had paused while the DJ spoke, and the din of lively chatter took over.

Nate walked by, brushing his hand on Alicia's arm as he passed. I watched as her eyes followed him toward the bar, her affection for him obvious in the slight curl of her lips. There was an intimacy in the simple gesture that I desperately missed having in my own life.

I bent down to pick up my backpack and wrap. "I think I'll take a walk around to look for Harmony. With Penny keeping Mackenzie company at the hospital, we're a little shorthanded, but I suppose it doesn't matter. Be sure to take some time to dance." The club had promised photos of the event, but with no dance partner of my own, I didn't mind taking on most of the responsibility. Not only would it help me feel less like a wallflower, but from the looks of it, the event promised lots of great candid shots. With our prompts in mind, I looked around the room. A shot of the DJ in action should cover the music cue.

I grabbed my backpack, ready to get to work. Straightening, with my bag in hand, I caught an exchanged glance between Alicia and Rose, one that looked clandestine. It wasn't normal for them to exclude me from their secrets, so I paused, waiting for them to share. They remained silent.

"Fine, don't tell me." Whatever it was, I'd find out sooner or later. I turned and stepped away, stopping abruptly when my foot hit a black dress shoe—belonging to a man. I breathed in a soft scent—clean and woodsy with a touch of spice—unfamiliar, yet undeniably pleasant. My balance teetered as I shifted my foot, and I let out a nervous laugh. The firm hand that grabbed my arm to steady me sent a shiver down my spine. It should have been a warning.

Regaining my balance, my gaze traced a path from the masculine hand on my arm, across a broad chest, dressed in a crisp white dress shirt, and straight to Ciarán Donovan's emerald green eyes. It had been four months since the night I first saw him at The Crow, but I would recognize him anywhere.

Chapter Fourteen

"I'm so sorry," I said with a gasp. Oh no, where did my throaty voice come from?

"My fault, entirely." He had a deep voice with a slight brogue, and his eyes twinkled with amusement. The hint of a smile played at the corners of his mouth. I found myself staring at his almost-smile, captivated by his lower lip, which was slightly fuller than the upper one. It looked—sultry.

Wait. No. Rewind!

"I'm Ciarán." His lips hitched a little higher—definitely a smile now. "I don't think we've officially met."

I did my best to disregard his hand—still on my arm—and the smoldering feel of it. "I'm Bobbie." My voice was a hoarse whisper, and I groaned inwardly. Was a whispery voice better or worse than a throaty one?

"It's nice to meet you finally. I was wondering if you'd like to dance."

Everything about him told me Nate was right. Ciarán was a nice guy. Even so...

"Oh... Well... I..." The pounding of my heart made it difficult to think. "That is—I need to..." What was I about to do? Something about my club. Harmony. I was planning to find her.

Alicia and Rose watched with interest, the meaning of their exchanged glance now clear. A warning might have been nice. To make matters more embarrassing, my mother came back with Mr. Miller. They'd retrieved the promised glass of wine and placed it on the table. But it was my mother's undisguised curiosity that made me wish invisibility were my superpower.

Alicia interrupted my internal stammering. "Ciarán, allow me to introduce our mother, Fiona Sullivan." I'd never been more thankful for her presence.

As they exchanged pleasantries, I took a step back from Ciarán's grasp. Several pairs of eyes bored into me as I willed my heart to slow down. As if my speechlessness wasn't bad enough, I also had an audience.

Alicia lifted her chin and aimed her *you're-making-a-fool-of-yourself* expression at me. But when I shot her with my harshest dagger-eyes, she only smiled back, not the least bit perturbed. I sighed, turning back to face Ciarán.

"I'm sorry," I said, gaining control of my voice. It had been a long time since a man had unhinged me the way he did. There was no way I could dance with him. My addled brain fumbled for an excuse.

"Perhaps another time," he said, graciously letting me off the hook.

My humiliation complete, Alicia's expression softened before shifting her attention to the impossibly handsome man with the lilting brogue and friendly smile who, for reasons inexplicable even to myself, I'd turned down.

"If you don't mind dancing with the wicked sister," Alicia said. "I'd love to join you." I envied her self-assuredness. Embracing her life as a goat farmer hadn't lessened her status as the more sophisticated sister.

"With pleasure." He offered his arm, and they walked toward the dance floor without a backward glance.

I couldn't seem to make my legs move, and I remained in place, tears threatening. Oh, please, not now. What was wrong with me? A man had asked me to dance, and I loved dancing. Yet there I stood, willing my ever-ready tears to stand back.

Rose gave my arm a gentle squeeze as she and William headed toward the dance floor, too. "Talk later?" she whispered in my ear.

I watched Rose dance her way to the other room and wished I could melt into the floor. "Shut Up and Dance" by Walk the Moon reverberated throughout the inn. Everyone, it seemed, was rushing to the dance floor—including Mr. Miller and my seventy-something mother, who was so much cooler than I.

Alone, despite the milling crowd around me, I blinked back tears and reached for the wineglass Mr. Miller had left on the table. I took a swig that burned my throat when I swallowed. It was time to get on with it. I opened my backpack to dig out my camera, and a warm hand touched my shoulder.

"Let's get some air." Nate's voice was low in my ear. He rested his hand lightly on my back while guiding me through the room.

As we passed through, I couldn't help peeking at Ciarán and my sister. They bopped to the lively song, obviously having fun. I wasn't sure whether I was relieved or irked. Probably, a little of both. It was relief I felt, though, when Nate opened the door and led me onto the porch, away from the merriment inside.

Fairy lights shone from the posts and ceiling, emulating the starlit sky. A variety of lanterns and heat lamps were scattered among pots of chrysanthemums. The effect was magical. I let out a long, calming breath and sat on a wooden bench. Nate rested his backside against the porch railing to face me.

I pulled my cashmere wrap around my shoulders and met my brother-in-law's eyes. "Are you going to tell me what an idiot I am?"

"You seemed upset," he said. "I thought you might want to catch some fresh air."

Tears stung my eyes, and I looked up at the twinkling lights above. "Why am I like this?"

"You need to give yourself a break."

I looked at him then, taking in his kind smile—the big brother I never had growing up. "Alicia will disagree with you." I swiped an escaped tear from my cheek.

"Yeah, well…" He spoke in a soft tone. "Alicia sometimes has a funny way of showing how much she cares. But she does."

"Maybe I'm just out of sorts with everything that's going on. Detective Cram told me Iris's death wasn't an accident."

Nate's eyebrows raised. His skepticism over the detective sharing information with me was apparent.

"Okay, he might not have meant to tell me," I said. "Did you know Iris was murdered?"

"I did." His voice turned wary. "I also heard you went to Harmony's house today."

No longer dwelling on my tearful awkwardness, I said. "She only wanted to talk. I also met her housemates, River and Tallulah."

Nate was slow to respond. "I'm surprised River was there. I heard he spent some time at the police station today."

Harmony hadn't told me about that. "Because of Iris?"

"That's right. The police found a note in Iris's room this morning. I haven't seen it, but from what I understand, Iris wrote River an apologetic note about her decision to take Saskia to France with her."

"If the note was found in Iris's room, it's possible she hadn't given it to River."

Nate shook his head. "He'd written a response at the bottom. It would seem his reply could be construed as threatening."

I was taken aback. Harmony had withheld this information while asking for my help? There had to be an explanation.

"You look surprised," Nate said. "Need I remind you that the police are on the case? This isn't a game."

"Need I remind you I didn't know Iris had been murdered when I went to Harmony's?" I didn't appreciate being treated like a child.

The sound of clapping came from inside the inn. The music, along with all the stomping and shouting, had ended. I rested on the bench, enjoying the moment of silence before hearing the door open. Ciarán walked onto the porch, his coat flung over his shoulder. He didn't seem to see us as he walked toward the stairs.

Nate called out to him. "Are you leaving, then?"

Ciarán stopped and turned, his gaze flicking from Nate to me. "I've got an early morning tomorrow."

"That's too bad," Nate said. "I was hoping you'd join me for a nip of whiskey later. It's a Crowley thing. Connor, I, and a few of our cousins. I thought you might enjoy it."

Ciarán hesitated, his eyes flicking to me, before returning to Nate. "Aye, that I would. But I wouldn't want to intrude on your family thing."

"You wouldn't be intruding. We'd consider you a welcome addition." Nate looked at me, chuckling. "Just a bit of guy fun."

"I see. A guys-only thing, huh?" I twisted my lips in mock disapproval.

Before Nate could respond, Harmony appeared on the inn's walkway. She glided toward us, her long skirt flowing behind her. "Sorry I'm late." Beautiful, as always, she'd completed her boho ensemble with a braided headband decorated with beads and feathers. "I hope I haven't missed anything. I was hesitant to leave home."

"How is Saskia?" I asked.

"Better than might be expected. Poor thing keeps talking about the lavender fields. She seems to think Iris went without her." Harmony shook her head. "River and Tallulah have settled in to watch a movie with her."

"Poor thing. She must be so confused," I said. "It would have been okay if you had decided to stay home. Penny is at the hospital with Mackenzie, but everyone else is here. We'll have plenty of photos."

"I don't mind," Harmony said before giving me a questioning look. No words were needed to understand her question about whether I would help her. She seemed reassured by the slight tip of my chin.

"Are you leaving?" She raised onto her tiptoes and planted a friendly peck on Ciarán's cheek. "Please tell me that's not so. I'm counting on you for at least one dance. It sounds downright raucous in there."

"It would seem you're staying," Nate said to Ciarán with a laugh.

The twinge of envy I felt over the easy familiarity between Harmony and Ciarán surprised me. They were friends, I knew. Last spring, when I first saw Ciarán at The Crow, he was with Harmony, his first Stonebridge client. Now, I couldn't help wondering if they were more than just friends.

Before I had time to figure out how that made me feel, Nate escorted Harmony to the door. As he opened it for her, Harmony said to Ciarán, "I'll be expecting a dance."

"And that whiskey I mentioned," Nate said, "I'll come grab you later."

Ciarán chuckled in response to both Harmony and Nate and moved to the porch railing where Nate stood earlier. I looked up from my lap and met his gaze. It would be so easy to get lost in his eyes, like meandering through the forest.

Oh, no. I groaned inwardly for the second time that evening. *Am I staring? I am, aren't I?* I jerked my head to the side.

"I feel terrible for Harmony." Ciarán's voice broke the silence. "It seems I missed the kerfuffle last night."

"Mmm." I looked up at him. "Where were you?"

His lips parted, and confusion swam in his expression. "If I didn't know better, I'd say you're asking me for an alibi. Didn't Harmony's friend die in a tragic accident?"

I shook my head. "Murder," I said. "Sorry, your whereabouts are none of my business."

"I can't help feeling a little shocked, like," he said. "But I wouldn't have thought myself a suspect."

"I suppose we're all suspects until the police find out more."

"Fair play," he said. "I was driving my last load of boxes from Boston."

"I'm sorry I was rude earlier." A wave of awkwardness washed over me again, but I managed to meet his gaze. Rusty didn't begin to describe my dating skills. Except—no. This was not dating. Not even the prelude to dating.

His lips twitched. "It's always the woman's prerogative to decline an invitation to dance."

"Still…"

"No explanation necessary." He had a relaxed manner that made it easy to understand why everyone liked him. No creaky hinges on his dating skills. He was probably used to women swooning over him.

I surprised myself by smiling. "I'm guessing my sister gave you an earful."

"Ah. That would be the older sister's prerogative." He chuckled. "I should know. I have three myself."

I laughed, loosening up, if only slightly. "Please don't tell Alicia. She's already an utter tyrant." I paused. "Three older sisters?" The mention of family always sparked my curiosity.

"Aye, and one younger," he said.

"That's a lot of sisters. Any brothers?"

The corners of his mouth lifted. "Two older brothers."

I couldn't even imagine having so many siblings. It had always been just Alicia and me. "Do they live nearby?"

"Ireland." He pronounced the country's name in the lilting way only someone who'd grown up there could. "Me siblings all live in Ireland." His brogue had thickened, underscoring his point.

"Ireland." My parents had taken us there once. Images of white sheep dotting green fields filled my mind. "You're a long way from home."

His shoulders moved in a non-committal shrug. He smiled his mesmerizing, barely-there smile while holding my gaze. No man should have eyes like his.

And no man should make my heart race like this.

Being near him felt dangerous. He had the power to unwittingly disrupt the delicate independence I'd worked so hard to build over the past year. I blinked, breaking the spell. Remembering my promise to Harmony to get the club together, I gathered my confidence and stood. "I'd better get back inside."

With a tip of his chin, he walked to the door and opened it. "Allow me." His fingers grazed the small of my back, sending another tingle up my spine. When I stepped inside, I was relieved to be back on familiar ground, surrounded by the clamor of the party.

I glanced over my shoulder to offer a belated thank you before rushing away. Ciarán stayed where he was, his hand on the doorknob. He watched me with a bemused expression, as if I were a riddle he needed to solve. I wasn't. I was simply a widow who wasn't ready for a handsome Irishman with hypnotic eyes and a barely-there smile to waltz into my life. I shrugged off the thought and focused my attention on the task at hand. It was time for the camera club to discuss Harmony's predicament. We had a murder to solve.

Chapter Fifteen

I t only took a few minutes to find each of my club members and ask them to join me in the parlor fifteen minutes later. I placed my camera strap around my neck and studied the room, looking for a place to hide my backpack. When Gino appeared behind the bar, I walked toward him and held up my bag. "Any chance you can stash this somewhere safe?"

"Anything for you, Baby Doll," he said. He took my backpack and disappeared into the kitchen, leaving me standing at the bar with Travis.

"The party seems to be going well." Small talk with Rose's ex wasn't our thing, but for reasons I couldn't explain, the silence seemed worse.

Travis gestured by tilting his head toward the far end of the bar. "Looks like there's a new guy in town." He sniggered. "And you've got competition."

I peered down the long counter to where Nate stood with Ciarán—and Muffy. The three of them were laughing, and Muffy's fingers brushed Ciarán's arm. Rose needn't have worried about her dress being over-the-top. I had to give Muffy credit; it took no small amount of savoir-faire to pull off a slinky slip dress in an attention-grabbing fire engine red. In the most un-Vermont way, she looked beyond sexy. When Alicia told me Muffy was on the prowl, she wasn't kidding. And from the looks of it, Ciarán wasn't minding her attention one bit.

"She'll get no competition from me," I said with a toss of my head meant to convey detachment I didn't feel.

"Right," Travis smirked. "Maybe this will help." He set a glass of white wine on the bar. I was grateful, even as I found it bothersome that he knew what I wanted before I did. My gratitude dissipated when he started whistling the melody to "Love Is in the Air."

Heat rose to my cheeks. "Has anyone ever told you you're excruciatingly irritating?"

"Too many to count." Travis shook his cocktail shaker to the beat of his song.

Gino's reappearance caught me mid-eye roll, but it couldn't have been better timed. "Your bag is safely tucked beneath my desk." He nudged Travis's shoulder. "Is this guy giving you problems?"

With a smirk of my own, I eyed Travis before answering. "On the contrary. I was just telling him how charming he can be."

"Glad to hear it. This place is a circus, and I need him to stay focused. No time to be flirting with the pretty ladies."

"No worries, there," I said while Travis snorted. "I hope you don't mind if my club meets in the parlor for a few minutes."

"Not at all. I'll bring you a plate of hors d'oeuvres. I outdid myself." He winked before bustling away.

"Let me guess," Travis said. "It's a meeting of the photographers-turned-Miss-Marple-acolyte club."

"Oh, good word. I'm impressed."

The corner of Travis's mouth lifted. "Little did you know I'm more than just eye candy."

After nearly choking on an ill-timed swallow, I stifled a snicker. Not a chance I was going to touch that one. "I take it you haven't heard Iris was murdered."

Travis's smirk disappeared, if only momentarily. "I guess I should join your little club so I can always be in the know."

Before I could plan a response, Harmony slid over next to me. Travis greeted her with a nod. "What can I get you?"

"Soda with lime." Harmony set her camera on the bar and leaned close so she could lower her voice. "Have you had a chance to look at Iris's sales ledger?"

I turned away from the bar. "Not yet," I said while making a mental note to study it when I got home. Still bothered by what Nate told me, I said, "I heard about River's trip to the police barracks."

Harmony's lips opened and closed. "Then you must know about Iris's note." She picked up her camera and drink while thanking Travis.

"Let's head over to the parlor."

Following me, Harmony said, "It was all a misunderstanding. She wrote it a few days ago. River and Iris talked it out since then."

"You should've told me. I felt blindsided. If we're going to work together, you need to be forthcoming."

"I thought you understood why I called you to my house. I didn't hide the fact that River is a suspect. He wasn't arrested."

"From here on out, let's be clearer with each other." We arrived at the parlor, and I dropped the subject, not wanting to argue in front of the other members.

Compared with the tavern area of the inn, the parlor was quiet. Clusters of chairs and sofas scattered throughout the room formed various conversation areas. There was only one other small group gathered nearby. Rose, Alicia, and Jackson sat on the couch and love seat, forming an L in front of the fireplace. As I sat down, Gino rushed over with the promised plate of appetizers.

"Let's call Penny," I said while we dug into the goodies. Gino hadn't been joking when he claimed he'd outdone himself. Along with the usual cheese and crackers, there was fresh bruschetta that smelled of garlic, miniature crab cakes, and a pastry steaming with spinach, artichokes, and goat cheese I guessed had come from Alicia.

The video chat connected, and my assistant's familiar somber expression filled the screen. I propped my phone on a coffee table so we could all huddle around it. There was no one else near enough to worry about eavesdropping.

"Harmony, why don't you start this off?" I suggested.

As Harmony described her experience with Detective Cram, I couldn't shake my sense of déjà vu. Alicia and Rose nodded along to her story, determination etched in their expressions. If I was reading the group correctly, the club was on board for a new investigation.

"I'll make a chart like I did the last time." Remembering that I'd mentally placed River and Tallulah on the suspect list, I didn't elaborate.

"How's Mackenzie doing?" Rose asked.

"Much better. She's coming home tomorrow." Penny peeked over her shoulder toward where I suspected her partner was.

"Do the doctors know what happened?" Alicia asked.

"They're running a toxicology screen," Penny said. "Mackenzie insists she picked a poisonous mushroom."

Rose leaned forward. "That's a relief. Was it just me, or did anyone else worry about a homicidal maniac running around Stonebridge poisoning and drowning people?"

In a dry tone, Alicia replied, "That seems a bit dramatic."

"It's possible." Rose crossed her arms and sat back.

"I'm relieved." I wasn't sure about a homicidal maniac, but I'd been worried about the timing between Iris's death and Mackenzie landing in the hospital. Rose seemed appeased, and I forged on. "I think we should all review our photos from last night. They could help us piece things together." My idea was met with nods. "Does tomorrow evening around six work for everyone?"

"I know it's late, but how about seven?" Alicia asked. "Tomorrow is Taste of Stonebridge, and it's going to be staggeringly busy."

"Seven," I repeated. "That will give everyone a chance to go home for a short break." No one objected, so I added, "Great, we'll keep it brief."

No sooner had I finished my sentence than Muffy slinked across the room.

"Hi, Harmony," she said in a soft voice. "Mind if I join you?"

I opened my mouth, then closed it without speaking. An image of her sidling up to Ciarán popped into my head, and I minded. I minded very much. Ugh—one more thought to examine later.

"Sorry, Muffy," Alicia said. "This is a camera club meeting."

Harmony looked sympathetic. "We're almost done. I'll come get you."

"Oh, okay." Muffy's head bowed slightly, making me feel guilty for not including her. I knew what it was like to be an outsider, and it wasn't like me to be unwelcoming.

Alicia glanced at me, her lips quirked, giving me the impression she didn't think much of the newest member of the Women's Guild.

Rose watched our wordless exchange and said, "She's really not all bad."

"Are you guys talking about Muffy McCain?" Penny asked. "That lady is whacked. She makes Mackenzie's life miserable with all her little protests at the library. Don't even get me started."

"Now's probably not the time, anyway," I said. "I think we're all set. Let's try to take a look at our photos before we meet up at my house tomorrow."

"Speaking of photos, no one has posted any pictures from the scavenger hunt to our online group," Rose said. Then she giggled. "Including me. So far, I've done *Silhouette* and *Landscape*."

"I've done all of them," Jackson said. "After I edit them, I'll post them on our site.

Harmony said, "I have *Music* and *Tradition*. Sorry about not posting."

Alicia shrugged. "I guess I need to get to work."

"Not tonight," I said. With the stress of Iris's murder, our photography prompts were the least of my worries. "You can all stash your cameras somewhere and dance the night away. I'll take over for the evening."

The rest of the party went smoothly. My camera club held me to my word, and while they danced, I wandered around, clicking photos and chatting. After snapping a few quick shots of the Crowley men—and Ciarán—enjoying their guy time, I had no trouble keeping my distance from the handsome Irishman. With Muffy hanging on his arm at the bar and dancing with both her and Harmony, I was sure my avoidance went unnoticed.

* * *

Later, snuggled beneath my covers with a cup of Iris's Sereni-Tea blend in hand and Darcy curled at my feet, the stress of the day faded. Emma was out with Connor, and I knew I wouldn't sleep soundly. It was one of those contradictions of motherhood. I rarely worried about Emma staying out late when she was in Boston, but when she visited my home, I was restless until I heard her footsteps in the hallway.

Lamplight from Main Street filtered through the crochet curtains on my windows, casting lacy shadows across my bed. Silhouettes of trees swayed outside. I sipped my tea and opened Iris's ledger. Her handwriting scrawled over the pages, filling them with loops and swirls. Everything seemed to be in code, and I thumbed through the notebook, trying to decipher it. Each page had two columns. One, I thought, was full of product names. But I wasn't familiar enough with the different herbs to guess their meanings. In the other column, I recognized abbreviations for several of her customers.

The first one I noticed was the abbreviation "MackzM." Mackenzie Miller, I assumed. Tracing the list with my finger, I found a name beginning with H and followed by musical notes. Harmony? On the next page, I landed on "TravL," "MuffM," and "GinoM." Travis Lavoie, Muffy McCain, and Gino Morelli were logical guesses. Iris had an interesting way of keeping records.

I thumbed through the pages, scanning the names. When the abbreviation "BoB" jumped out at me, I checked the column next to it. "SereniT" it read. I guessed I was BoB. Both Travis and Gino were listed again, leading me to believe they were regular customers. Somehow, I doubted Sereni-Tea was their thing, so what was? Were they using Iris's supplements?

To make heads or tails out of the scribbled notes, I needed to learn more about herbs and their various remedies. I made a mental note to research them, along with the ailments they treated. It amazed me to think people would use unfamiliar supplements, but I also acknowledged there wasn't a huge difference between my tea blend and other concoctions. I hadn't heard any complaints about Iris or Wild Meadow Herbs in the village, but what if a supplement didn't work? It made sense that any business could have dissatisfied customers.

I finished my tea and placed my cup on the nightstand, thoughts swirling in my mind. Iris was sweet and soft-spoken. Villagers adored her. Just about everyone at the masquerade party had the means and opportunity. What I needed was a motive. Was the answer resting in my hands?

My eyes grew heavy as I turned the pages. The tea was working its magic. My last thoughts as I turned off my lamp were about Travis and Gino. If supplements were a motive for killing Iris, I needed to add both men to my suspect list, alibi or not.

Chapter Sixteen

The next morning, after attending service at our village's non-denominational church, I drove Emma and Darcy up the long, winding driveway of the Crowley Farm. I parked my car beside an unfamiliar, newer-model Subaru. My sister's home sat in a grassy valley, bordered by forest and nestled in the mountains. A broad porch stretched across the front of the sprawling house. Once, it had been a modest New England farmhouse. But over the years, numerous additions had been built to accommodate the growing family. Near the kitchen door, a porch swing hung, and a scattering of rocking chairs swayed gently in the breeze, as if occupied by the ghosts of ancestors content to watch the goings-on of their beloved farm.

This was Nate's childhood home, and the home where he and Alicia raised their two sons. It was also the home where Dan and I had spent countless weekends with Emma, escaping our city lives, if only for a couple of days at a time.

Darcy whined from the backseat, his tail thumping against the door in excitement. He loved Sunday dinner as much as I did. While I enjoyed a warm home-cooked meal in the company of Nate, Alicia, Connor, and whomever they'd invited, Darcy ran about the farm, playing with Nate's hunting dogs, Harry and Sally.

"Sundays on the farm are the best," Emma said, opening her door.

"Alicia warned this wouldn't be a normal dinner. She needs help prepping for the festival. Taste of Stonebridge is the main event this afternoon." I let Darcy out of the car, and he wasted no time running to the porch where the black labs were lazing in the sun.

"Sounds like fun to me. Besides, Auntie always has something to munch on." Emma jumped from the car.

"Without a doubt." I laughed. "No one ever goes hungry here."

Emma's blue eyes shone. "Connor is already here."

"Mmm." I'd dozed off the night before, Iris's ledger in hand, only to be awakened by Emma's footsteps in the hallway shortly after midnight. She and Connor had likely headed to The Crow after the party. Less than twelve hours later, her excitement to see him reminded me of when Dan and I were first dating.

Emma ran up the stairs and disappeared into the kitchen almost before I had the chance to shut my car door. While stepping onto the porch, I soaked in the warmth of the morning sunshine. Darcy and his doggy cousins were already barking and jumping on the lawn. In the distant field, the red barn provided a bucolic backdrop to the grazing goats.

Alicia appeared in the doorway, blocking me from entering.

"What's up?" I asked.

She looked uncharacteristically hesitant, and before she had a chance to speak, I raised on tiptoes to see what she was hiding from my view. Standing at the oversized butcher block counter, chatting with my mother, was Ciarán. I crossed my arms and waited for an explanation.

Hands on her hips, Alicia said, "This isn't about you, Bobbie. Ciarán and Nate are good friends. And since Ciarán is new here, Nate wants to make him feel welcome. You're going to need to deal with it." Although she'd kept her voice low, I hadn't missed her reprimand.

"Fine." I let out a slow breath. "Far be it from me to break up a budding bromance."

Alicia's lips twitched, and Nate appeared in the doorway. "Is there a problem?"

I reached past Alicia and grabbed Nate's arm. "We need to talk."

With a roll of her eyes, Alicia said, "Don't be long. I need all the help I can get."

Nate nodded before stepping onto the porch. "What is it?" He shut the door behind him.

"I have something for you. But first, I want to know what you've learned about Iris's death."

"Bobbie…" Nate's voice filled with exasperation. "The police are working the case."

"I'll find out anyway."

Nate let out an agitated sigh. "Okay. I'd rather not have you poking a hornet's nest." He paused. "The autopsy found bruises that looked like fingerprints on the sides of Iris's neck. There was also a large bruise on her forehead. The marks on her neck and forehead make it appear that she was approached from behind, and her head was slammed into the stone edge of the fountain. She was probably unconscious and left to drown."

My hand flew to my mouth. "How brutal."

"This isn't a game. The way she was killed was a sign of extreme rage." The intensity of his gaze bore into me. "I know Harmony asked for your help. I also know she's your friend. But, for what it's worth, getting involved is a bad idea. A witness placed her near the scene right before Iris was killed."

"Harmony would never hurt Iris." There was no imaginable scenario where she slammed her friend's face into a fountain.

Nate's patience seemed to be wearing thin as he drew in a long breath. "You said you have something for me?"

"I have Iris's sales ledger," I said. "What if someone murdered her because of her supplements?"

"It's a thought," Nate said.

"I haven't had much time to study it, but I recognized what I think are abbreviations for a few of her customers."

"It's not for you to study. You know what you need to do with it." When I didn't answer, he continued. "You're not a detective."

He was right. I needed to give it to Detective Cram. "Yeah, fine."

"Okay, we'd better head inside before Alicia comes back out. That wife of mine—she's on a mission, and we both know it's best to fall in line."

"I'm here to help," I said. "I hope there's something to eat, too. I'm starving." My stomach grumbled on cue.

We entered the kitchen to the sound of rollicking laughter. Everyone was working and seemed to be having a good time. Once inside, Alicia paired me with Ciarán to cut and wrap miniature logs of herbed chèvre. On Ciarán's other side, Nate and my mother were assembling tasty-looking goat cheese and fig tarts. Emma and Connor were rolling a mixture of goat cheese, honey, and spices into bite-sized balls before coating them with chopped nuts and dried cranberries. A platter of sandwiches sat in the center of the island. I grabbed one and bit off the corner before braving a glance at my partner. Of course, Alicia had paired me with him.

Without a word, Ciarán and I went to work, rolling and wrapping bite-sized logs of chèvre. I worked quietly, listening to the others as they bantered, telling jokes and stories. I was the brunt of some good-natured ribbing, mainly because of my tendency to be nosier than some people might like. *Ahem.*

At one point, after hearing stories of Ciarán's childhood in Ireland, we persuaded him to sing an Irish folk song. It wasn't long before he was leading us in a lively chorus of "Molly Malone." He sang with confidence—his brogue stronger than when he spoke—enjoying the song. I loved singing, despite my inability to carry a tune. Growing up, I was teased far too many times to not feel self-conscious. Thankfully, my father's and my tone deafness skipped Emma. It was with no small amount of envy that I watched her belt out the chorus along with Alicia and Fiona.

After the song, we fell into a busy silence, working on our assigned tasks. With their heads nearly touching, Emma and Connor talked softly, their conversation a background hum I paid little attention to.

"She was so cute," Connor was saying. "Those blonde pigtails of hers bouncing as she skipped along beside her father. I think she wanted to join the party."

"I feel so bad for her," Emma said. "I can't imagine what she must be thinking, losing her mom that way."

I looked up from the log of chèvre I was rolling in the snipped herbs. Connor and Emma must have been talking about Saskia. Before I could butt into their conversation, an elbow tapped my side. I slid my gaze toward

Ciarán. Between his fingers, he held a misshapen lump of herbed goat cheese.

He chuckled. "What is this meant to be?"

I suppressed a smile and took the cheese from him, a zing rushing up my arm when our fingers touched. *Dang.* Heat flooded my cheeks, and what had been a comfortable silence suddenly felt awkward.

Unable to endure my discomfort, I filled the silence by asking, "Did you have a good time last night?"

"That I did," Ciarán answered. "The dancing was good *craic.*"

I recognized the Irish term for *fun.* Then, remembering all the photos I'd taken near the dance floor, I said, "From the looks of it, you had no shortage of dance partners." *Smooth, Bobbie. Smooth.*

Ciarán's grin widened, and he pinned me with his glittery-eyed gaze.

"I mean…I was taking pictures. I wasn't…" I gave up. Honestly, I hadn't been keeping track of him. I blamed it on Muffy's eye-catching red dress—a shade that would likely go well with my cheeks.

"How about another song?" Alicia said, casting a sly glance my way.

Big sister for the save. I busied myself with fixing my misshapen wad of chèvre.

It didn't take much coaxing before Ciarán launched into a charming rendition of "When Irish Eyes Are Smiling." He had an unsettling way of looking at us, one by one, as if the song were meant for each of us alone. The sound of everyone's voices singing the chorus nearly raised the roof. I had to admit to myself—and only myself—that, like it or not, I found the man beguiling. The thought felt irrationally dangerous.

"You don't enjoy singing?" Ciarán asked me as we resumed our tasks.

"Oh, I do," I said. "Alone in the shower. I can't carry a tune."

He raised a questioning eyebrow, but when my mother, Alicia, Nate, and Emma all nodded agreement, he chuckled. "I think I'd like to hear it someday."

I laughed. "Trust me, you wouldn't. My voice is something no one should be subjected to—ever."

We got back to work, and with all of us contributing, Alicia's appetizers for the Taste of Stonebridge were nearly done. In no time, it seemed, we'd assembled enough food to send Alicia off to the festival. I'd even been comfortable working next to Ciarán—in between the many side-eyed glances Emma threw our way, that is. I was especially cautious not to produce any more malformed lumps, avoiding troublesome zings.

When it was time to leave, Emma took off with Connor. The camera club was contributing a photo booth that Jackson and William were setting up. Before heading to the festival, I needed to stop at home to change out of my cheese-smeared clothing and pick up the box of props I'd left in my foyer. Hats, boas, plastic sunglasses, and clunky costume jewelry would add to the picture-taking fun.

"You can leave Darcy here," Nate said after stepping onto the porch to see us off. "I'll be in and out most of the day, running around for your sister. I'll drop him by your house on my final trip."

I agreed, knowing my rambunctious dog would rather chase after Harry and Sally than lie around our empty house. I pivoted then and almost stepped on Ciarán's shoe for the second time in as many days. With his hand on my arm, he steadied me again, but this time I was prepared and managed to suppress my shiver.

"My feet seem to be making a habit of getting in your way," he said, his voice filled with humor. "Will you be at the festival?"

"Yes." I squeaked out the word—and awkward Bobbie was back. I paused to gather myself. "That is, my club is running a photo booth."

Ciarán chuckled. "I'll look forward to seeing you there." He strode to his car and drove away.

I bit my lip and turned to Nate. His friendship with Ciarán presented me with an unexpected and unwelcome challenge. I wanted to ask him to stop inviting his new friend to everything, but I wasn't being fair. He couldn't know how difficult the last year and a half had been for me. Every step I'd taken, learning to appreciate my unrequested independence, had been hard fought. If I had to face Ciarán every time I visited the farm, I was afraid I'd regress.

"All set, Bobbie?" Nate asked.

"Yeah." I squared my shoulders and summoned composure. This was a challenge I needed to accept. "I'm good." I walked to my car and opened the door. "I'll see you at the festival."

"Don't forget to bring Iris's ledger," Nate answered. "If you want, I'll walk it to the station with you."

"Sounds good." I got into my car, shifting my thoughts back to Iris. I needed a second pair of eyes on her ledger before I handed it over to the police. Rose's coffee shop would likely be slammed with customers, but I hoped to steal her attention for a couple of minutes. Time was ticking, and Iris's notebook might be the crucial piece of evidence we were searching for.

Chapter Seventeen

G lad to get out of my messy clothes, I changed into a clean pair of jeans, a crisp white tee, and a faux leather moto jacket in a soft blush pink. I tied a silk scarf around my ponytail and stashed Iris's ledger in my backpack. After setting the box of props on my front porch to retrieve later, I hightailed it to the Rosebud Café. Still unmoored by my morning at the farmhouse, I needed the dose of grounding Rose was so good at providing.

The place was swamped with customers. Filtered sunlight streamed through the tall, narrow windows of the Victorian-era home-turned-coffee shop, casting a warm glow that was enhanced by noisy chit-chat and the heavenly aroma of coffee. I made a quick check, hoping to sit at the counter. A man was about to leave his stool, and I hurried to snag his seat. In my haste, I failed to notice Travis slumped over his coffee on the next stool.

"We need to stop meeting like this." He faced me with his customary smirk.

I groaned. "Just ignore me."

"I usually do," he muttered, before gulping his coffee.

A snort of laughter escaped my lips before I could stop it. "Touchè."

"Hey, girl." Rose wiped the counter before plunking a latte with a cute heart design on the clean spot—a perk of being the best friend of the barista. In a bright orange sweater that matched her hair, she reminded me of a fall pumpkin—an especially adorable one. "Wasn't last night so much fun?"

"Mm-hmm," I hummed with a non-committal nod. *Fun* wasn't the word I'd use to describe watching everyone else dance. But I'd enjoyed taking pictures and chatting with friends. The inn had gone all out, and Gino's glowing reviews were well deserved.

Travis scowled. "I'll leave you hens to your clucking." He guzzled the rest of his coffee and stood. "I'm out."

"Even better," Rose said, sotto voce. She leaned on the counter. "Dancing with William was like a dream."

"I'm glad you had such a good time. You deserve it," I said. "And I'm sorry I didn't get a chance to tell you how beautiful you looked."

"Aww, thanks." Rose's cheeks flushed. "William thought so, too." She paused, her smile twisting into something more mischievous. "You looked pretty, too. I happened to notice that *someone* hardly took his eyes off you."

Was she joking? *Someone* had spent most of the night dancing with the red-dressed siren. Doing my best to keep my voice light, I said, "Can we do this another time? I'd rather not rehash my complete lack of social grace." I rummaged through my bag and pulled out Iris's ledger.

"All I'm saying is I'm having so much more fun since I started dating William." She let out a sigh. "I only want the same for you. And Ciarán seems so nice."

"Yes. He does. Extremely nice." *Much nicer than I'm ready for.* I didn't mean to sound curt, but I hoped my brusque tone signaled the end of the topic. I opened the ledger. "Nate insists that I hand this over to the police, and I need help decoding it before I do."

"Aye aye, captain." Rose took the notebook and squinted at it while flipping through the pages.

While she studied it, I surveyed the scene around me. Even with the festival going on across the street, the demand for Rose's coffee hadn't lessened. Apart from a few missing regulars, the café bustled with the usual Sunday mob.

"I hate to admit it, but it's kind of weird without the Righteous Sisters." Rose looked up. "Right? Only Vickie Sue stayed home."

"And Muffy," I said.

"Oh yeah. If we're calling her a Righteous Sister, that is." Rose set the ledger on the counter and pointed to an entry. "I can guess some of the names and maybe some herbs." She pointed to Iris's loopy scrawl. "C-

H-M-L, Chamomile? S-J-W, Saint John's wort? But I think some of the other abbreviations must refer to herbal blends. You'd need to know her recipes."

I stared at the page. "You're right. There's too much to figure out quickly. I'll snap photos." I dug my phone from my pocket and took images of several pages, knowing I needed to hand the notebook over to Detective Cram.

"Good idea." Rose flipped the notebook and did the same.

"What do you think of a dissatisfied customer as a motive?" I asked. "The murderer could be hidden in this book."

Rose's eyes widened. "Oh my gosh, what a scary thought. But it's as good a motive as anything I can think of." Rose ran her finger down the page before looking up at me. "Would it help to visit Iris's garden? You know, see for ourselves what she was growing?"

"Her garden was unbelievable," I said. "Everything is tidy and well-marked. Taking another look is a good idea. But when?"

"Maybe Harmony would let us come visit?"

I tapped my finger on the counter. "I'm not sure why, but I'd rather she not know."

"You can't think Harmony had anything to do with Iris's death," Rose said. "That's totally not possible."

"I agree, but let's keep it between us for now."

Rose held my gaze. "I suppose we could sneak over there. I feel so bad for Iris. She was so nice."

"I feel bad for Jackson, too," I said. "It can't be easy to be in his position."

Rose averted her gaze.

"Something's bothering you," I said.

"I've been meaning to say something." Rose seemed hesitant to continue. "I know how you are about our club, and I don't want to diss anyone..."

"Spill it," I said while thumbing through the ledger.

Rose took in a long breath and let it out with a gush of words. "It's Jackson. I just think...I mean, there's something off with him."

"His girlfriend was murdered," I said. "Grief is different for everyone."

"I want to think that's it. I do." She paused. "But he's been kind of weirding me out."

My mind flashed back to when he arrived at my house before the party. It was a bit unusual, I supposed, but he'd been anxious to find out if I knew anything about Iris's death.

"It could just be me," Rose continued. "But maybe we should be careful about what we share with him?"

"You think I should add him to my suspect list?" I let out a slow breath as Rose gave a tentative nod. "What would be his motive?"

"That's my stumbling block. Forget I said anything."

I thought it unlikely Jackson was involved, but I couldn't dismiss Rose's instincts. With reluctance, I made a mental note to add him to my chart.

* * *

The second full day of the festival was even busier than the first, with the Taste of Stonebridge being a popular draw. After leaving Rose, I went back to my house to grab my box of props. Balancing it in my arms, I started pushing my way toward our booth before I paused to check myself. The box was more bulky than heavy, so I reined in my hurried city-girl attitude and slowed down enough to enjoy the variety of delicious aromas wafting from the food tents.

When I arrived at our club's photo booth, I was glad to see everything was set up and in order. The booth was like a tall box with a flat roof and three sturdy sides. A curtain covered the front. An open canopy offered extra protection in case the weather turned. Penny stood beside a table covered with a meager assortment of hats and scarves.

I dropped my box on the ground. "How's Mackenzie doing?" I asked Penny.

"So much better." Penny treated me to one of her infrequent smiles. "She wanted to hang out at the festival, but I talked her into staying home with Hope and taking it easy. I'm guessing she'll get antsy and will drop by after Hope's nap."

"I'm so relieved she's better. She had me worried." I turned to where

Harmony ushered a young family into the booth before returning to rummage through my box.

"These are great." Harmony put on a hot pink boa and a pair of purple heart-shaped sunglasses. "How do I look?"

"We're supposed to be working." Penny emptied my box and added my props to the others on the table.

Ignoring her, Harmony stood on her tiptoes and waved her fluffy boa to someone in the crowd. "Over here," she called.

"Aren't you glamorous?" A deep voice replied, teasing her. I spun to see Ciarán approach us. Looking exceedingly natty in his tweed flat cap, his eyes met mine. "Hello, again."

I smiled in greeting as Harmony grabbed a green bow tie and a feathered top hat. Before Ciarán seemed to know what was happening, she'd fastened the bow tie around his neck and replaced his cap with the top hat.

"Let's do this." She took him by the arm and guided him to the booth.

"I don't think so." He chuckled.

"It's for a good cause," she coaxed. "I've got plenty of tickets." She placed several tickets in the box and opened the booth's curtain.

I couldn't help but laugh at the beseeching glance Ciarán threw my way. "It's best not to argue with a yogi. Bad karma."

Their disappearance into the booth gave me the perfect chance to slip away. "You seem to have this under control," I said to Penny as I turned to leave. "I'll be back in"—I checked my watch—"about an hour or so."

"Sounds good. I'll be here."

I took off to explore the nearby food stalls. With time to kill, I intended to make the most of the many delicious choices. Wandering from tent to tent, I filled my plate with tasty bites from several of our village's talented chefs. Laden with a mini chicken kebab, a couple of Alicia's goat cheese tarts, a small cup of cheddar-ale soup, and some delicious-looking pastry filled with a gooey chocolate concoction, my flimsy plate threatened to spill. While searching for a place to sit and enjoy my finds, someone tapped my shoulder.

"Excellent choices, Baby Doll." Gino regaled me with a wide grin. "I highly recommend your sister's tarts. I've eaten three, myself." He patted his stomach while pulling me toward an empty picnic table, where he plopped onto a bench.

"You approve, do you?" I settled on the bench across from him. I took a bite of Alicia's tart. The goat cheese was warm and creamy, while the fig gave it a touch of sweetness. Gino was right; it was delicious.

"You seemed busy last night," he said. "I would have thought you'd be dancing. Did you get to enjoy the party at all?"

"More or less," I said. "The food was outstanding. Over-the-top deliciousness."

"It was, wasn't it?" He grinned. "It was fun to stretch my culinary muscles for all you Stonebridgians? Stonebridgites?—no matter. You're a fantastic crew to cook for. So willing to try new things. This festival has been great fun. Big parties are kind of my thing."

"And yet, you relocated from New York to Stonebridge." I was joking, but he didn't look amused. His reaction made me wonder if there was something secretive behind his career change.

"Hey, there," Gino called out to someone, interrupting my thoughts. "It's good to see you again."

River and Tallulah ambled past us with Saskia flitting circles around them, flapping her butterfly wings. River nodded in greeting, and Tallulah said in a soft voice, "It's good to see you, too."

"You know Harmony's housemates?" I asked after they passed by.

"Not really," Gino responded. "I ran into them on Friday night while traveling between the inn and the masquerade party. I was carrying a tray of appetizers, and since they said they didn't have a ticket to the party, I tucked a few in a napkin for them."

I froze, my fork midway to my mouth. "They were on the village green during the masquerade party?"

The news sent my mind spinning. Their proximity to the fountain gave them both the means and opportunity to kill Iris. As soon as the thought formed, it vanished with a poof. They'd been with Saskia. I couldn't imagine either of them hurting Iris in front of her.

Gino's fingers reached across the table and tapped mine. "Hey, you seem like you're somewhere else. Does it matter that they were here?"

"I don't know," I said, trying to reason it out. Then, meeting Gino's gaze, I wondered again about Iris's supplements. Choosing my words, I asked, "Did you know Iris sold herbal supplements?"

"Did she?" Gino's attention shifted to the crowd behind me.

"So it seems." Certain he'd been in the ledger, his evasiveness made me curious. "She had an extensive clientele within the village."

"I really wouldn't know." He stood. "What I do know is my cheddar cheese puffs won't make themselves. They're selling like hotcakes, and it's time I brought another batch down here." With that, he turned on his heel and lumbered back to the inn.

Hmm. I stared at my plate and lifted the kebab to my lips, my mind wandering. Gino and I had formed a quick friendship, but I realized I knew little about his past. His nervous reaction wasn't wholly unexpected. I was familiar with how personal supplements could be. After Dan died, I'd been secretive about taking melatonin—as if trouble sleeping after the death of a loved one was something to be ashamed of. But if customer dissatisfaction was a possible motive, I needed to add Gino to my chart, whether I wanted to or not. He'd been running back and forth between the inn and the party all evening, giving him ample opportunity to kill Iris.

Chapter Eighteen

While savoring the impressive variety of appetizers on my plate, I contemplated my suspects. River and Tallulah had been on the green during the party, Gino was acting cagey about the herbal supplements, and Jackson was weirding Rose out. But did any of them have a motive strong enough to kill? Preoccupied, I walked back to the photo booth, arriving at the same time as Jackson. We were next on the schedule.

"Reporting for duty," Jackson said to Harmony and Penny, who were talking near the table of props.

"I don't mind staying," Penny said. "I've been absent from everything so far. I want to make up for it."

Jackson and I exchanged a glance, silently deciding who would get the out. The truth was, I wanted to stay. I still needed to run the ledger to the police station, but there'd be time for that later.

"I guess you're free for the rest of the afternoon," I said to Jackson. "Besides, you and William set up the booth, so it's my turn."

"Cool." Jackson held up a strip of tickets. "That'll give me a chance to partake in all this wonderful food." He seemed to be planning his strategy when Connor walked by, carrying a heavy tray.

"Where's Emma?" I asked him.

He slowed down just long enough to reply. "She said she was *festivaled out*—her words. She went back to your house." Giving his tray a slight lift, he added, "I'd better get these to Alicia. Her tent is mobbed."

As he rushed away, I considered Emma. Being festivaled out seemed about right. Like her father in many ways, Emma liked social activities in small doses. Over the years, Dan and I had gone to many functions and events. Some were necessary for his research foundation, others were for fun, mostly mine. He'd always worked the room like the best of them, but he never truly enjoyed it the way I did. As a compromise, we created a signal. When Dan pressed a finger to his chin, I knew he was ready to leave. When I responded the same way, it meant, *message received.* Connor was a Crowley—an extrovert through and through. I guessed he and Emma would create a signal of their own someday.

"Bobbie?" Harmony's voice pulled me from my thoughts. "Are we on to review our photos at your house tonight?"

"Seven o'clock," I said.

"I looked through my photos this morning," Jackson said. "I didn't see any smoking guns, but I'll look again."

"I'll set up my widescreen. Hopefully, more sets of eyes will help." I made a mental to-do list for the meeting. Then, pulling my phone out of my pocket, I entered the list into an app I shared with Penny.

"I appreciate everyone's willingness to help me out," Harmony said.

"We're here for you." Jackson's words, though condescending to my ears, were met with nods. I made another mental note—to stop being so hard on him. This note, I didn't add to the app, even though I suspected Penny could use the reminder, too.

"I guess I should check on River and Tallulah," Harmony said before turning to me. "But first, do you have a minute?"

"Sure thing." I followed Harmony around to the side of the photo booth.

"Did you get a chance to ask Jackson if Iris talked to him about the trip?" Her voice was little more than a whisper.

"He claims Iris was still planning to go to France," I said. "And to be clear, that's the assumption I'm going on, too."

"Because of the note? I explained that."

"Not just the note," I said. "Iris was making deliveries that afternoon. She mentioned preparing for a trip, and Saskia seemed excited about it."

Harmony rubbed her forehead and sighed.

"We have Iris's ledger to consider." I mentioned it to reassure her that I was looking at every angle. "I'm planning to take it to the police barracks this afternoon, but I took pictures so I can study it for clues later. The whole thing was written in some sort of code."

"Probably more shorthand than code," Harmony said.

"Either way, figuring it out will take work. Our killer could be in those pages." I was relieved to see her relax, because I knew she'd be unhappy with my next question. "Did you know River and Tallulah were on the village green the night of the masquerade party?"

"They mentioned going out for maple creemees." Harmony crossed her arms over her chest. "Why do you ask?"

"Alicia's market is the only place nearby that sells creemees." The mention of Vermont's creamier version of maple-sweetened soft serve made my mouth water. "They also ran into Gino on the other side of the green, which puts them near the murder."

Aggravation flashed across Harmony's expression. "River would never hurt Iris. Never. Just because they weren't together romantically doesn't mean he didn't love her. He's not a killer."

Her indignation reminded me of the time she told me my aura was red. If red meant anger, she'd been spot on. But I couldn't help wondering what color she'd assign to hers. That was, if I believed in that kind of thing.

I swallowed, thinking back to my earlier conversation with Nate. Someone saw Harmony by the fountain. "Where were you when Iris was killed?"

"Surely you don't suspect—" Harmony's dark eyes blazed. Red. Without a doubt, her aura was red.

I interrupted her. "I don't. Truly. But I can't help you if I don't have all the facts. And if you were nearby, you might have seen something."

She let out a slow breath. "When I asked for your help, I expected something different. First River, and now me?"

Stunned, I watched her walk away, realizing she hadn't answered my questions. I was sure she hadn't killed her friend. But there had to be a reason she wasn't being forthcoming.

When I moved around the photo booth to join Penny, I was surprised to find Jackson hanging around. He sidled up to me. "I'd say Harmony needs a calming mantra." Jackson scoffed at his joke. He made no secret of his disdain for her new age philosophies, which made me wonder why Iris, with her passion for alternative remedies, had been attracted to him.

I wasn't in a joking mood. In my head, I heard Rose's voice saying Jackson was weirding her out.

"What did Harmony want?" Jackson asked. "I heard her ask about me."

"It was nothing. Don't worry about it." I didn't want to get stuck in the middle. We were all meant to be working together. "I should be helping Penny. We can talk more at our meeting tonight."

His hand skimmed the side of his head. For a moment, he seemed to want to protest. "Okay, then," he said. "*À bientôt.* I'll see you tonight." With his tickets trailing from his hand, he turned to leave.

I returned to the table to neaten the props. As I sorted through the collection of colorful accessories, I put aside my conversations with Harmony and Jackson. The festival was going full-tilt, and it was hard not to get caught up in the upbeat atmosphere. One look at our box of tickets told me we'd be making a sizable donation to our local animal shelter. Apparently, the lure of goofy pictures, taken behind the privacy of a curtain, was too tempting to resist.

A teenage couple exited the booth, snickering at their strip of photos. They dropped their props on the table and left without a word.

"Thanks," I called after them.

With Penny talking to a potential customer, I ducked inside the booth to check for abandoned accessories. It was the first time I'd been inside, and the dimness surprised me, making me feel claustrophobic. The walls, though thin, were solid enough to block out most of the noise outside. Being alone in the little cubicle, removed from the festival's activity, felt almost eerie.

I spied a string of beads on the floor. When I bent down to pick them up, a loud bang startled me. I froze. After a moment of stillness, I stood back up before taking another look at the floor. Tucked into a dark corner was a feather boa. As I stooped to pick it up, I heard another bang. This time it was louder, causing the booth to tip slightly, as if someone had fallen against it—or was pushing it.

What the...?

"What's going on?" I called as I straightened, holding the beads and the feather boa. The booth swayed, making a strange creaking noise. I clutched the curtain, and a hand grasped my arm, pulling me away from the teetering walls.

Boom. The photo booth crashed to the ground.

I stood in a daze, stunned by the sight of the fallen booth, its walls collapsed on top of one another. I'd nearly been crushed.

"I heard you call out. Are you okay?" Connor's hand gripped my arm in a tight hold.

Too stunned to speak, I twisted to check that no one had been pinned beneath the fallen walls.

"*Mon Dieu*," Jackson said with a gasp, appearing from what should have been the back side of the booth. "You could have been killed."

"Did you see what happened?" I asked. "Did someone fall into the back of the booth?"

Connor released my arm. "It would take a lot more than a fall to knock it over. Someone must have pushed it."

"Intentionally?" Rubbing my hand over my arm, I looked at him with a slow realization. Someone tried to hurt me. If it hadn't been for Connor, they might have succeeded. But surely no one was brazen enough to push the photo booth over during a busy festival. My eyes followed Connor's to the area behind the booth. Tents set up in rows formed a sort of alley where many of the vendors kept their back flaps closed, and some had crates of food and supplies stacked as high as my chin. It made for an easy place to hide—and an easy place from which to rejoin the crowd.

Curious onlookers gathered near our fallen booth, and I turned to face them. Both Tallulah and River were at a nearby tent, with Saskia dancing circles around them. Muffy appeared, too, from where I couldn't tell. Everyone looked as stunned as I felt.

"Are you okay?" Muffy asked.

"I think so." I put on a brave face. Later, when I had time to reflect, I'd question Muffy, Tallulah, and River's whereabouts when the booth crashed. Jackson's too. They'd all arrived so quickly. But the cacophony made it impossible to form a coherent thought. One thing was certain: this had been no accident, and I'd been targeted.

Again.

Soon, Nate, Alicia, and my mother were standing beside me. Ciarán had followed along, concern etched in his creased forehead.

"I'm afraid to ask how this happened," Alicia said as my mother wrapped an arm around my shoulders and gave me a quick squeeze. It was an oddly affectionate gesture, but I leaned into it.

"Thank goodness you weren't hurt," Nate said. He looked at Connor, and through some unspoken agreement, he, Connor, and Jackson attempted to stabilize the booth. The ceiling had caved in, and the walls were unstable, but it stood.

"We need to check the camera equipment," Penny said.

Still holding a wall steady, Jackson said, "I can help with that."

Snippets of conversations surrounded me, making my head buzz. Amidst the chaos, time seemed to freeze. Images flickered in my mind, disjointed and scratchy, like an old home movie: Emma, holding Iris's limp body; Mackenzie's pale face, ghostly under the dim glow of the street light; headlights glaring in my rearview mirror; Jackson standing on my porch; and Muffy's red dress. I shuddered.

When I looked up, River, Tallulah, Saskia, and Muffy were gone. The gravity of the situation hit me with a force that left me feeling breathless. I squeezed my eyes shut. Someone was out to get me, but it wasn't like I knew anything.

Or do I?

The filmstrip playing inside my head came to a halt. Everything around me had gone eerily silent.

"This is a mistake." Harmony's voice drifted through the quiet. "You don't need handcuffs. I'm not resisting."

Handcuffs? Handcuffs on Harmony?

"Good heavens. Is that your yogi friend?" I'd forgotten my mother was standing next to me.

My eyes snapped open, and three things struck me. First, and least significant, Ciarán had vanished. Second, the crowd had parted, and everyone was watching an improbable spectacle, which was the third and most significant thing. Detective Cram had a firm grip on Harmony's shoulder, and he was leading her to the police barracks.

Chapter Nineteen

"Wait." I snatched my backpack and chased after Detective Cram and Harmony.

"Bobbie, hold on," Nate called after me.

The sound of Nate's voice only pushed me to run faster. I wouldn't let him stop me. When I got within earshot of the detective, I shouted. "You can't take her!" Even as I said it, I knew Detective Cram wasn't about to take orders from me. But when he turned to me with a sneer, I became even more determined to catch up.

"You need to stay out of this, Mrs. Brooks," he called over his shoulder. His long legs made for a fast pace. Harmony appeared to be struggling to keep up with him.

By the time we reached the police station parking lot, the havoc of the festival was behind us. Even with my head start, Nate had no trouble catching up. Detective Cram paused as he opened the station door. With his beady eyes boring into me, he said, "Run along now. I'm sure you have a good Miss Marple story at home to read."

My jaw dropped. "I'm not going anywhere."

"Bobbie…" Nate's voice was low, issuing a warning.

"No," I said. "He's making a mistake, and he knows it."

As Detective Cram used his keycard to open the security door, Harmony turned to look at me with an oddly calm expression.

Okay…

I was following her when Olivia rose from her seat behind the window. "Oh, you can't go in there."

The heck I can't. The door hadn't fully closed, and I reached to grab it, but Nate's firm grip pulled me back.

"Oh, hello Mr. Crowley." Olivia twirled her ponytail. I stiffened at her obvious flirtation.

"Hello, Olivia," Nate responded in his usual friendly manner. "Any chance I can speak with the detective?"

I glanced from the flirty receptionist to Nate. Satisfied that Nate's expression was all business, I relaxed. I pulled my arm from his grip so I could turn to face him.

"We need to help Harmony," I said.

"There's nothing you can do. You must know that."

I blanched at Nate's dismissive tone. "Don't you dare tell me what I can't do." I knew I sounded like a petulant child, but I was so tired of being told to let the police handle it. Everything about this case left me feeling frustrated, and Nate's telling me to back off only made it worse.

Then, I saw Ciarán standing next to Nate, and my frustration hit its peak. His habit of constantly turning up was beginning to wear on me. I glared at him, but he wasn't paying attention. That was when it came to me—he'd come out of concern for Harmony. As Alicia had said earlier, it wasn't always about me. Feeling mollified, I took a shaky breath and turned to Nate.

"There must be something we can do," I said.

Nate lifted his palms in surrender. "Tell you what, I'll offer to sit in with Harmony."

"Thank you," I said. When Olivia returned with Detective Cram, I shot a sharp glare at him and bit my tongue. Unleashing my jumbled thoughts wouldn't help my friend.

Nate greeted the detective and informed him he'd be providing Harmony counsel.

Detective Cram tipped his head. "You know which room. Olivia can buzz you in." With a widened stance and arms crossed in front of his chest, he turned to look at me.

"You may as well leave. We'll be keeping Ms. Santos for the foreseeable future." Cram turned his attention to Ciarán. "Are you here for Ms. Santos also?"

"I'll wait over there," Ciarán said. He strode to the visitor's lobby and seated himself.

"Why have you arrested Harmony?" I asked the detective in a calm voice.

"She's not under arrest," he said. "Yet."

"You caused quite a spectacle at the festival for someone who isn't under arrest."

The detective hissed out a breath. If he was trying to hide his irritation, he needed to try harder. "Something has come to our attention," he said with a note of resignation in his voice. "Bringing in witnesses is never convenient, especially when they resist."

"She's a witness, then? Not a suspect?" I searched the detective's eyes for answers.

"At this point in the investigation, there's little difference between the two." His stare didn't waver. "You should go on with whatever you have planned for the day."

My shoulders sagged as the truth of his words sank in. But knowing what it was like to be in his interrogation room, I felt terrible at the thought of leaving Harmony behind.

Without saying another word, I walked to the lobby and sat in a chair in the waiting area, across from where Ciarán sat. I leaned forward, resting my elbows on my knees.

"Today took an unexpected turn," Ciarán said in a low voice.

"It did." I looked up. Trying to lighten the mood, I said, "It seems you made it through your photo session. Do you get to end your modeling career now?"

The tips of Ciarán's ears reddened. "Photo booths aren't my thing. But as Harmony said, it's for a good cause." He paused, regarding me. "It seems *you* made a rather harrowing escape yourself."

"Thank goodness for Connor." I settled back into my chair. "We're donating our funds to provide food for the animal shelter."

Ciarán hesitated before nodding. "Aye. Then it's a good thing I endured. I can't bear the thought of hungry dogs and cats." He reached into his jacket pocket and pulled out a photo strip. With a chuckle, he handed it to me and said, "I guess I'm supposed to hang this on my refrigerator."

I skimmed the images. Harmony and Ciarán's goofy poses and expressions made it seem like photo booths were, indeed, his thing. He and Harmony had certainly been hamming it up behind the curtain. In one photo, Harmony and Ciarán looked at each other with wide, ear-to-ear grins. No barely-there smiles for Harmony, apparently. If I didn't know better, I'd think I was jealous. But that was absurd.

Mustering nonchalance, I met his gaze. "You should definitely hang it on your refrigerator. It looks like you were having fun."

He took the strip and glanced at it with a shrug before stuffing it back into his pocket. "Harmony has been a good friend to me."

"I'm supposed to be helping her," I said. "I'm afraid I'm not doing a very good job."

"I'm not sure what any of us can do," Ciarán replied.

Footsteps sounded in the hallway, and Nate appeared. "There's no sense waiting here," he said. "She could be here all night."

Ciarán's expression mirrored my surprise.

"You must be kidding," I said.

Nate shook his head. "Harmony is refusing counsel. She claims she doesn't need it."

"But…" I was incredulous. Surely Harmony was smarter than that.

"I can't force her to accept representation," Nate said. "Detective Cram went in to question her."

"But, how is she?" I remembered all too well what sitting across the table from Detective Cram was like. Having Nate by my side had gotten me through the ordeal. It was foolish to refuse help.

"When I left, she appeared to be meditating." Nate chuckled. "You know Harmony."

If I weren't so wound up, I might have found the image that came to mind amusing. Harmony, sitting cross-legged on the metal chair with lashes lowered, while Detective Cram questioned her. I could picture his bulging eyes and flared nostrils.

"We should go now." Nate turned to me. "But first, don't you have something you promised to hand over?"

It took me a moment to remember Iris's ledger. I dug into my backpack and retrieved the notebook. "I almost forgot." I handed it to Nate.

Nate turned to walk to the reception desk, and I was left sitting in the small waiting area with Ciarán. I attempted a smile.

"I've been meaning to ask you…" Ciarán sounded uncertain. "What I mean is, I've been wondering if you'd like to grab a coffee sometime." He seemed to sense my reluctance and added, "After the festival is over, of course. Perhaps next week?"

"Umm…" I crossed my arms over my chest in a defensive gesture that probably looked unfriendly. What was it about him that completely unsettled me? He was handsome, but handsome men were common enough. Most didn't make my heart race.

I wasn't ready. Not even for a cup of coffee. I uncrossed my arms and dropped my hands onto my lap, hoping to soften my refusal. "I don't think so," I said. "I really can't." It felt harsh to stop there, but surely I wasn't required to give a long, personal explanation about my husband's death and why I wasn't ready to date. There was nothing else to say.

"Oh." He paused. "Okay, then." He leaned back, drew his phone from his pocket, and shifted his attention to it.

Nate ended his conversation with Olivia and walked across the room. "I explained the ledger to Olivia. She'll make sure Detective Cram gets it."

Still shaken from my talk with Ciarán, I only nodded.

"Is everything okay?" Nate's glance skipped from me to Ciarán and back to me. "If it makes you feel better, I'll stop by the station in a couple of hours to check on Harmony."

"I'll be here," Olivia piped up. I turned to find her watching us. Again, I noticed her bright-eyed, pink-cheeked face and wondered at her obvious crush on my brother-in-law. Hadn't she gone to school with Nate and Alicia's twins? In fairness, even with the considerable age gap, Nate was crush-worthy, oblivious or not.

"Thanks, Olivia," Nate answered her before turning to look at Ciarán and me. "Let's head out."

I stood. "I guess there's no sense in staying."

"Go on without me," Ciarán said. "I think I'll wait a while."

"Harmony's not coming out anytime soon," Nate said to him.

"All the same." Ciarán crossed his ankle over his knee, avoiding me as he returned his attention to his phone.

As the door closed behind Nate and me, another one closed in my thoughts—the door I'd just shut in Ciarán's face. It was for the best. Stringing him along would be wrong. I was doing him a favor, really. Alicia's insistence that I should be ready to move on didn't make it so. Not that a cup of coffee was a real date or anything. Still. With so much going on, I had more than enough on my plate. I let out a long breath and gathered my thoughts. The truth was simpler. To start dating again meant shutting Dan out of my life. I couldn't do that.

I started walking, leaving all thoughts of Ciarán behind me. Nate kept pace as we strode back toward the village green. "What's the new information about Harmony?" I asked.

"She wasn't sure," Nate said. "Something about text messages between her and Iris."

"Text messages? Not that she was seen near the fountain when Iris was killed?"

"That's what Harmony said, but I don't think she knew for sure."

"I guess I'll have to wait to ask her." I headed back toward the festival to see how Jackson and Penny were doing with the camera equipment.

"Bobbie." Nate's voice sounded tired. "I can tell you have no intention of heeding my warning. It's only been an hour since someone tried to hurt you, and you're planning to forge ahead?"

I stopped walking. There was truth in what he said, but I was in danger, regardless. The only way to get back to safety was to find the killer. Since Detective Cram would be tied up with Harmony all afternoon, it wouldn't be him.

"All the more reason to find out who's behind this." My conviction was unshakable.

Chapter Twenty

When I returned to the photo booth, both Penny and Jackson were there, testing the cameras. Surprisingly, they seemed to work. With the walls back in place, we debated reopening the booth, but decided against it.

Jackson sidled up next to me. "So, Harmony is a suspect?"

"Not a suspect." I didn't appreciate the smugness in his voice. "She's being questioned for information."

"If you say so."

I was exhausted, and it was time to go home. I looked out over the festival and spotted River, Tallulah, and Saskia sitting on a blanket near the gazebo where a band was setting up for a concert. They seemed to have gathered everything needed for a picnic supper from the various food tents. I checked my watch. There was no one at the commune, and plenty of time before the camera club meeting.

After pulling my phone from my pocket, I typed a message to Rose.

Commune is empty. Can you get away?

Her response was immediate.

Perfect timing. Closing up the café. Ethan can handle it.

Through a series of texts, we agreed that Rose would pick me up on the sidewalk outside the Rosebud. I hoisted my backpack onto my shoulder and said goodbye to Penny and Jackson. "Don't forget, camera club meeting at seven."

After pushing my way through the throng and crossing Main Street, I found Rose waiting for me. "Bobbie!" she said as soon as I stepped into the car. "I heard you almost got crushed in the photo booth. Holy schmoly, what happened?"

"I'm still processing it." I clicked my seat belt. "Let's get out of here."

Rose pulled into the flow of traffic. "Did someone push the booth over on purpose? Did they know you were in there? How could they? Maybe we should back off."

I waited her out before speaking. "I don't think backing off will help. Whoever is doing this isn't going to stop."

Rose's cheeks puffed, but she kept her eyes on the road ahead. "Okay, so what's our plan?"

I laughed. "Like I devised a plan in five minutes?"

"You're sure no one's home?"

"They're sitting on a blanket with a spread of food and watching the band. We should be good."

"They didn't know about Harmony being arrested?" Rose asked.

"Not arrested," I said. "She's being questioned." I looked out the window. From the look of things, everyone in Stonebridge was on the village green. It'd been a beautiful day and promised to be a beautiful evening as well. With winter nearing, we all knew to soak up whatever sun we could.

"Don't you think it's screwy they aren't checking up on her?"

"It's possible they did." I lifted my phone to suggest they could have called or texted.

"Yeah, okay." Rose's hands gripped her steering wheel as cars wove in and out of traffic from the side streets, presumably looking for a place to park. "So, I think when we get there, our best strategy is to split the garden between us and take pictures. No way we'll remember everything."

"Good plan," I said. "We'll also need to be quick about it. We have our meeting tonight, remember?" I checked the time. We had less than two hours before we were expected at my house. I sent a text to Penny, asking her to set up for the meeting. If Emma wasn't home to let her in, Penny knew where I kept a spare key in the studio.

"Even without the meeting, we'll need to work fast," Rose said. "The sun will set soon, and it gets dark fast."

Rose turned onto Harmony's street, and I pointed out a small parking area near a trailhead where Rose's car would go unnoticed. After parking, we followed a narrow footpath that led directly to Harmony's backyard.

The garden was as neat as I remembered it. Wordlessly, Rose and I each chose opposite corners and started taking photos with our cell phones.

"Echinacea," Rose said as she snapped a photo. "Isn't that used for colds?"

"You're asking me? It sounds right, I guess." I leaned in to get a closer look at one of the plant stakes. "Foxglove. Why do I think foxglove is poisonous?"

"Because it is," Rose said. "Digitalis. It's used to regulate a heartbeat or something like that."

I snapped the photo. "Would you trust an herbalist to regulate your heartbeat?"

Rose stood, placing her hands on her hips. "Nope. Was Iris doing that? It seems dangerous."

"Agreed. Lots of people grow foxglove for its pretty flowers. Maybe Iris's is decorative." I moved to the next stake and snapped another photo. "Calendula. That's pretty benign, right?"

"Yes." Rose ran her hand over a plant before lifting her fingers to her face. "Lavender. Mmm. That smells good." She turned to me. "This is crazy. We're going to have lots of research to do."

The variety and volume of herbs overwhelmed me. Rose had a point. Even if we took pictures of every plant, what did we know about them? I could spend the entire evening on my computer, looking up information, and come away knowing only a fraction of what I needed to learn. I straightened, scanning the garden and the woods surrounding us. Nodding to the clump of hemp, I asked, "What do you think of CBD products?"

"They're super popular." Rose laughed. "Maybe I should sell CBD coffee."

"Something about the combination seems contradictory." The sun had dipped behind the forest. It hadn't set, but the light had dimmed to a pale gray. I inhaled the pot-scented air.

"CBD is totally legit," Rose said. "Pot, on the other hand. What if she had something going on the side?"

"Harmony said Iris was licensed. Besides, I got the impression Iris took her business seriously. I doubt she'd jeopardize it." I was starting to feel frustrated. "Is this going to help us?"

Rose stood. "What else can we do? I'm almost finished taking photos of this section."

"And I've taken pictures of all of these." I thumbed through the photos on my phone. There were too many to count. "I'm thinking we need her formulas." I shifted to look at the house. It wasn't that I wanted to break in, but having an album of plant photos felt inadequate.

"I bet they're in the house."

I nodded. "Unless she kept them on a computer."

"I don't know how to break into a computer," Rose said.

"Iris kept her sales ledger in a notebook." I kept staring at the house, wondering how hard it would be to get inside.

"True," Rose said. "If she were computerized, you'd think her sales records would be first."

"She's been doing this for several years." I didn't relish the idea of creeping around the old house, but conceded it was the only way to find what we wanted. "Should we take a quick peek?"

"I bet the door's unlocked." Rose walked across the garden toward the house.

"Stop," I said. "Do we want to do this?"

"What's the harm?" Rose asked. "We're not going to steal anything." She grasped the doorknob, twisted, and pushed the door open. "Voila!" I didn't need to see her eyes to know their twinkle. Always up for an adventure, Rose loved this kind of thing.

"Umm… okay…" I bit my lip. "But let's make it snappy. If we don't find anything, we bug out."

Inside, the kitchen smelled of fresh-baked rolls, coffee, and something more earthy. Patchouli, I thought. Pausing, I remembered when Harmony retrieved Iris's ledger for me. She'd gone through the door to my left. Presumably, Iris had an office or apothecary.

"This way." I led Rose down a narrow hallway. About halfway down, I peeked through an open door that led into a small room lined with shelves of jars. The scent of dried plants and flowers grew stronger. The breeze rattled a window, making the room feel forbidden.

"Wow." Rose's voice echoed my awe.

"Where to begin?" I'd never seen anything like it. It felt like stepping back in time, like entering a cross between an old-time pharmacy and a witch's lair.

Rose, who hadn't moved since entering the room, snapped out of her trance. "I'll put my phone on video and scan everything. You search for the formulas."

The room was tidy, with everything appearing to have its place. A large wooden desk took up the middle of the room. Its scratched surface showed years of use, but it was also bare. I walked over to a cupboard and opened it to survey its contents. Empty jars, measuring cups, and a scale. I closed the door and moved on to the next. More supplies, based on what I saw. The desk's file drawer was filled with bank statements, receipts, and tax records, but nothing that looked like formulas. As I prepared to move to open another drawer, I heard the kitchen door slam shut.

I stopped, my heart hammering in my chest. Rose must have heard it too, because she turned with a start, her mouth a circle. "Who?" she mouthed without making a sound.

A light came on in the hallway, adding a faint glow to the room. The wooden floor creaked with the sound of footsteps.

"Wait till I show Harmy and Lula," a little voice said. Saskia? What was she doing at home? Just minutes ago, she'd been picnicking with River and Tallulah.

Rose and I both turned, colliding and nearly knocking me off my feet. She grabbed my arm and pulled me to the floor. "Under here," she whispered.

The space beneath the desk was small, hardly large enough for one person, let alone two. Crouching, we squeezed ourselves into the tiny space, our arms and legs tangled together.

"No, Sassyfrass," a man's voice said. There was affection in the low, gruff voice, an endearing tone I wouldn't have associated with River.

Rose's eyes met mine, only inches apart. I shook my head, wordlessly expressing my confusion.

"But I want to show them," Saskia replied to her father with a stamp of her foot. It sounded close. Much too close.

"I said no," River said. "Remember what I told you about surprises? We keep them secret."

"Like at the big party?" Saskia asked.

"Yes, Sassyfrass," River said. "Like at the big party."

The relief in his voice put me on edge. I wondered if by *big party*, Saskia was referring to the masquerade. She was on the green that night. What sort of surprise did River need to keep secret? Before I could think about it, the quick sound of little footsteps came closer.

I jerked and hit my head on the underside of the desk. Without thinking, I followed the first bump with another when I lifted my hand to my head. In the otherwise quiet room, the knocks on the desk seemed to echo. Rose's finger shot to her pursed lips, shushing me.

"What was dat?" Saskia's footsteps came to a halt.

Rose grasped my hand, and we stared at each other, not daring to breathe. Although creepy, I was thankful for the dimming light. As long as Saskia didn't look under the desk, she wouldn't see us.

"What was what?" River asked.

"I heard a noise," Saskia said. "Come here, Daddy."

"What did I tell you about making up stories?" River's voice drew closer. Heavier footsteps stomped into the room. It was one thing to hide from a child, but being caught by River would be perilous. The footsteps stopped near the desk. "You know you're not supposed to be in here," River said.

I jolted, almost bumping my head again. For a second, I thought he was talking to me. But he couldn't possibly see through the solid wood of the desk. Letting my breath out slowly, I slouched back again.

"Mommy used to let me," Saskia whined. "Poppy needs her blankie. She's cold."

Rose's nails dug into my hand as she squeezed it. *Ow.* I tried to shake my hand from her grasp, but she wasn't letting go. Even over the pounding of my heart, the sound of Saskia's skipping seemed loud.

"Poppy is only a doll," River said. "She doesn't get cold."

"She does too," Saskia said.

"Fine. Grab the blanket and be quick. I'll get our jackets. Lula is waiting for us."

"I want my puffy pink one," Saskia said, her feet visible near the opening beneath the desk.

"Puffy pink, it is," River said. "No more stalling. Poppy's blanket is right over there. Go on now. Pick it up, and let's get going. We told Tallulah we'd only be gone a minute."

"Can't we just stay here?" Saskia stomped her foot.

"And miss the music? You know you love to dance."

The room was silent for a moment, and I didn't dare exhale.

"One, two…" Like a parent who didn't want to punish their child, River counted slowly but firmly.

I heard Saskia's feet scamper across the floor. "Got it," she said.

"Good girl." River sighed heavily. "Let's move along now."

The sound of their footsteps faded, and Rose's grip on my hand loosened. We both held our breath until we heard the kitchen door close.

"Holy cannoli," Rose said on a long exhale. "I thought we were goners." Her face broke into a wide smile before she crawled out from underneath the desk. "That was so much fun!"

I followed her, arching my back as I stood. "Sometimes I wonder how we can be such good friends when our ideas of fun are so different."

"You'll be laughing later," Rose said.

She might've been right, but my mind was still on our eavesdropping. "Did you hear what River said to Saskia?"

"About getting the doll's blanket? Totally understandable," Rose said.

"Not that," I said. "The part about their secrets. Do you think he's keeping something from Harmony and Tallulah?"

"It could be anything."

"Saskia wanted to show them something," I said.

"When Ethan was little, Travis used to buy him Hot Wheels whenever they went somewhere. Ethan was supposed to keep it a secret from me."

Rose snorted. "I guess Travis thought I wouldn't notice the sharp pain in my feet when I stepped on them."

"I guess it could be like that," I said. "Were they talking about the masquerade party?"

"It was a big party," Rose said.

"I don't like it. I'm going to tell Harmony."

"Won't that give us away?"

"I'll figure something out." Stopping to look around the now-dark room, I wondered where the formulas could be. "Did you get the video?"

Rose fumbled with her phone. "Yep. Should we keep looking?"

I glanced at my watch. "It's time to get back. Camera club meeting in fifteen."

"Whoa, how did it get so late so fast?" Rose asked. "It's just as well. In the dark, this place is totally giving me the creeps."

"Yeah." A chill ran down my spine. "I'm not sure our pictures will help. But we learned River is keeping things from Harmony and Tallulah. We need to find out what that's about."

Chapter Twenty-One

As we drove back to my house, I couldn't stop thinking about River's secrets. What—besides Iris being murdered—happened at the big party and was secret-worthy? I was still puzzling things out when Rose pulled her car into her driveway.

After a quick walk across our front yards, we entered my house to the sound of Penny setting up for our meeting. Darcy ambled into the foyer to greet me, but seemed more interested in whatever was happening in the kitchen, and he soon retreated. Notably absent were Harmony and Alicia.

"So glad you could join us," Penny said with a smile that hinted she was only joking. "Were you checking up on Harmony?"

"Something like that," I said.

"I can't believe Detective Cram." She gave her tongue ring a couple of loud taps.

"It must have been quite the scene," Rose said.

"It really was," I agreed. I turned to see Emma enter, carrying a fresh pitcher of iced tea from the kitchen. Across the room, Jackson sat calmly on the couch, stuffing a huge chunk of muffin into his mouth. It wasn't that I thought he was glad Harmony had been hauled to the police barracks, but I couldn't forget his earlier self-satisfied comment about her being a suspect.

Penny placed the memory cards we'd given her on the table next to my laptop and said, "Fortunately, Harmony gave me her card when we were at the photo booth. I have everyone's, except for Alicia's. She texted to say she'll be here soon."

"Let's get started," I said. "It's been a busy day. I'm sure you all have something you'd rather be doing tonight."

"Yeah, like sipping a glass of wine with my feet up," Rose said. "The café was a madhouse all day."

"Alrighty." Penny inserted a card and projected images from the masquerade party. We sat quietly, studying them as they appeared one after another on my wide-screen TV. Occasionally, one of us would ask Penny to go back to the previous image, but we found nothing amiss.

After reaching the last image on a card, Penny ejected it and inserted the next. The pictures on the screen took me back to the party. I could hear the sound of the band and feet stomping on the makeshift dance floor. I remembered how amazed I'd been by the creative costumes and the many cheerful smiles. As the kickoff of the much-anticipated festival, it was supposed to have been a fun evening.

We'd viewed four of the five cards, and a sigh escaped me. My eyes felt tired as I watched images flicker on the screen. It didn't seem possible that it had only been two nights since Iris was killed. Also beyond belief, Harmony was being held at the police station. I'd failed her.

"Last card," Penny said as she inserted it into the computer. She flashed through the remaining images, and I was convinced this was a useless exercise.

"Hold on. Go back." Jackson's voice broke through my mental fog. "What's that?" He stood and pointed as he walked toward the screen.

My jaw dropped when I noticed what Jackson was pointing to.

From the other end of the couch, Rose groaned. "He just can't get out of his own way."

"Wait, are these my photos?" I asked. "I'm surprised I overlooked this when I reviewed them."

Penny shrugged. "That's why we're doing this."

"Good eye, Jackson." I moved in closer. "What, exactly, is Travis doing?"

Rose groaned again. "Who knows what he does? It looks like he's dropping a capsule into the drink."

"It's sure not a garnish," Jackson said.

I tried to remember what had been happening when I snapped the picture.

Nate and Alicia were standing at the bar chatting with one of Nate's many cousins. Travis was behind them, his hand and whatever he'd dropped into the drink were blurred by the aperture setting I used to create the shallow depth-of-field. Jackson was right. There had been apple slices in the cider, but whatever Travis was dropping into the drink was no piece of fruit.

"Only a few more images on this card," Penny said.

I nodded for her to continue. The image of Travis had perked me up. I was so engrossed in studying the pictures that I didn't hear my front door open.

"Sorry I'm late." Alicia handed her memory card to Penny with one hand while balancing a foil-covered casserole dish in the other. "Mom is going to pop this in the oven."

My glance flitted between my mother and sister, trying to dig up any hint that might remind me of making plans for the evening. The scent of whatever tasty concoction Alicia was holding seemed to have reached Darcy's nose. He appeared by her side, his snout pointed at the casserole dish.

"Sorry, Darce." Alicia rubbed my dog's head. "This one isn't for you."

"Hello, darling," my mother said. "We haven't had the chance to spend time together, so I thought this evening would be nice. Alicia was gracious enough to provide us with dinner."

"Oh." It seemed I was spending the evening with my mother. Unsure how I felt about my new plans, I forced a smile. "Make yourself at home. We're almost done."

"Hey, Gran." Emma entered from the kitchen, appearing excited by the unexpected visit. "Come on back." My mother took the casserole from Alicia and followed Emma out of the room.

"Okay, where were we?" I returned my attention to the meeting while Alicia slipped onto the couch.

"All we have left are Alicia's photos." Penny inserted the card and clicked on the first one.

It didn't take long to view the pictures Alicia had taken. Nothing about them, except for the terrible close-up of me, captured our attention the same way the image of Travis had. Penny suggested she keep the memory cards for the time being, and she handed out new ones. I suspected something was churning in her mind, and I trusted her instincts.

"Sync the photo of Travis to the cloud," I said, unable to hide the heaviness in my voice. "I'll need to send it to Detective Cram."

"Shouldn't someone talk to Travis first?" Rose asked. "But to be clear, I don't want it to be me."

"I'll do it," I said, my mind conjuring images of another sparring match with Rose's ex. "We can do both."

"What do you need to talk to Travis about?" Alicia asked.

We explained the photo showing Travis dropping a capsule into a drink.

"Okay, but am I missing something?" Alicia asked. "Even if Iris was drugged—and we don't know that yet—doesn't Travis have an alibi for her murder? The only way this works is if he was in cahoots with someone."

Alicia had a point. "I admit it seems unlikely. The way Iris was killed doesn't suggest that kind of pre-planning. But the picture looks suspicious, and it merits a follow-up."

"Freakin' fantastic." Rose puffed out a breath.

"Okay, let's check it out," Alicia said. "What else are we doing to help Harmony?"

"Do you have any ideas?" I asked.

"I could stop at the police barracks on my way home," Alicia offered. "There's always a slight chance they'll let me talk to her."

"Good idea," Rose said. "Detective Cram can't stand Bobbie, but he might let you in. I'll keep working on cracking the code in Iris's ledger."

"I have to admit, I was hoping we'd find something revealing tonight," I said. "I'll follow up with Travis and see where it leads. I can also touch base with Nate; he seems to have contacts inside the police." I had my suspicions about his contacts, but I kept them to myself.

"Better you than me," Alicia agreed. "It's best to keep him in the dark about my involvement."

Penny lifted her bag. "I'll review all the photos again when I'm in the studio tomorrow."

CHAPTER TWENTY-ONE

"What about me?" Jackson brushed a crumb from his chin.

I thought about my failed mission to get hold of Iris's formulas. "Any chance you have access to Iris's apothecary?"

"What do you have in mind?" Jackson asked.

I told him about our efforts to decipher Iris's ledger. "I wish I had her formulas."

Jackson's brow furrowed. "Too bad you didn't just ask Harmony. But sure, I can tell River I left something behind—or something like that."

Too bad, indeed. At least we had something to propel our investigation forward. "Let's all keep our eyes open and cameras focused. If you discover anything, text the group or post it to our Facebook group along with your photos for the prompts."

"Great job on the scavenger hunt, by the way," Rose said. "Especially Jackson. You're killing it with your interpretation of the prompts. My favorite is the one where you caught everyone dancing at the wine and cheese party. I could almost hear the music!" Before allowing Jackson to preen too much, she turned to me. "Everyone has posted photos except for you."

"Sorry," I said. "I've done most of the prompts—*Sparkling, Motion, Tradition,* and *Silhouette.*" After a year-long respite from social media, reactivating my accounts was a big step. Actually posting something would be another tremendous leap.

"Then post them already." Rose wasn't letting up.

I resisted the urge to sigh. "Will do." I gave a quick salute before changing the subject. "At our next meeting, we'll learn about masking."

Without looking up, Penny said, "Masking? Cool. I don't know what that is, but I'd like to help you set it up."

"It's an editing technique," I said. "Basically, masking is a way to apply edits to a photo selectively. I'll be happy to go over it with you in more detail later." I was tired. The day had been emotionally draining, to say the least.

As the members rose to leave, my thoughts shifted to my mother, who was waiting for me in the kitchen. I'd been looking forward to relaxing and maybe studying Iris's ledger again. Instead, it seemed I'd be hosting Fiona. I could only imagine what she had in store for me.

Chapter Twenty-Two

No sooner had the front door closed behind my club members than Emma walked through the room to grab her jacket and say a quick goodbye before rushing out the door. Plans with Connor, it seemed. Alicia left with the others, claiming the festival was wearing her ragged. She'd made a date with a bathtub full of bubbles and a scented candle from Hazel and Bee.

I met my mother's eye as she entered the room, Darcy on her heels. She stood, nearly as tall as I, with a confident posture that showed no signs of surrendering to age. I admired her, even as she intimidated me.

"It's you and me, darling." Her voice held a hint of amusement. She appeared to be enjoying the discomfort I was doing a poor job of hiding. "Your new home is thoroughly charming." Her gaze swept my living room.

"Thanks?" I hadn't intended my response to be a question. I gave myself a mental shake. "Let me show you around." My home was small and simple, nothing like the Beacon Hill townhouse I'd grown up in, with all its many levels and heavy antique furniture. There wasn't much to show, so I swept my arm in a wide circle, feeling somewhat embarrassed. "Well, this is my home."

"Yes, I can see that," my mother said. "It looks like you."

Small and simple? I let out another sigh and forced a smile. "Thanks?" This time, I meant it as a question.

"Yes, darling. Your home has a lovely open feel to it. It's bright and airy with cheerful pops of color and meaningful mementos scattered about." She strode to the fireplace and lifted my favorite photo of Dan and Emma from the mantle. Her eyes met mine. "Your home has a lot of heart."

"Oh…" I closed my mouth before my jaw could make good on its threat of dropping to the floor. "Thank you."

I didn't need to look at the picture in my mother's hand. I'd memorized every pixel. It was a photo from a happier time, one I'd snapped of Dan and Emma horsing around on the beach. Taken the summer before Dan died, it was one of the last carefree days we'd had as a family, a rare day when we'd all played hooky from everyday life.

Tears threatened, and I turned toward the kitchen before my mother noticed. The delicious aroma of whatever Alicia had prepared filled my kitchen. Chicken and mushrooms with garlic, herbs, and goat cheese, if I were to guess. I squared my shoulders and gave my cheek a quick swipe.

"I'm guessing dinner needs a bit more time in the oven. Why don't I give you the rest of the tour?" I gestured for my mother to follow me.

After a quick trip to view the two upstairs bedrooms, one of which looked like a tornado had blown through, tossing Emma's clothes everywhere, I suggested we head out to my studio behind the house. I was proud of my barn-turned-photography studio. The barn itself was nothing special. It had likely been built so a family could keep a horse and carriage for transportation, and possibly a cow for milk. Much smaller than the dairy barn at Crowley Farm, this was a barn for a family who lived in town. As I unlocked the door, I pointed to the flower bed along the side of my studio. Last spring, I'd learned the first rule of gardening: weeds are relentless. Many hours I'd spent kneeling in the mud, nearly pulling my back out, along with the unwanted vegetation.

"It's not much yet," I said. "Alicia is helping me plant a perennial garden here. Someday, I hope to use it as a backdrop for photos. For now, I take my clients to Alicia's farm. She has beautiful gardens."

My mother chuckled. "It amazes me how your sister took to farming."

"I know, right?" I laughed. "I doubt I'll ever love gardening the way she does, but I'm learning." I gave my mother a playful nudge. "And you always thought Alicia was the more city-savvy sister."

"You were both much too savvy for your own good. How a daughter of mine—now both daughters—wound up in Vermont is beyond me." Her voice sounded cross, but a playful glimmer danced in her eyes.

I opened my studio's door and flipped on the lights. "Welcome to my new photography studio."

My mother's appraising gaze swept through the space. Once dark and dusty, the old barn had new windows to fill it with natural light. Near the door, I'd created a small sitting area for clients where they could browse through albums of my work. Penny's desk faced the front and was tidy, with papers organized in trays. Behind it, she kept a shelf of toys and baby blankets for days when she needed to bring Hope to work. There was studio space, too, hidden behind a closed door at the far end of the room.

I loved my new studio. It wasn't until my mother murmured her approval that my body began to relax. I hadn't realized how much it meant to me.

"This was once an old barn." Amazement sounded in her voice. "You've done a wonderful job with it." She scanned the studio once more, glancing up at my loft-office, then turned on her heel. "We'd best check on Alicia's chicken."

Again, my mother had left me speechless. A slow smile spread across my face as I flicked off the lights, closed the door, and locked it. Walking across the patio to my kitchen, I tried to imagine the evening ahead. Maybe being alone with my mother wouldn't be so difficult after all.

A mouth-watering aroma greeted us when we entered the kitchen. Lying in front of the oven, Darcy guarded our dinner. I praised him for his successful efforts. Seemingly satisfied, he ambled over to the table, where he settled on the floor. He was no dummy.

Fiona opened the oven. "The casserole is bubbling. I suppose that means it's ready?"

"I think so?" I was surprised my mother was as clueless as I was. "Let's set it on the stove while I make a salad."

"That sounds lovely." She rummaged through my utensil drawer and pulled out a corkscrew. "Meanwhile, how about a glass of wine while I set the table?"

"I have a bottle chilling in the fridge." I pretty much always had a bottle in the refrigerator, but I didn't need to tell her that. I handed her the bottle while rummaging for ingredients for a tossed salad. My mother opened the wine and poured a glass for each of us.

"It's a good thing Alicia is such a wonderful cook," I said, laughing. "If it were left to me, this salad would be all we'd have to eat."

My mother set the plates on the table. "I suppose you get that from me. I can just about boil myself an egg." She chuckled. Then, probably noting my surprise, she added, "Surely you don't have any memories of me in the kitchen. Why do you think we had Mrs. O'Toole?"

"I figured you were too involved with your charity work," I said.

"That too." My mother's voice was dismissive. "I can't help it, but I've always admired your lack of interest in cooking. It was like you refused to conform to gender roles. From what I could tell, Dan didn't mind." My mother's eyes lit with her wicked smile. "It makes me believe I've done something right."

I lifted my wineglass, lost in thought. All my life, I'd put my mother on a pedestal. To be sure, she was a smart woman with a commanding presence. Even after moving to Florida, she kept her leadership roles on several charitable foundations, working tirelessly as an advocate for victims of domestic abuse. When Fiona Sullivan spoke, people listened. It didn't hurt that my father had been an influential attorney, but my mother never needed coattails to ride on. Born into a working-class family of nine and raised by an alcoholic father and overwrought mother, she earned her way through Radcliffe College with a combination of scholarships, smarts, and hard work. It never occurred to me that there was something she couldn't do.

I clinked my wineglass with hers. "To women who don't cook." My grin spread from ear to ear. "I've always wanted to take after you in *some* way."

With a tilt of her head, she placed her glass on the table. "It's true, you've always been more like your father. You remind me so much of him," she said. "Always leading with your emotions. I suppose that's why you insist on getting involved in these murder investigations. You have a deep-seated need to set things right."

"That's not true." I let out a nervous laugh, knowing deep down it was true. I could tell myself I was getting involved because Harmony had asked me to, but I knew better. The image of Iris's limp body filled my mind. She hadn't deserved whatever happened to her. Neither did Saskia.

My mother's somber expression made it clear she wasn't buying my denial. "Tell me about the young woman who was so brutally killed."

In a gush, I spilled everything—Iris's upcoming trip to France and her relationships with Jackson and River. I voiced my worries about Emma finding Iris's body and the confused atmosphere of the masquerade party. I mentioned the ledger and the possible connection with Gino. I'd almost forgotten about him and how he clammed up like he was hiding something.

With hesitation, I told her about being chased home from the hospital, about hearing River tell Saskia to keep something secret while being stuck beneath the desk, and then nearly being discovered. Throughout my monologue, we worked side by side before sitting down to eat. Between bites of Alicia's delicious chicken dish and sips of the cool, crisp wine, my mother listened and offered insights. She was the perfect sounding board for my spilled thoughts, helping me dig more deeply than my hectic day had allowed. When I finished, I was both drained and energized.

"I have to say, this camera club of yours sounds more like a detective club." My mother set her fork on her empty plate with a clink.

"We're learning about photography, too," I said, trying to keep the defensiveness out of my voice. A glint of mischief played in my mother's eyes, and I relaxed. I'd always felt her judgment, but maybe I had it wrong.

"I'm sure you're aware of what my instincts tell me." My mother's words broke through my haze.

I nodded absentmindedly. Her experience with victims of domestic abuse would lead her to think of Iris's partners, both current and former. Then, with a shake of my head meant to clear my mind, I asked, "But which one? River or Jackson?"

"I'm uncomfortable with a little girl keeping secrets." I could almost see the gears turning in my mother's mind. "Do you think she's in danger?"

I thought for a moment, then shook my head. "It didn't seem that way. If it had, I would have confronted River." There was obvious affection between him and his daughter. My thoughts shifted to his secret. "But what if the big party he was referring to was the masquerade party, and River did something the police should know about? What if Saskia saw whatever it was, and she's keeping it secret?"

"That doesn't sound like much of a surprise."

"I'm sure he wouldn't hurt Iris in front of Saskia." This was something I didn't question for a minute.

My mother seemed to mull over my words. "You're sure the young woman was planning to take her daughter abroad?"

"Pretty sure," I said, remembering Iris's deliveries that afternoon. "If she changed her mind, it would have been at the very last minute."

"That gives River a powerful motive." My mother sipped her wine.

"Definitely," I said. "I have to consider Tallulah, too. I have a feeling she's got a crush on River."

It took my mother a moment to answer. "Wasn't Iris already involved with the man she was planning her trip with?"

She was, which made Tallulah's motive weak. I wasn't ready to dismiss it entirely.

"All this talk about murder makes me worry about you," my mother said. "You've been threatened twice now. Considering how truly horrendous your roads are, I'm amazed they failed."

I scoffed. Long winding roads without traffic lights every few feet were what my mother considered horrendous.

"This isn't a laughing matter, Bobbie Ann. While it might be intriguing to solve a puzzle, you should leave the legwork to the police.

Uh-oh, Bobbie Ann... My mother meant business. No matter, I couldn't let whatever happened to Iris go.

"So like your father. Passionate to a fault." She shook her head. "I miss him every day."

Thoughts of Iris's death faded as I noticed my mother's wistful tone. "How do you do it?" My voice dropped to a whisper. "How do you live with missing him?"

"One day at a time," my mother said. "It's been more than five years, and I take it day by day."

Those dreaded, always-ready tears of mine surfaced, and I looked at my mother with bleary eyes. There was so much I wanted to ask her. We'd never had that kind of relationship, though.

"I'm so sorry this happened to you." My mother's low voice soothed me. "To receive a call at work informing you that your husband had collapsed is unthinkable. You're far too young to be a widow."

I lifted my shoulders in a weak shrug. "Aneurysms don't care about age," I said. "Are you ever afraid you'll forget Dad?"

She shook her head and gave my hand another squeeze. "Never. Just as you'll never forget Dan." My mother's smile was soft. "All you need to do is look at Emma."

I brushed my cheek and sniffed. "Everyone seems to think I should be ready to move on. That I should start dating." I paused. "But I'm so afraid I'll lose Dan." It was a thought I'd hardly admitted to myself. It felt good to let it out.

"I hope you'll date again." Although my mother spoke in a gentle tone, there was a firmness in her voice. "When you're ready."

I couldn't imagine ever being ready, regardless of a certain green-eyed man who crept into my thoughts unbidden. "What about you? Will you date again?"

My mother let go of my hand, and her devilish smile returned. "What makes you believe I don't?"

"Really?" The easy way she'd formed a friendship with my neighbor was surprising, but that wasn't the same as dating.

Her hand waved, dismissing my surprise. "Nothing more than a bit of fun, darling. Male companionship is enjoyable from time to time. I may be old, but I'm not dead yet."

Oh...*Oh!* I snapped my mouth shut. Something in her expression warned me not to think, not even for one second, about what she meant by *a bit of fun.* Sure, my mother, with her upright posture and active lifestyle, was young for her seventy-plus years. Even so—*TMI.* I observed her—her stylish blouse and jeans, her expertly streaked silver-blonde hair, and understated makeup. She was beautiful. "You've never seemed old," I said finally.

"Thank you for that," she said. "And neither are you. Being a widow is something you'll always carry, but you have to remember it's not *who* you are. You have a lot of life to live, and I firmly believe Dan would want you to."

I couldn't help groaning. "Now you sound like Alicia. She said something similar…something about being a widow not defining me."

"Did she?" My mother chuckled. "Alicia is smart, but she doesn't know everything. She knows nothing about losing a husband, and thank goodness."

Losing Nate would be devastating for all of us. "I'm really glad you came over tonight."

"So am I." She gave my shoulder a squeeze before standing to carry her plate to the sink.

Darcy, who'd been lying quietly during our dinner, got up to follow us. I picked a couple of morsels of chicken from my plate and handed them to him. Although I tried not to feed him from the table—and was mostly successful—I couldn't deny him the treat. I wasn't sure he even tasted the food, but he seemed appreciative.

With a raised eyebrow, my mother watched me as I fed Darcy. "He's been such a good boy, I almost forgot he was lying on my feet." She bent to pat Darcy's head. "And now, I must leave you. I promised your next-door neighbor I'd stop by."

I blinked. "Mr. Miller?" Pushing thoughts of male companionship aside, I suppressed a shudder and walked my mother to the front door.

Fiona stopped my spinning thoughts with a pointed stare. "Don't be silly, Bobbie Ann. I just met the man. He's lovely to chat with. He tells such charming stories about growing up in Stonebridge. Woodchucks, swimming holes, and sleeping under the stars. This village of yours is a whole different world."

I laughed. "I don't think he's talking about woodchucks, as in the animal." Vermonters with several generations of Vermont ancestry wore the term like a badge of honor.

"No, I rather got the impression he was referring to himself. Quite proudly, I might add." She raised her eyebrows as though bewildered. "Like I said, a whole different world. I'll probably visit with him for an hour or so before I retire to my beautiful room at the inn."

"The rooms at the Mill House are as nice as they say? It just reopened over the summer."

"It's lovely," my mother said. She put on her jacket and gave me a quick wink as she left.

Pulling Darcy's leash off a hook, I said, "Just a quick walk tonight. I've got a long night ahead—lots of plants that need researching."

Chapter Twenty-Three

I had just put on my pajamas and was about to crawl into bed with my computer and the photos of Iris's ledger when my phone buzzed. It was Rose.

Fascinating stuff. Lots of poisonous herbs.

So Rose was doing the same thing I was. I texted back.

I was just about to get started

A thought occurred to me, and I shot off a second text.

Want to research together? I have an open bottle of rosé

Rose's response was immediate.

You sure know how to tempt a girl

I'm in my PJs

I laughed as I gazed at myself in the mirror. No makeup. Hair wound into a messy topknot. Rainbow unicorn pajamas.

Me too - Pajama party

I watched the dots wave across my phone's screen until her message appeared.

On my way

By the time I'd taken my computer back downstairs and poured two glasses of wine, Rose's voice called from my open front door. "Hey, you. This is going to be so much more fun than doing it alone."

I handed my friend a glass of wine while trying to suppress a laugh. Only Rose would wear fuzzy, bright pink, footed pajamas, covered with smiling monkeys.

"Do those have a drop—" I couldn't finish the sentence without bursting into laughter.

"A drop seat?" Rose's eyes twinkled. "You're covered in unicorns, and you're laughing at me?"

"Good point," I said, still laughing. I locked the front door, and we moved to the living room where we sank into my comfy couches.

"How'd your evening with Fiona go?" Rose's nose crinkled.

"Amazingly well. We had a fantastic conversation." I couldn't get over it. There'd been no criticism of my move to Vermont, which I knew she considered a bad decision, not to mention impulsive. But then, she wasn't entirely wrong about the second part. I felt like we'd had a breakthrough, and part of me wondered if our lack of closeness was my fault rather than hers.

"Really?" Rose's widened eyes reflected the surprise in her voice. "I've always been curious about Emma and your sister being so close to her."

"Oh, you know, Alicia and Fiona are two peas in a pod. And Emma…" I paused. "She and my mother are nothing alike, really, but Emma's the granddaughter. My mother dotes on her in a way she never doted on Alicia or me."

"I'm so relieved it went okay. I felt terrible leaving after our meeting. Seriously, Bobbie, your mother has presence. She's wicked intimidating."

"Any news about Harmony?" I asked.

"Did you see the latest post in the Stonebridge Scandal?"

I groaned. "You know I don't read that."

"You really should," Rose said. "It can be super entertaining."

"Hard pass." I sipped my wine.

"Anyway, it claims that Harmony's whole new-age persona must be a ruse for her murderous temperament. Their words, definitely not mine."

"Poor Harmony. I know how that feels." I thought back to when Detective Cram led her into an interrogation room. She'd seemed calm, which had nothing to do with her persona being a ruse.

Rose opened her computer. "This is what I have so far."

"I'm listening." Next to me, Darcy crawled onto the couch, and after a few turns and a loud groan, he settled into a big yellow ball. I stroked his fur.

"So, echinacea," Rose said after waiting for Darcy to settle. "It turns out, it's not only good for colds, but it's used for sore throats, burns, and toothaches. And Saint John's Wart? It helps with insomnia and depression. I mean, who knew?"

"Okay, but what about adverse effects?" I asked. "If someone was angry enough to kill over a supplement, something must have gone wrong."

"Well, in the article I read, some people reported stomach aches and dizziness. Not much of a reason to kill anyone." Rose paused. "Oh, but wait. You know the video I made of Iris's jars? There was a jar of nightshade. That stuff is way toxic. Like, deadly toxic."

"Nightshade? I've heard of it. Are there any non-toxic uses for it?"

"Maybe, but I haven't found any," Rose said. "How about I do more research on it while you look up digitalis?"

"On it," I said.

"When do you plan to talk to Travis?" Rose asked as she tapped her keyboard.

My screen filled with search results. Distractedly, I said, "Tomorrow morning, I guess. He'll probably be at the festival for closing ceremonies."

"I can't see Travis poisoning anyone," Rose said. "And, so far, this nightshade stuff is looking worse and worse. So deadly."

"Travis's alibi for Iris's murder is rock solid." I clicked one of the search results for digitalis, then looked across the coffee table to where Rose lounged on the couch opposite mine. "Unless we can connect Travis with a murderer, I think he'll be a dead end. But whatever he was putting in that drink, it sure looked suspicious."

"I wonder how Alicia made out at the police barracks," Rose said. "Is there any chance Detective Cram allowed her to talk to Harmony?"

"I'm guessing no, but thanks for reminding me that I need to ask her about it." I stopped talking to read the information on my computer screen.

"Find anything good?" Rose asked.

"This confirms what we already suspected. Digitalis—or foxglove—messes with a person's heartbeat. It says here it's used for conditions such as congestive heart failure or heart rhythm problems. If dosed improperly, it causes abnormal heartbeat, nausea, and confusion." I stopped reading and looked at Rose. " I wonder why Iris grew it in her garden. Surely she wasn't using it in her supplements."

"Good question," Rose said. "I'll look up valerian."

"I'll take elderberry."

We continued researching and chatting for another hour, refilling our wine glasses as we worked. The list was long. Chamomile, feverfew, ginkgo, ginseng, goldenseal, saw palmetto, milk thistle, and more. The range of ailments they were said to treat was even broader. Asthma, nausea, inflammation, sex drive, tinnitus, sleeplessness, anxiety, energy… And, they all seemed to have reported side effects ranging from mild headaches or stomach upset to heart attacks. I couldn't imagine how Iris learned everything she knew.

Rose yawned. "We'd better pack it up. I'll try to look up a few more herbs tomorrow."

"We're learning a lot, but without Iris's recipes, it will be almost impossible to track the side effects to a specific customer."

"Hopefully Jackson can get his hands on them." Rose yawned again, stretching as she stood. "Thanks for the wine. This was way more fun than researching alone."

"I'm glad you came over." I walked her to the front door and stood on my porch to watch her scurry across our lawns to the safety of her home.

* * *

The next morning, I rolled out of bed to find the sun streaming through my open curtains and chickadees chirping sweetly in the tree outside my window. Emma's bedroom door was shut, and the house had the calm, early morning stillness I'd finally learned to love after more than a year of living alone.

While getting dressed, my mind wandered back to the night before. First, there was my surprising evening with my mom. Then, I'd learned more about herbs than I thought possible, but I still felt like I knew nothing. When

I'd finally dropped into bed, I fell into a deep sleep.

Lost in thought, I walked to the kitchen, where Darcy whined at the door. I let him out and made myself a cup of coffee. Next door at The Rosebud, caffeine-seekers were already spilling out the doorway and heading toward the village green with to-go cups in hand.

After letting Darcy back in and pouring my coffee into a thermal mug, I walked to the front door to grab my jacket and backpack. Tail wagging, Darcy pulled his leash down and looked up at me with eyes that made me melt. "Not today, buddy," I said, my heart breaking as he dropped his leash and plopped down on the floor with a beleaguered moan. Not risking a backward glance, I walked outside feeling contrite.

Sipping my coffee as I went, I walked straight to Alicia's market. If there were any news about Harmony, she'd have heard it. Gossip flew through her market at a speed rivaling social media, and with Alicia mediating, it was somewhat more credible. I wasn't buying the story about Harmony hiding murderous intent behind her new age serenity.

"Hey, Sis," I called as I entered the shop. The Stonebridge Country Market was undeniably the heart of the village. Despite the many modern updates, entering Alicia's market felt like stepping back in time. In rural Vermont, country stores served the community's every need from groceries to baked goods, and from clothing to farming supplies. Crammed aisles brimmed with an array of boxed and canned goods. In another corner, sweatshirts, mittens, and woolen caps were piled high on tables with boxes of snow boots stashed beneath. But it wasn't the merchandise that transported me so much as the aromas of aged wood mingling with the spicy-sweet scent of cinnamon rolls cooling on the bakery counter.

From behind the cash register, Alicia looked at me with one eyebrow raised. "How did it go with Mom last night?"

"Not bad," I said. I wasn't in the mood for an *I told you so*, so I got to the point of my visit. "Did you get to talk to Harmony?"

The corner of Alicia's mouth lifted. "What do you think?"

"It was worth a try," I said. "Have you heard anything new? Other than the nonsense in the Scandal, that is."

"I heard it was late when Cram let Harmony go. Unfortunately, that's all I know. People seem to be eating up the story about her false persona. They don't truly believe it. It's all just fun to them."

I scoffed at the idea of finding gossip fun. I stepped aside as a customer approached the counter with a basket of goods. Alicia lifted her cherry-red reading glasses from the chain around her neck. With quick, efficient motions, she poked the buttons on the cash register while boxing the items.

"Have a great rest of your day," she said to the customer as they lifted their box from the counter. Turning back to me, she said, "The festival's closing ceremony starts soon."

"I'm surprised you aren't there."

"I'm leaving now. Hopefully, we'll find Harmony there." She pressed the bell on her counter, signaling for one of her clerks to step in.

As if summoned, the door swung open, and Harmony walked inside.

Alicia's glance slid from Harmony to me. "I'll see you there," she said as she slipped out the door.

Harmony pulled me to a side aisle. "I'm so glad I found you." Her hair was smooth and shiny, and she looked amazing for someone who'd spent most of the night at the police station.

"I'm so relieved to see you," I said. "When did they let you go?"

"Last night," she said. "I wasn't under arrest, but oh man, Detective Cram was relentless. He kept asking the same questions repeatedly."

"Tell me about it," I replied. "What did he want to know?"

"Someone claimed to see me near the fountain shortly before Iris was killed," Harmony said. "Their timing must be off."

"Did he say who saw you?"

"That's the problem." Her expression tightened. "He said he needs to protect his sources."

Not for the first time, I had the feeling Harmony was being evasive. "You know how I feel about Detective Cram, but I can't help thinking there's more to this. Even he wouldn't keep you that long over something so iffy. "

Harmony sucked in air. "Text messages." She paused, gathering her thoughts. "The police have Iris's phone, and they read all her messages.

We have a group chat—River, Iris, Tallulah, and me."

I waited a moment for her to keep going. When she didn't, I couldn't hide my exasperation. "And?"

"He claimed some of them were incriminating. It's truly absurd."

My patience was wearing thin. "If I'm going to help you, I'll need you to tell me everything."

"You're right." She blinked. "One of River's messages may have sounded intimidating. He wasn't happy about Iris taking Saskia to France. Any parent could understand that. He said something to the effect that there was no way he'd let Iris take her."

Words I never thought I'd say came out of my mouth. "I'm going to have to agree with Detective Cram on this one. That sounds pretty incriminating."

"You don't know River," Harmony said. "He's rough around the edges, but he certainly didn't mean he wanted to kill Iris. Did the camera club photos show anything?"

I lacked Harmony's confidence in her housemate, but hounding her wouldn't get us anywhere. I told her about the photo showing Travis dropping something into a drink and explained that I planned to talk to him about it.

"I don't get it," Harmony said. "What do you suspect him of doing?"

"Nothing yet," I admitted. "We know he didn't kill Iris, but what if he was helping someone?" I rubbed my temple. "This whole thing has me running in circles."

Harmony nodded. "I wish we could get to the bottom of it. Detective Cram's aura made me uncomfortable. It was such a dark shade of purple, it was almost black. Obviously, he wants to solve this case. All I want is to clear my housemates and get justice for Iris."

"Agreed." I checked my watch. "I'd better run. Closing ceremonies are starting soon, and I need to be there to take photos." As well as questioning Travis, hopefully for the last time.

Chapter Twenty-Four

No sooner had I stepped onto the sidewalk than I ran into Nate. He appeared to be coming from the police barracks, but he could have simply parked his car in the area. "You look like you're in a different world," he said.

"You know me." I gave him an impish grin. "Head's always in the clouds."

"Ha," he guffawed. "If that's where it was, I wouldn't worry. But we both know your head is where it shouldn't be. What has my intrepid sister-in-law stuck her nose into so early in the day?"

With an upward tilt of my chin, I sniffed. "I'll share if you do."

He raised his brow. "Let's hear it."

I told him about the photo of Travis, River's threatening text message, and overhearing him ask Saskia to keep a secret. What I didn't tell him was where I was when I was eavesdropping. If he didn't ask, there was no reason to share. "Are any of these things important?"

"It's possible. It would be a leap to assume Travis had an accomplice. What would his motive be?" He paused as a voice echoed over the speaker system on the green. "Let's walk," he said. "The closing festivities are about to start. Alicia and I were nominated for the costume contest, and she'll have my head if I'm not there."

I laughed along with his joke, sure he wasn't at all worried about his head. As pushy as my sister could be, Nate was meeting his wife out of respect, not fear. With his hand on my elbow, we walked through the flowing crowd toward the event tent.

"I'm convinced Iris was planning to go to France," Nate said when we reached the other side of the street. "The police have a string of text messages between Iris and Harmony from Friday morning."

"Harmony told me about them," I said.

Nate gave me a disbelieving look. "Did she also tell you she and River were pressuring Iris to change her mind? One text seemed to insinuate that Iris owed her."

"Owed Harmony? For what?" I couldn't believe what he was saying. "That doesn't sound like her."

"I agree. But I read the entire string—in black and white." His lips were set in a grim line. "After being chased home by a mysterious truck and nearly crushed in a falling photo booth, I'd think you would be more cautious." He raised his hand to stop my inevitable protest. "I know Harmony is your friend, and I know she practices yoga, but none of that makes her innocent."

I huffed as I sought words of rebuttal. Of course, Harmony was innocent. She wouldn't hurt Iris. "Did Detective Cram share all this with you?" I knew Nate had his sources, but I doubted the detective was one of them. As much as I hated to admit it, I was sure the detective was too competent to be leaking information.

"He told me they were questioning Harmony about some text messages."

"But he wasn't the one who showed them to you." It wasn't a question. I took a moment to study Nate, but he gave nothing away. I pictured the police station. I was pretty sure I knew who his source was. "It was Olivia."

"Please don't say anything," he said in a low voice. "I don't want her to get into trouble."

"Nate! You know she's crushing on you."

He barked out a laugh. "That's ludicrous. She's the same age as the twins." He sounded genuinely taken aback. "Aiden took her to their senior prom, for Pete's sake."

"Men." I shook my head. "Are you all so oblivious? I'm telling you what I observed."

"You have to admit, your observations aren't always spot-on." Nate chuckled in a way that said he hadn't quite brushed my words away. "We can take this up another time. But now, we need to find Alicia."

The chairperson of Stonebridge's Selectboard was speaking when we joined Alicia and Fiona under the event tent. As she droned on about another successful harvest festival—like a murder hadn't happened at the opening event—I sidled up to Alicia.

"I hear you and Nate are up for the best couples costume."

"Meh." Alicia's voice was dismissive. "We're nominated almost every year. We've even won a couple of times. *I Love Lucy* was fun, but I don't have high hopes for this year." She raised an eyebrow. "Speaking of costumes, you might have been nominated in the individual category if anyone had known who you were supposed to be."

"Who did you dress as, darling?" My mother asked.

"Annie Leibovitz," I whispered back. "She's an extremely talented—"

"Photographer. Yes, I know." My mother nodded. "Excellent choice."

"Thanks." I beamed under her praise while shooting Alicia with a sisterly *so there* look.

The chairperson's speech ended, and we clapped as Alicia handed her camera bag to our mother and stepped up to the podium. As the head of the festival committee, she expressed her thanks to all who'd participated. I was only half listening to her reiteration of the many contest winners for events I'd missed when Ciarán joined Nate. They were laughing about something I couldn't hear, and I felt embarrassed over the way I'd treated him.

I slouched beside my mother, leaning just a little so that I could secretly watch him. He had an easy manner, but I couldn't help thinking that behind those gorgeous green eyes and his barely-there smile, there was something deeper. Something hurtful from his past. Something that, like me, induced him to leave Boston to move here. Or, maybe I was projecting.

Another round of applause erupted when Alicia announced the preliminary estimate of dollars raised for charity. I clapped while scanning the area until my eyes landed on Travis, who was standing behind the concession stand.

"I'll be right back," I said to my mother before walking away.

"And now, the moment you've all been waiting for." Alicia's voice echoed through the speakers. "It's time to announce the winners of the costume contest. This year's theme was *Arts and Entertainment*. With so many creative interpretations, it was difficult…"

I stopped listening.

Travis met my approach with his usual one-sided grin. "Don't tell me," he said. "Jessica Fletcher hasn't solved the crime yet, and I'm a suspect again."

"Something like that." I leaned my hip against the counter, trying to adopt a casual stance. Judging from the look in his eye, it wasn't working.

"Let's have it. What did I do this time?"

There was no point beating around the bush. Travis would be Travis, and he'd either answer my questions or he wouldn't. I opened my mouth to speak, but was drowned out by another round of whoops and clapping as Jackson was awarded the prize for most creative costume. I raised my hands above my head and clapped for my fellow club member. He'd made an excellent Napoleon Bonaparte.

"You were saying?" Travis's voice cut through the racket.

"Right." I pulled my phone from my pocket and opened the camera roll. "We have a photo that shows you putting something into a drink. It definitely wasn't the usual apple slice."

Travis leaned to take a glance. "You're kidding." He snorted. "So…what? You suspect me of drugging someone? Come on, Bobbie, I know you think I'm pathetic and all, but I swear I'll shoot myself if I ever get so desperate that I need to drug a woman for a night in the sack."

"I could have done without the imagery—thanks so much." I blinked. "You can't deny the photo looks suspicious."

Travis raised his hand like he was trying to push me away. "Oh, no, you don't. What reason would I have for drugging anyone?"

Alicia's voice caught our attention. "And in the couple's category, our nominees are—" When she paused, Travis and I both turned to look at Rose and William, who'd just arrived. Even from halfway across the marquee, I could see Rose's excitement. "Nathaniel and…" Alicia chuckled. "Well, and me, as Lucy and Ricky Ricardo from *I Love Lucy*." Alicia went on to recognize the other nominees. The costume contest was easily the favorite event among locals, and the cheers were deafening.

I glanced at Travis, who'd busied himself by wiping the counter. His jealousy over Rose's new relationship was evident, and I couldn't blame him. Rose looked radiant with excitement.

"And the winner is…" The crowd fell silent. "*The Great Gatsby*—William Johnson and Rose Lavoie!"

Rose's squeal filled the tent as she jumped up and threw her arms around William. Happy for my friend, I clapped so hard my palms turned red. When the cheering finally died down, I looked back at Travis. His eyes were cast downward, and a memory of the masquerade party came back to me. Rose had caught Travis's eye, and I'd teased her about making her ex-husband jealous. Sometimes my observations hit the bullseye.

Any thoughts of making a snarky comment vanished. Travis looked up. "We both know I was a lousy husband. She deserves this."

His reaction caught me off guard. "She does," I agreed.

The corner of his mouth hitched upward, and the old Travis was back. "Okay, so, no way I drugged anyone."

"If you want me to stop bugging you, I'll need a better explanation."

"Because I'm feeling magnanimous today—" He smirked. "And because I really do want you off my back once and for all, I'll show you what you think you saw."

I leaned against the counter. "Please do. Oh, and good word." I imitated his smirk.

"You'd be surprised at my vocabulary." He scoffed as he drew a small capsule from his pocket. "Ginger, and I'm not sure what else. Mostly ginger. Iris made it to help me with my indigestion and nausea, among other things." He wiggled his eyebrows. "You might have fun researching ginger's many benefits." He poured cider into a cup and emptied the capsule's contents. "And since your presence is making me nauseous, I don't mind if I do." He gulped the cider and wiped his chin with the back of his hand.

"Right." I deflated. Another dead end. With all the nonchalance I could muster, I ignored his triumphant grin. "See you around."

After making an about-face, I strode back to my friends to offer my congratulations on their winning costumes. After giving Jackson a thumbs up, I pulled him aside to ask about Iris's formulas.

"I didn't have the chance," Jackson said. "I hear Harmony was released. Maybe you can get them from her."

To avoid showing my frustration, I turned to Rose and drew her into a congratulatory hug. As I released her, my phone buzzed in my pocket. Rose, Alicia, Jackson, and I reached for our phones at the same time. Our screens showed a group text from Penny.

I found something. Come to the studio asap

Chapter Twenty-Five

R ose's eyes widened. "It's from Penny."

"What do you think she found?" Jackson asked.

I was as befuddled as they were. "She wants us at the studio." I scrolled through my calendar to check our club's schedule. The only event remaining was the festival committee's closing skit. I needed one photographer to stay behind to capture it. "Jackson, you're on photography duty this morning. Do you mind taking photos of the skit?"

He shifted from one foot to the other and rubbed his hand along his bald head. "But what if Penny found out something about Iris? I should be there to see it, too."

"I can stay," Alicia offered. "I need to be here with the committee when they do their skit."

"But aren't you in it?" I asked.

"Be real. I'm directing." She gestured with air quotes on her last word.

"Perfect," I said. "We'll be sure to text you if there's anything to report."

She took her camera bag from our mother and hung her camera around her neck.

* * *

When we arrived at my studio, Penny looked up from her seat behind the computer.

"Penny, what in the world are you doing here?" Rose asked. "You should have been at the festival. You and Mackenzie were nominated for best

161

costume."

"Awesome," Penny muttered. "Did we win?"

"Well, no…" Rose's cheeks flushed.

"Rose and William did," Jackson said. "I won in the individual category."

Penny's glance darted between Rose and Jackson. "Awesome. Congrats, then." She couldn't have sounded less interested.

"Has anyone seen Harmony?" I asked. "She wasn't with us at the closing ceremonies."

"Not yet." Penny shook her head. "She's part of the group text, so I'm sure she'll get here when she can. Come around behind me. This may be nothing, but I want you all to see."

We moved behind the desk to peer over her shoulder at the monitor. Penny looked at me. "What did you learn from Travis?" she asked.

"Ginger." I sighed. "For his nausea."

"Drat. I was hoping it would make what I'm about to show you easier," Penny said as she turned to the computer and opened the photography software. "There was something about the way we viewed everyone's photos individually that bothered me. I could hardly sleep thinking about it."

"Okay." I wondered where she was going with this.

Penny clicked the mouse and opened the first photo in a series. "Mackenzie has the holiday off and agreed to stay with Hope, so I came in early to load everyone's photos into our software. Then, I sorted by timestamp. Now, all the photos are combined to make a complete timeline—everything in chronological order."

"That's brilliant," I said. "I'm so impressed by your initiative."

Penny's lips parted into a tentative smile.

Jackson tapped his toe. "Let's see it, then."

Penny flashed him with a steely glare, and her tongue ring clicked from behind closed lips. "I'll scroll through and pause on the photos I found interesting. But if you see something, let me know."

She clicked through several photos, which captured Iris in her black hooded cloak from different angles. In one picture, Iris had her back to the camera and appeared to be talking to Jackson. His expression was neutral.

From a different angle, the next photo showed Iris talking to Mackenzie while Travis handed her a mug of cider. After viewing a few more images of various party-goers, she paused on one of my early shots. Jackson was standing at the bar with two hooded figures. In the background, his scowl was visible. I remembered there'd been an argument, and Jackson looked annoyed about something. To avoid reading too much into his expression without context, I pushed my thoughts to the back of my mind.

"Make note of the time on this one," Penny said. "It was shortly after seven-thirty. Still fairly early." Penny continued to scroll through the images, pausing at a picture of me with Penny, probably discussing my website's flawed scheduling software.

The next photo was of Alicia and me, and my expression showed surprise. Or was it alarm? Alicia and I were looking at each other with wide eyes and parted lips.

"This was taken right after I heard the scream." A shiver ran through me as I murmured, "Iris must already be dead."

In a hoarse whisper, Rose said, "This is giving me the heebie jeebies."

Penny's voice was all business, though. "The photo was taken around seven-forty, and we can assume Iris is already… You know." The click of her tongue ring filled the silence in my studio.

Jackson groaned, and I wondered whether he should have stayed at the festival after all.

The studio door opened, and Harmony breezed in. "I got here as fast as I could." She sounded as though she'd been running. "What's going on?"

"Penny put together a timeline," I said.

Harmony joined us to watch as Penny scrolled through more photos. The commotion at the party wasn't yet obvious, but I could sense it coming. In the next photo, Penny paused. Alicia was grabbing my arm while Nate laughed in the background, and Jackson stood near the edge of the tent. Emma told me Jackson had been outside, so the picture didn't surprise me. I stole another glance at him.

Several more images showed a group of party-goers leaving the marquee. Then there seemed to be a gap in the timeline. When the photos resumed several minutes later, the party appeared considerably more somber.

"Stop. Go back," Rose said.

Penny clicked on the previous picture and looked at Rose.

Rose squealed at a shadowy image of William and her. "Our costumes really were fabulous. Dressing as Daisy was so much fun."

"Can we stay on track?" Penny turned back to her screen.

"I'm just saying," Rose sniffed. "Whoever took this one should post it to our group. It's a good fit for the silhouette prompt.

"That would be me," Penny said. "Moving on."

After viewing a few more images, Penny paused again. She exchanged glances with each of us, and we leaned forward to get a closer look. Penny stayed silent, as if waiting for us to catch up with her.

It was Rose who spotted it first. "Wait. That can't be," she said. A hand flew to her mouth as she pointed at a hooded image.

I took in a quick breath. "Are you sure the timestamp on this photo is correct?"

Penny nodded and clicked to the next image.

"*Impossible*," Jackson said, using the French pronunciation. "Iris can't possibly be at the bar."

It was like seeing a ghost. No one seemed to know what to say. We were like zombies, staring at Penny's screen.

Penny clicked on the next photo. The same hooded figure had turned sideways, and a shock of bright pink hair spilled from the side of her hood.

"It's Mackenzie." Jackson let out a gust of air before gathering himself. "So what?"

Rose slumped, visibly relieved, and Harmony stared at the screen. My mind raced. What didn't I understand?

"Good heavens," Harmony finally said, her voice little more than a whisper.

With a jolt, it hit me. "Iris was killed from behind." The implication was staggering. "And from behind, she and Mackenzie were identical." I thought back to my early photo of two hooded figures who looked alike. Why hadn't I noticed it before?

Penny nodded, prodding me to continue.

"And Mackenzie was suddenly sick…" I grasped the back of Penny's chair, fighting off sudden dizziness. "No…" My initial thoughts about Mackenzie's illness came back to me. Maybe she'd been intentionally poisoned, after all.

"There must have been several costumes with black hooded capes." Rose sounded confused.

"There were," Penny said. "And I'll gladly show you all the hooded costumes I found. There were some notable differences. Most capes were shorter, a few had designs like stars or squiggles, and some were worn by taller, broader men. From what I could see, Iris and Mackenzie wore the only full-length, black hooded cloaks. They are—were—of a similar height and weight. Even though their costumes were very different from the front, they looked alike from behind."

"Oh, good heavens," Harmony said again. "Did the killer make a mistake?"

Jackson dropped into a chair with a guttural wail. *"Ma chère,"* he keened. With his elbows on his knees, he buried his face in his hands.

The room fell silent. There was no right way to respond. I edged over to where Jackson sat, shaking his head and mumbling to himself, and I placed my hand on his shoulder. "I'm so, so sorry."

He looked at me with red-rimmed eyes. "How could this happen?"

"We don't know anything for sure." I gave his shoulder a gentle squeeze. "This is only a theory." A theory I needed to share with Detective Cram.

Stunned, we absorbed the possibility that Mackenzie was the intended victim—that she'd been poisoned. I was still missing the pieces I needed to connect the events. The killer had slipped Mackenzie something poisonous, but then what? They thought they saw her alone at the fountain and chose the quicker—though wrong—solution?

Mistaken identity. Sitting apart from the rest of the club members, Jackson muttered to himself, lamenting the unfairness of his girlfriend's death and how it wasn't Iris who was supposed to be dead.

There was little more the club could do, and everyone left, leaving Penny and me to close up the studio.

"I wanted to slap him." Penny's voice was so low I barely heard her.

I stroked my scarf's silky tail. "Jackson is insensitive even in the best of times. He's grieving. We need to cut him some slack."

"I guess. But the way he went on and on about how no one would ever kill his poor, sweet Iris—and yeah, Iris was sweet. She didn't deserve to die. But it was like he wished Mackenzie had been murdered instead." She gave her tongue ring a couple of loud taps.

"I really don't think he meant it that way." I pulled a chair next to Penny so we could review the photos again. Jackson's anguish had seemed genuine, but the pictures of him returning to the tent right after Iris's murder bothered me. There had to be an innocent explanation.

As Penny clicked through the images, I noted which ones would be most important to support our theory. As much as I dreaded it, I had to tell the detective. It would be easier to make our case if I had pictures to show him. I gave Penny a list of the ones I wanted. "Create a new collection with these photos and be sure everything syncs to the cloud. That way, when I go to the police barracks, I'll be able to pull them up on my phone."

"Will do," Penny answered with a nod.

"Can you think of any reason someone would want to poison Mackenzie?"

"None," Penny said. "Mackenzie is awesome."

I smiled. "If we're to take this theory seriously, we need to think beyond her awesomeness."

"I so wanted to believe Mackenzie had picked the wrong mushrooms. She's not very experienced."

"She said she was out foraging for butternuts." I thought back to our conversation at the hospital. "What made her decide to pick mushrooms?"

Penny groaned. "I don't know." She leaned on her elbows. "It's all my fault. I should have checked them over. I'm not an expert either, but I used to forage with my mom."

I rested a hand on her back. "It's not your fault. Besides, since we don't know what made her sick, we can't rule them out." I paused. "Any idea when the tox screen will be ready?"

"We haven't heard anything. It could be weeks," Penny said.

"Mistaken identity seems like a good theory," I said. "It links Mackenzie's illness with Iris's death. I'm not ready to throw out my suspect chart just yet, but I'll create a new column. The problem seems to be finding a motive. It's baffling."

"The only person who doesn't like Mackenzie is Muffy."

"There aren't many photos of her in our timeline. Do you have a sense of Muffy's movements that night?"

Penny's mouth opened, then closed, and she shook her head. "Mackenzie would've been avoiding her."

I remembered what Alicia said about the sudden death of Muffy's husband. There'd been no hint of foul play, but now I wondered. I had to admit my personal feelings were coloring my judgment. "If Mackenzie was poisoned, someone was trying to harm her."

Penny tapped her tongue ring. "I can't see Muffy doing that. It must be Jackson. You heard him. It's like he wanted Mackenzie to be dead instead of Iris."

"That's not a motive," I said.

"No, but can we be sure he wasn't acting?" Penny asked. "You know, to make him look innocent."

I didn't think so, but Penny was distraught, and I didn't want to argue with her. If someone tried to kill Mackenzie, I was worried about her safety. "I think you should go home."

"We have another consultation appointment booked for later this afternoon. I also wanted to go over what I should prepare for our next meeting. You said it was about masking. It's part of photo editing?"

"I can take care of the consultation," I said. "And we can discuss the details of masking later. The condensed version is that creating a mask while editing enables the photographer to isolate a specific portion of the photo. With a mask, adjustments can be applied to the selected area."

"That sounds so cool," Penny said. "But it also sounds a little like cheating."

"People often think of photo editing that way. What they don't fully comprehend is that the human eye adjusts to lighting changes, but a camera lens can't. So, a face we see clearly in real life might be heavily shadowed in the photo. Or, we might remember seeing a blue sky with fluffy white clouds, but the photo only shows a pale, blank space. As long as the exposure isn't too far off, masking helps us recover some of these details."

Penny turned thoughtful. "I guess I never thought of it like that. I usually think of all the airbrushed models."

"Masking is used for that, too. Why do you think celebrities have smoother skin than everyone else? Other than plastic surgery and high-end skin care, that is." I chuckled. "I'll send you links to more information so you can study at home. What time is our consultation appointment?"

"He's coming at four," Penny said.

I checked my watch. "That should give me time. First, I'd better take these photos to Detective Cram. Then, I want to talk to Mackenzie."

"She'll be home babysitting. I'm working at The Crow tonight."

"Any chance you can call in?" I asked. "Mackenzie shouldn't be alone—for now, at least."

"Are you saying Mackenzie is in danger?"

"If someone tried to poison her, yes." Something was bothering me, but I couldn't grasp what it was. Poisons, Mackenzie, Iris... An image of Iris's apothecary swam in my head. Herbs, formulas, customers... I opened the photo app on my phone and thumbed back to Iris's ledger. I was certain I'd seen Mackenzie's name.

"What are you looking for?" Penny asked.

I continued to search. "Mackenzie was one of Iris's customers."

"Iris made a tea blend she liked," Penny said. "It was her afternoon pick-me-up."

"Iris was making deliveries the afternoon of the masquerade party." I skimmed each page as I scrolled. "Do you know if Mackenzie got a tea delivery too?"

"You're making me nervous. I...I...don't know."

I clicked on the last page of Iris's ledger. The last entry, written in Iris's loopy handwriting, was for MackzM. Something about it was different. It took me a moment, but then I saw it. Each of the previous entries had a check mark next to it, but Mackenzie's was marked with a red *X*.

Chapter Twenty-Six

My mind spun. Why was the mark different? Why a red *X*? While Penny synced the photos, I texted Nate to meet me at the police barracks. Without asking for an explanation, he agreed to meet me in fifteen minutes. The station was just a short walk down Main Street, but, worried about Mackenzie being alone, I drove Penny home first.

Nate was waiting outside when I pulled my car into the parking lot.

"What's going on?" he asked.

While explaining our new theory, I couldn't help but read the skepticism in his raised eyebrow. "I know it sounds like a long shot," I said. "But, think about it. What if the killer poisoned Mackenzie, but then they got impatient? Later, they thought they saw her alone by the fountain. With most of the village at the party, the green was pretty deserted. The main tent was just far enough away that the fountain wasn't visible." I paused, giving him time to process what I was trying to say. "The killer was presented with an opportunity they couldn't pass up."

"Mistaken identity." Nate rubbed his chin. "I'm not sure I buy it, but if we're to assume Mackenzie was poisoned, your theory creates a possible connection to Iris."

"That could explain the red *X*. Someone other than Iris could've poisoned Mackenzie's tea."

"All right, let's present the idea to Detective Cram. Just don't be surprised if he's less than enthusiastic about it. It's his decision whether to pursue it." He fixed me with a stern stare. "Understood?"

I met his stare with one of my own. It wasn't my fault if he misinterpreted it as agreement.

After entering the police station, I watched the tips of Nate's ears redden from Olivia's flirtatious greeting. It seemed that this time, even he had noticed her coquettish smile and ponytail twirl. Hopefully, I hadn't inadvertently ruined a good thing. The information she fed Nate was helpful. It wasn't like we'd get anything from Detective Cram.

"To what do I owe this dubious pleasure?" the detective asked as soon as he spotted us from behind Olivia's desk.

"Bobbie has something she wants to share with you," Nate said.

"Oh, goody." Detective Cram pressed his palms together in a mocking gesture.

Or, I can solve this by myself. I held back a huff.

Nate's expression remained impassive, but I couldn't stop myself from glaring. I was not to be cowed by the detective's sarcasm.

"As you know," I said, "the camera club took photos at the masquerade party. We put together a timeline you might find interesting."

"Let's see it," he said. He disappeared for a moment, then reappeared as he walked through the security door to join us in the lobby.

"I only have a few of the more interesting photos with me. I can send the entire timeline later."

Nate, Detective Cram, and I formed a huddle as I clicked on the collection of pictures. Holding my phone so we could all view the screen, I swiped through the photos Penny had synced to our software. I showed him images of both Iris and Mackenzie from behind, explaining our theory as I went.

"They do look identical," Nate said, and I felt encouraged. He seemed to be chewing over our theory.

"Mistaken identity." Detective Cram seemed to be considering it as well.

"There's one more thing." He needed to know about the entry in Iris's ledger.

Cram cocked his head, looking more impatient than curious. No matter.

"You have Iris's ledger," I said. "Turn to the last page. There's an entry for Mackenzie that doesn't match the rest of Iris's entries." I explained about the red *X*. As I said it out loud, it didn't sound like much, and I could tell

Detective Cram wasn't impressed. "Iris kept poisonous herbs at her house. Someone could have tampered with Mackenzie's tea."

"I'll take a look," the detective said. "Send me whatever photos you have. It's a long shot, but contrary to what you seem to think of me, I leave no stone unturned."

That wasn't how I remembered him, but I might have had some tunnel vision of my own. If he were serious about looking into it, I'd accept the olive branch.

"I'll do it this afternoon," I said.

We turned to leave, but Detective Cram's voice stopped me in my tracks. "Oh, and Mrs. Brooks," he said. "From what I'm hearing, I think you should consider yourself in danger, too. After the incident in the photo booth, I was informed about the truck that followed you home. You should have told me yourself."

"I…umm…" I wasn't sure what to say. Not in a million years had I expected the detective to listen to me. "I didn't know what to make of it at the time."

"Back off and let me do my job." And there it was—the arrogant glower I was so familiar with.

As we left the station, Nate said, "You heard him." We stopped next to my car. "It's time you backed away from this. The more involved you get, the more dangerous it becomes. If Mackenzie was the target, the killer isn't done."

"I heard him," I said, swallowing my annoyance. Nate had my best interests in mind, but I didn't need him telling me what I already knew.

"Please tell me you're listening," Nate said. "If you get in the killer's way, there's no reason to think they won't do whatever it takes to get rid of you."

Nate and I parted in the parking lot after I assured him I was planning to come to the farm for dinner. My mother was leaving to fly back to Florida the next day, and this would be her last evening in Stonebridge. I was more than a little surprised to realize I would miss her. Her visit to Vermont had flown by.

I checked my watch. I had almost two hours before I needed to return to the studio for the consultation appointment. It was time to find out why someone might want to kill Mackenzie.

* * *

I parked my car in Penny's driveway and reached for my backpack. From across the street, the burbling of the river greeted me. Penny's expansive front lawn sat on the corner of River Street near the village's iconic covered bridge. The small ranch-style house needed a fresh coat of paint, but the purple and yellow chrysanthemums in terra-cotta pots lining the front walk were a welcoming touch.

As I knocked, I took a peek at the house next door. It had been empty for the last few months, but I'd heard rumors of a new renter moving in. It looked like the lawn had been mowed, and blinds replaced the old curtains in the windows. Since empty houses attracted squatters, I thought Penny and Mackenzie must be glad to have neighbors again.

Penny appeared in the doorway with her nine-month-old daughter, Hope, resting on her slim hip. She was dressed in a red polo and black slacks, the uniform of The Mad Crow Tavern. To answer my questioning glance, she said, "I'm only going in for an hour. There's a large party at the bar that should be leaving soon."

With a nod, I stepped inside the living room, relieved to see Mackenzie on the couch, looking like herself again. A healthy glow colored her cheeks, framed as they were by her colorful, shoulder-length hair.

"Hey, Bobbie," she said. "Penny says you want to talk to me?"

I sat on a chair next to the couch and got straight to the point. "Penny told you our new theory?"

Mackenzie bit her lip. "I can't believe anyone poisoned me."

Penny placed Hope in Mackenzie's lap and handed her a bottle. "I'll be back as soon as I can." She walked to the door and grabbed a jacket from the coat hook.

As Penny left, my thoughts shifted to Iris's ledger. "Penny says you used to buy tea from Iris. Did you receive a new bag on Friday?"

"Yes," Mackenzie said. "It was unexpected, but I knew she was preparing to go away for a while." She tipped Hope to feed her.

"You knew about her plans?"

"Oh, sure. She's been planning for weeks now. Her housemates were none too happy about it, but it was an exciting opportunity for her."

I'd almost forgotten that until recently, Mackenzie lived in Harmony's house. The thought took me back to the earthy aroma of the farmhouse kitchen and to River stirring a steaming pot of soup: wild rice and *mushroom* soup.

"I'm curious about the mushrooms you picked. Penny says you're not experienced at it."

"I'm not," Mackenzie said. "I hadn't planned on picking them, but after filling my bag with nuts, I ran into River. He had a basketful of mushrooms and pointed me to where he'd found them."

"He was making soup," I said. "It smelled good." My mind raced with the thought that River might be involved.

As though reading my mind, Mackenzie said, "No way. River showed me the mushrooms he'd picked and what to look for. If I picked a poisonous one, it wasn't his fault."

I wasn't convinced. If Mackenzie had been the killer's intended target, her poisoning had been intentional. I shifted gears. "Tell me about living in the commune."

"Commune?" Mackenzie scoffed. "I guess that's fair. I'm not sure what I can tell you. When I came back to Stonebridge, the idea of moving in with my aunt felt like a step backward. Harmony offered me a place to crash."

"So you must have known Iris and River pretty well."

Mackenzie bit her lip. "I guess so. I'd just started my job at the library, and was super busy. I had tons of ideas for new programming, but there were so many political hoops to jump through." She let out a soft laugh.

"I can imagine." Small villages, I was learning, had big politics. "What was it like to live there?"

"Harmony and Iris were great. They were both so welcoming. I didn't have a lot to contribute, so I helped where I could. I paid rent, too. But I have to admit, what Harmony charged me was super low." Mackenzie turned her attention to Hope and placed the bottle on the coffee table. She lifted the baby to pat her back and kiss her chubby little cheek.

"Who would have thought I'd be here, taking care of a baby? I never expected to have kids. I'm so lucky to have Penny and Hope in my life."

Her words turned me into a gooey mess. I remembered when Emma was a baby—the feel of her downy head against my cheek. Back then, Dan and I had planned to have a house full of children. After several miscarriages, we gave up and counted our blessings. We had Emma, and we had each other. In our own way, we were fortunate.

I blinked away the memory. "Was Tallulah living there?"

"We only overlapped by a couple of weeks." Mackenzie lifted Hope's bottle and settled the baby back to feed her the rest. "Tallulah was super eager to fit in. I kind of think she has a thing for River, but I'm probably not the best judge. River is so not my type."

I laughed. "I get that."

"Anyway, except for some tension over Iris's plans to take Saskia to France, I'd say everyone got along pretty well."

"River was okay with Iris dating Jackson?"

Mackenzie shrugged before shifting Hope again. "River could be possessive. Toward the end of my stay, tensions were growing. I don't think it was about Jackson, though. River and Iris argued about Saskia a lot."

"That's understandable." I couldn't imagine anyone taking Emma from me, even temporarily.

"I made the mistake of agreeing with River's concerns. Iris didn't seem to appreciate it. Not that she said anything to me. It was more like she quietly froze me out."

My thoughts flitted back to Iris's ledger. It bothered me that Mackenzie's entry was different from the others. There had to be a reason. I looked up and realized that Mackenzie speaking.

"…into a whole big thing," Mackenzie said. "Iris must have told Jackson, because he confronted me earlier this week, telling me to stay out of their business. He has quite the temper." Mackenzie stood and bounced Hope on her shoulder as she crossed the room to look out the window. She groaned.

CHAPTER TWENTY-SIX

"You've *got* to be kidding me. That woman…"

I turned to see what had raised Mackenzie's hackles. Out on the street, Muffy was bent over a stroller. She retrieved a toy from the ground and handed it to her child.

"First, she bothers me at work. Now she knows where I live?" Mackenzie stepped back and returned to the couch.

"Maybe she's out for a walk?" I suggested. "Your road makes a loop with Bridge Street and Main Street. Darcy and I walk it almost every day."

"I guess." Mackenzie let out a long breath, like she was trying to calm herself. "You've heard about the uptick in book banning, right?"

I nodded.

"Muffy thinks—very loudly—that some of our picture books are inappropriate. It's not like toddlers come to the library and check out books on their own. I trust their parents on this."

Alicia and Penny had both mentioned Muffy hassling Mackenzie. But stalking her at home was ratcheting things up a notch. As I watched, Muffy turned to head back the way she came. So much for walking the loop. I stepped back from the window just as I saw Muffy look up. I didn't need to worry about being caught. She was looking at the house next door.

"Have you noticed her outside your house before?" I asked.

"No, but Penny has. Yesterday."

"I think she was checking out the house next door, too. Have you met your new neighbor?"

"Not yet. I keep meaning to make them a casserole."

"Muffy hanging around your house is kind of creepy. Do you think she could have poisoned you?" It was worth considering.

"I doubt it," Mackenzie said. "She and my aunt are friends, which I'm not crazy about. But Vickie Sue has the right to choose who she hangs around with."

I walked back to the chair I was sitting in, but it was getting late. I needed to get back to the studio.

"One last thing," I said. "You said Iris was upset with you. How was she when she delivered your tea on Friday?"

"Oh, she didn't deliver it," Mackenzie said.

"I thought—"

"Right, I got a new bag. But Jackson delivered it."

I couldn't help taking a big gulp of air. "Was that normal?"

"Not at all. I usually picked up my order at Iris's house. She made such a great blend. No caffeine, but somehow it perked me up. It was perfect for getting through the afternoon."

"Did you drink any of it?"

"Oh, sure. I knew the masquerade party would run late into the evening, so I made a big pot as I closed up the library." Mackenzie's eye grew wide. "You don't think…"

My mind spun with possibilities. "Have you had any since?"

"No. I keep it at the library. I haven't been back since going to the hospital."

"Maybe you should take it to the police? Have it tested?"

"I can't believe Iris would poison my tea."

Not Iris. But, as much as I'd been avoiding it, it was time to think more seriously about Jackson.

Chapter Twenty-Seven

I returned to my studio to meet the client who'd booked an appointment through my website. I let myself in and turned on the lights. Sitting at the front desk, I powered on the computer while reflecting on my talk with Mackenzie. The day had taken quite a turn. It didn't help that Nate's and Detective Cram's warnings played in my mind, and I knew they were right. I was in danger and should consider backing off.

Even as I considered dropping the investigation, I opened my photography software and opened Penny's timeline. With my focus on Mackenzie as the intended victim, I felt like I was viewing a new set of photos. I scrolled through each image, carefully examining them from corner to corner. When viewing pictures, it was natural to ignore elements lurking in the background. This time, nothing was beyond my notice.

I clicked on the image of Jackson entering the marquee from the village green, and I couldn't help but wonder where he'd been. I enlarged the image to examine his face more closely. His lips were turned up slightly. A smile or a grimace, I couldn't tell. I checked for clues in his posture, but he looked natural enough.

My eyes felt tired, and I blinked, trying to stave off my growing frustration. Outside, the light had dimmed. A quick check of my watch told me my client was thirty minutes late. I looked toward my door, as if doing so would conjure my tardy customer. No such luck. These no-shows were becoming a tremendous waste of both Penny's and my time. While I'd been focused on the mystery of Mackenzie's poisoning, I should have been concentrating on the real mystery: our troublesome scheduling software.

I hated to think it, but it was probably time to hire Ciarán. I pictured the way he'd avoided me since I turned down his invitation. I couldn't fault him, but the next image that popped into my mind was one I didn't like—me groveling. I hoped to delay that for as long as possible.

After shooting off the package of photos I'd promised Detective Cram, I turned off the computer and stood. At this point, my appointment was unlikely to show. There was still a little time to kill before I was due at the Crowleys' for my mom's farewell dinner. I could use it to catch up on my much-neglected paperwork. I shut off the studio lights and strode up the stairs to my office.

Sticky notes framed my monitor, reminding me of invoices and proposals awaiting my approval. This was the necessary, but mundane, part of running my business. Fortunately, Penny kept everything neatly organized.

As I flicked on my desk lamp, I opened the first file that appeared on my desktop. The proposal, on a standard form Nate had helped me create, was already completed and signed. As I looked through my notes, I checked the proposed pricing and the client's chosen locations for their engagement shoot. They were a cute couple from New Jersey, excited about their spring wedding on Stratton Mountain, and I was looking forward to working with them.

As I opened my calendar to double-check the dates, I heard a thump below. I moved to the railing and peered over, hoping my appointment had arrived after all. All was quiet below. Even though I'd turned off the lights, it wasn't yet evening, and the dim afternoon sun filtered through the windows.

"Hello?" I called out.

No answer. I stayed still, sure I heard footsteps. Thinking my client might be looking for me, I took a step forward, but not before grabbing a heavy stoneware mug from my desk. It wasn't much of a weapon, but it was silly to think I needed one. I started down the stairs and heard another thump. This one was more like a crash, something falling to the floor.

I called out again. "Hello?"
Silence.
Clutching the mug to my chest, I leaned my back against the wall and took

one slow step after another. My voice trembled. "Is anyone there?"

Behind the wall separating the staircase from the kitchenette, footsteps plodded across the rustic wooden floor. The door creaked open, and a gust of wind blew into the studio, ruffling papers on the front desk.

I rushed down the remaining steps to the studio's entrance and found the door wide open. After running outside, I scanned my driveway and patio but saw no one. Then, I turned toward the line of woods behind my studio. The setting sun cast heavy shadows on the trees. It wouldn't be the first time someone had hidden back there.

I shivered and walked back inside, slamming the door shut behind me and securing the deadbolt. Nothing looked amiss. The ruffled papers had remained secure beneath the camera-shaped paperweight Alicia had given me as a studio warming gift. If someone had been at the desk, I would have seen them from the loft. That left the kitchenette beneath my office.

A flip of the light switch illuminated a stoneware mug, shattered on the floor.

Huh...

While inspecting the tiny room, I bent down to pick up the broken pieces. The kitchenette contained little more than a countertop with a sink, a microwave, an electric kettle, and a single-serve coffee maker. Tucked in the corner by the door, a small, little-used table with two chairs sat, with an empty box and a box cutter on top. We kept mugs on a shelf above the counter, along with a stash of coffee pods and tea bags. Aside from the broken mug, everything looked tidy.

I was certain Penny hadn't come in to restock, accidentally pushing a mug from the shelf. I texted her anyway. While waiting for her reply, I debated calling Detective Cram. With my door unlocked, no one had broken in. What would I report? A broken mug? As far as I could tell, nothing had been stolen. I hadn't even been threatened. If I called the detective, he'd just blow it off the same way he did once before.

It was getting late, and I had a dinner to get to. I trudged back up to the loft, where I shut down my computer, turned off my lamp, and checked my phone for Penny's reply. The paperwork could wait until morning. I shook off a sense of unease. Penny was usually quick to respond.

Chapter Twenty-Eight

It wasn't until I'd walked into the warmth of my kitchen that my body relaxed and I realized how tense I was. I didn't have time to think about it, though. My mother was waiting for me to pick her up at the inn, and I knew all too well what a stickler she was for punctuality.

I rummaged through my closet and pulled out the sweater dress I'd originally planned for the wine and cheese party. I put it on and smoothed the soft knit over my waist. Both cute and casual, the hem hit my tights right above my knees, and the soft cashmere skimmed my curves without being clingy. It was warm and familiar, like a hug, one that helped settle my nerves. After freshening my mascara with a quick swipe, I wove a scarf into my hair, creating a long braid, and gave myself a glance in the mirror. Satisfied I didn't look as anxious as I felt, I was ready to go.

I walked downstairs to grab my coat and backpack, and my phone buzzed. I was relieved to see a text from Penny. As I expected, she was at home with Mackenzie and Hope. She was clearly upset about the no-show as well as the intrusion into what she seemed to consider *her* space. Her annoyance was evident in her string of texts, as was her scolding over my neglect to lock the studio door.

R U serious?

Someone barged into our studio? WTH?

You left the door unlocked?

What were you thinking?!?!?!

Sheesh. Sometimes I wondered which one of us was the boss.

After finishing our text exchange, I was late, if only by a few minutes. I shot off a quick text to Alicia and my mom.

Running late. On my way.

Alicia's reply came almost immediately.

Everything okay?

I fiddled with my phone, deciding to tell her what happened. I typed, deleted, retyped, and finally sent a message about the intruder in my studio.

Her response was alarmed.

Inviting Rose for dinner—we need to talk!!

I replied.

Harmony and Jackson, too?

The undulating dots appeared, disappeared, then reappeared. I waited as patiently as I could, using the time to text my mother to let her know I'd be on my way in a few minutes. The dots were replaced by Alicia's message.

Better not tonight. Nate will be suspicious.

Full house already.

Did she mean Connor and Emma? I assumed Emma was already there. I responded with a question mark. Alicia replied.

Ciarán and Muffy—will explain later.

I resisted the temptation to reply with a string of symbols and exclamation points. Ciarán and Muffy? Together? Then, I considered sending a long rant about how her house used to be my safe place. I didn't, knowing how selfish that would be. It had only been a day since I declined Ciarán's invitation. I'd made the right decision. At least, that's what I told myself. Despite my conviction, dinner would prove to be more awkward than I needed. I calmed down enough to text my sister a reply that was considerably more mature than I was feeling.

K. Picking up Mother

I gave Darcy a quick pat, certain I read betrayal in his brown eyes. Guilt for leaving him behind sat heavy in my gut. He couldn't possibly know I was headed to the farm. "I'll take you for a walk when I get back," I promised, convinced I read treachery in his doleful gaze.

As I drove around the village green toward the inn, I was amazed at how quickly the festival tents had been disassembled. Once again, Stonebridge was a peaceful little village. My mother and I exchanged our usual greetings as she got into my car—complete with air kisses. Beyond that, we had little to say, but our silence was comfortable enough. When I drove up Alicia's long driveway, there were several cars parked near the house, including Rose's and Ciarán's. I took a moment to gather my wits before getting out of the car and walking to the porch.

The kitchen door swung open. "Come in, come in." Alicia sounded cheerful as she held the door for our mother. She turned to me, her eyes wide and intense as if asking, *What the heck is going on?*

I twisted my lips to the side in an expression I hoped said, *We need to figure this out, STAT.*

Boisterous laughter and a spicy aroma that made my mouth water greeted me as I stepped inside. Nate rushed over to hug both my mother and me. He took our coats as Connor stepped forward, holding cute cactus-stemmed margarita glasses filled with a slushy, pale-green liquid. I accepted the much-needed, nerve-calming cocktail and spotted Ciarán and Muffy over his shoulder.

Ciarán greeted me with a quick nod, not allowing me time to nod back before he widened his smile for my mother. Then, he resumed his conversation with Muffy, who offered me a sweet smile. I had yet to figure out Muffy's game, but Ciarán's slight had been clear enough. Knowing I'd earned it, my cheeks heated with chagrin.

"We're celebrating the end of another harvest festival with a Mexican fiesta." Alicia's voice rang through the commotion. She held her glass aloft. "*Olè.*"

"*Olè,*" we chorused. I clicked glasses with everyone before downing a huge gulp of my drink. While I savored the slow burn of the tequila, Alicia nodded her head toward the dining room. Rose's hand touched my arm, and we slipped out of the kitchen, leaving the rest of our party to their nachos, margaritas, and carefree chatter.

Still feeling the chill of Ciarán's rejection, I glared at Alicia with all the annoyance I'd been holding back. Her house was supposed to be my refuge, my hideaway, my sanctum. I railed in my mind, indignant over the injustice of it all.

"Stop it, Bobbie." Alicia cut my internal rant short. "We didn't know about you turning Ciarán down."

Rose's mouth dropped open. "He asked you out?"

I waved my hand at her. "Just for coffee. It's not important."

"Then stop being mad," Alicia said. "Ciarán thought Nate was inviting him to a casual dinner. When he got here and found out the whole family was coming, he offered to leave. Nate wouldn't hear of it, of course. This is uncomfortable for Ciarán, too."

"And Muffy?" I asked, annoyed despite myself.

"She was hanging around Ciarán when Nate invited him. You know Nate; he'd invite the whole village if our house were big enough."

"Fine. Whatever." I'd given up the right to care who Ciarán had on his arm, even if she was young and cute and made me feel like a big oaf.

"You seriously turned down a date with Ciarán?" Rose asked. "But why?"

"Not a date," I said. "Just coffee."

"Then why turn him dow—"

"We've got more important things to discuss," I said. "Like Mackenzie."

"And your intruder," Alicia said.

Rose frowned, looking offended. Thankfully, she let the topic drop.

"I've got to show you what I made." Alicia slid something that looked very poster-like from its hiding place behind the sideboard.

"Is that what I think it is?" Rose clapped her hands together. "A murder board? I always wanted to do one of those."

Alicia took a peek toward the kitchen doorway before flipping it around. "I took a slightly different approach from your chart."

"This reminds me of *Death in Paradise*." Rose nearly squealed. "A picture for every suspect."

Alicia had drawn lines connecting each suspect to the victim, and in some cases, to each other. "I drew the connections we knew about, and added motives and whatever additional information I could think of."

"I like it." I smiled. "It's a great visual. And, I have something to add."

Alicia handed me a marker. I set my margarita glass on the table and removed the marker's lid before drawing a line between Jackson and Mackenzie."

"What's that for?" Alicia asked.

"Mackenzie got a tea delivery on the day of the masquerade party," I said.

"And?" Rose asked.

I took a moment before responding, enjoying the drama. "Iris didn't deliver it. Jackson did."

Rose's eyes widened. "That seems weird."

"Agreed," Alicia traced the line with her finger. "What do you think it means?"

"Mackenzie received the tea that morning," I said. "It's her afternoon pick-me-up, and she brewed a large pot for herself that afternoon. She was severely sick that evening." I paused. "Maybe the tea was tampered with."

Rose clamped her hand over her mouth. In a muffled voice, she said, "I told you Jackson was creeping me out."

"It's a big jump to assume Jackson poisoned her tea. I can hardly imagine it. But, I also can't ignore the possibility." I lifted my margarita glass and took a sip before stepping back to the murder board and drawing another line.

"You're full of information," Alicia said. "What's this one for?"

I smiled. "River is the one who showed Mackenzie which mushrooms to pick."

Alicia paused for a moment. "And Mackenzie said she sliced mushrooms on her salad that day."

"Exactly." The added lines to Alicia's board felt like progress.

"So, we're focusing on the mushrooms and the tea as potential sources." Alicia peered at the lines I'd drawn. "What are their motivations?"

"That's where things get sketchy," I said. "It seems Jackson was angry with Mackenzie." I told them about how Jackson confronted Mackenzie after she sided with River about taking Saskia to France. "As far as motives go, it seems weak."

"Jackson has a temper," Rose said.

"That's exactly what Mackenzie said." I sipped my margarita.

Alicia let out a long breath. "Maybe you should tell us about your intruder."

With a slow shake of my head, I relayed the whole story, starting from when I sat at Penny's desk to wait for my no-show client. I could tell they wanted to jump in with questions when I mentioned hearing the thump, but they listened as I spoke. My knees felt like jelly.

"You had a break-in at your studio?" Nate walked into the room with Ciarán behind him. Immediately, he zeroed in on Alicia's poster. "What is that?"

"It's nothing." Alicia slid it back behind the sideboard. "I'll show you later."

I sipped my cocktail, doing all I could to hide my face behind the oversized glass.

I wanted to tell Nate this was a private discussion. I wanted to ask him to leave. I wanted to stop being painfully aware of a tall, handsome Irishman standing in the doorway. But I knew none of these things were possible; instead, I took another throat-burning gulp of my icy tequila-laced lime juice.

Alicia sighed, meeting her husband's stare. "Bobbie's break-in just happened a little while ago." There was a note of defensiveness in her voice. "We're trying to figure it out."

"By not calling the police?" Nate shifted his attention from Alicia to me.

"We're not doing that." I was adamant, and no amount of surprise in Nate's eyes would make me budge. "There's nothing Detective Cram can do about it. And whoever it was didn't threaten me. For all I know, they came into my studio by mistake. I often have walk-ins."

An eyebrow inched up his forehead. "That seems unlikely, don't you think?"

"Okay, yes." I conceded the point but held my ground. "What would you have me say to Detective Cram? That I was in my unlocked studio and heard someone come in and then leave?"

"Bobbie has a point," Rose said.

Nate ran his fingers through his hair. "All right. I can see what you're saying. I still don't like it."

Alicia placed a hand on her husband's arm while looking at me. "You said there was a broken mug on the floor?"

"When I looked over the railing of my loft, I couldn't see anyone." I paused. "They'd gone into my kitchenette."

"But why?" Rose asked. "They went looking for you when you weren't at the reception desk?"

"That's what I thought," I said.

Nate looked thoughtful. "Other than the broken mug, was anything out of place?"

"Not that I could see," I said. "I didn't spend much time looking around. I was running late, and to make matters worse, I felt creeped out. But everything seemed okay."

"Take a closer look tomorrow," Nate said. "And I shouldn't have to tell you this, but you need to be more careful."

"Agreed," Alicia said. "What was going through your head, not locking your door?"

"That my client was late and might still show." We seemed to be at a stand-off, and I looked down at my feet, thinking about my situation. Alicia and Nate were right. Of course they were. I should have locked up the studio before going to my office. But scolding me for my mistake wouldn't solve the problem.

"These no-show clients, how do they make their appointments?" Ciarán's voice broke our silence. He'd been so quiet during our discussion, I'd almost forgotten he was there. Almost.

As he spoke, Muffy sidled up next to him, pressing herself against his side. If he noticed, he didn't show it. Begrudgingly, I admitted that despite their age difference, they made a stunning couple.

I forced myself to meet his gaze. "Through my website," I said. "We allow initial consultation appointments to be set up online."

"It could be a problem with your software." His voice was professional.

"I suspect you're right." I didn't want to think about what it would take to overhaul my website. It was beyond my capabilities.

"Aunt Alicia, a timer in your kitchen is buzzing." Emma peered over Muffy's shoulder and blinked. "Oh, sorry. I didn't mean to interrupt."

"Not a problem." Alicia's expression relaxed. She let go of Nate's arm and headed toward the doorway. "It's time for the fiesta to begin. Enchiladas and make-your-own tacos in the kitchen, complete with rice, beans, guacamole, and all the fixins." She squeezed through the doorway, signaling the end of our discussion. She didn't need to ask twice.

As everyone turned to follow her, drawn by the smoky, spicy, cheesy scent, I grabbed Rose's arm and whispered, "If this is about Mackenzie rather than Iris, I'm putting Muffy back on my list. But if she was here, I don't see how she could've broken into my studio."

"She only got here about two seconds before you did." Rose's eyes widened. "Do you think it's her?"

I didn't. Not really. But, before I could manage a weak shrug, Alicia came back to get us. "Hey, you two. Come eat."

Dinner conversation was lively, as it always was at the Crowleys'. Emma and Connor chatted away, while Fiona and Ciarán seemed to be deeply engaged in a lively discussion about food in Ireland, with Muffy hanging on their every word. Rose, Alicia, and I sat together at the other end of the table. Still, we didn't dare continue our earlier conversation.

When it was time to leave, I turned to offer Emma a ride home while my mother and I put on our jackets.

"Connor and I are planning to head back to his place to hang out for a while." Emma smiled at Connor.

"If that's okay with you," Connor said.

"I don't need my mom's permission," Emma said. I wasn't sure if her words were for my benefit or Connor's, a reminder that she was no longer a little girl. Connor didn't need reminding, that much I was sure of.

With a shrug, Connor offered his good-natured smile.

"Of course, you don't," I said. "Have fun. I'll see you in the morning."

Chapter Twenty-Nine

The moon shone above the trees in the inky black sky. I turned on my high beams and squinted to navigate the Crowleys' dark driveway back to the main road.

"Emma will be out for a while." My mother broke our silence. "I'm not yet ready to retire. Why don't you come into the inn with me? We can have a glass of wine."

No. My reaction was automatic.

It had been a long day. I could almost hear my couch calling to me. I wanted nothing more than to burrow beneath a warm throw and snuggle with my dog. But I knew better. My reaction had nothing to do with soft cushions or Darcy's calming presence, and everything to do with my mother.

Our conversation from the other night gave me a glimmer of hope. It wasn't that we'd ever been antagonistic toward each other—nothing like that. And, I was beginning to feel that something new was growing, an understanding of sorts. Maybe we still had time.

"A glass of wine sounds nice," I said. As I pulled my car into a parking spot, another idea occurred to me. With the holiday weekend behind us, the inn would be quiet. Gino would be there. And he seemed to know Muffy.

* * *

The light inside the Inn's rustic tavern was dim. Its rough-hewn beams, olive-green walls, and flickering candlelit tables gave it an intimate ambiance. Soft music played from speakers on the wall, making the murmurs of a couple at one of the small tables inaudible. Otherwise, the room was empty. To my surprise, my mother strode past the tables straight to the bar, where she settled on a stool. Huh. The bar was almost always my preference, too.

"I have to admit, this bar is altogether charming," my mother said.

"Look at you, complimenting Vermont." I gave my mother a gentle nudge, which made her chuckle.

As we draped our jackets over the backs of our seats, Gino came through the kitchen doorway. "Baby Doll," he said with a broad grin before leaning across the bar to peck my cheek. "And the lovely Fiona." His eyes sparkled as he lifted my mother's hands to his lips. "This is an unexpected pleasure. What can I get you?"

We both ordered chardonnay, and as Gino poured wine into our glasses, my mother said, "Tell me about the break-in at your studio."

"What's this?" Gino's hand froze mid-pour. "Someone broke into your studio? Aren't bartenders supposed to be the first to hear about such things?"

"Umm, you might want to…" I pointed at the wineglass that was about to overflow. He startled, lifting the bottle, and I started telling my tale. For the second time—or was it the third?—I rehashed everything that happened. Even in the retelling, nothing seemed clearer.

"And you can't guess who it was?" Fiona asked.

"Nope." As far as I knew, neither Gino nor my mom had heard our latest theory—the one where Mackenzie was the intended victim. "There's been a twist in the investigation."

"Do tell." Gino pushed our filled wineglasses across the counter.

I launched into our latest camera club theory.

"The woman with the pink hair? The one who left the party in an ambulance?" Gino's eyebrows nearly met his hairline. "She's the village's librarian, right?

"You haven't met her?" I asked.

"I have," he said. "But we only met for the first time at the masquerade party."

Changing the investigation's focus to Mackenzie gave it a brand new feel. If Gino didn't know Mackenzie—and I was willing to take him at his word—

that should let him off the hook. I no longer needed to understand the purpose of the supplements he bought from Iris. The thought offered relief.

"You mentioned running into Tallulah and River on the village green the night of the masquerade party."

"Yep," he said. "And the cute little tyke with the blonde pigtails."

"She's the monkey wrench in my theory," I said. I refused to believe that either River or Tallulah would've murdered Iris in front of Saskia, even if they thought she was Mackenzie.

"Lay it on me," Gino said. "What's kicking around in your pretty little head?"

"I'm working the timeline," I said. "You must have been on the village green around the time Iris was killed. Do you remember seeing anything?"

Gino appeared to think about my question before shaking his head. "Nothing unusual comes to mind."

"But that was around the time you met River and Tallulah and gave them appetizers?"

"Sounds right. It was the little girl who caught my attention. I offered her a bite-sized fruit tart, and that's when I met River." Gino laughed. "Not exactly the jovial type, is he?"

I snorted. "So, it's not just me." Cheerless would be a better description for him.

"What did you think of Tallulah?" I had yet to remove her from my list. Motive unknown.

"She seems somewhat…vanilla," Gino said.

"Okay, so bad analogy. Vanilla is my favorite flavor." I chewed my lip and met Gino's gaze. "What do you know about Muffy?" I twisted my lips. "You know, the Audrey Hepburn look-alike who has a major crush on you."

My mother startled. "You mean the young woman who was draped all over Ciarán this evening?"

"The very one," I said. "It seems she's unhappy with Mackenzie's choice of children's books. And before you tell me it's a weak motive, I'm going to add that I saw her skulking around outside Mackenzie's house."

"Pfft," Gino said. "She's harmless."

"Flashing you with her big, round goo-goo eyes doesn't make her harmless," I said.

"That seems rather a waste of time," my mother said.

"Mom!" I gasped, suppressing a laugh.

With an amused grin, Gino seemed to be doing the same. That Gino was gay wasn't a secret, but my mother's matter-of-fact observation took me by surprise. Gino and I burst out laughing, our heads thrown back.

"You're not wrong, there," Gino said, fighting to catch his breath.

"Oh, for heaven's sake," my mother said, a sly smile sliding across her face as she looked at me. "If I'm not mistaken, that was the first time in many years that you called me *mom*."

My laughter stopped. Was it? And my mom noticed? Fiona gave a slight nod, like she was reading my mind.

Before I could get lost in the maze of my thoughts, Gino cleared his throat. "Anyway, I stand by my statement about Muffy."

"Yeah, Muffy is a long shot," I said. "I wish I knew more about her husband's death. That was what, three months ago?"

"She had a husband who died recently?" My mother pinched her lips in a disapproving gesture I knew all too well.

"A very wealthy, much older husband. He wasn't much younger than you," I said with a satisfied nod.

"How did he die?" my mother asked.

"Natural causes, apparently," I said. "But, he had no underlying health issues."

Gino was silent, a faraway look in his eyes.

"Earth to Gino," I said. "What are you thinking?"

With a jerk of his head, Gino's eyes cleared. "I was just remembering something," he said. "It was right after I started here. Early June, I'd say. Muffy was in the bar alone, sitting at the table over there." He nodded toward the back corner of the tavern. "She had a stack of library books in front of her and was reading. When I brought her the wine she'd ordered, I joked around about a pretty young thing being at the bar alone"—he narrowed his eyes—"studying herbal medicine." Gino paused. "This was the week before her husband died."

"One week?" I shuddered.

"I didn't think anything of it," Gino said. "She said she preferred doing research in the privacy of the bar, that she was looking for the fountain of youth. Pretty as she is, it's not surprising she'd want to stay that way."

"Quite the interesting development," my mother said, lifting her wineglass to her lips.

"And these were library books?" I asked. I exchanged glances with both Gino and my mother. "That means Mackenzie would know about it."

We were silent for a moment, and I sipped my wine while pondering the implications of Gino's revelation. Muffy might've been telling the truth. I didn't know her age. Early thirties was my guess. Wanting to stay youthful was nothing new. I could relate. But I was growing wary of coincidences, and this was a weird one.

The couple who'd been talking quietly stood up to leave, and Gino chatted with them while cashing them out. My mother hummed along to the tune of some pop song I was surprised she knew. I was starting to realize that everything I thought I knew about her was probably wrong.

Gino returned and leaned against the bar. "I admit, Muffy makes for an interesting suspect."

No sooner were the words out of Gino's mouth than something crashed in the kitchen. He jerked to look behind him. "Can I get you ladies anything before I go mitigate whatever disaster just happened?"

I turned to my mother, and we both shook our heads. "You'd best run," my mother said to Gino.

"I should probably head home, too." I drained the last sip of my wine. "I promised Darcy a walk."

"Will he hold you to it?" My mother shot me an amused look. Then, she turned serious. "I worry about you, Bobbie Ann."

"What? Don't be silly. I'm perfectly capable of taking care of myself."

In answer to my protest, her eyebrows arched. "A mother never stops worrying. I'm sure you're familiar with the concept."

"Emma is only twenty-three," I said. "By the time I was her age, I was already married."

My mother wasn't buying it. "You were married to a graduate student, with a baby on the way, not a dollar between the two of you, and trying to live on Dan's stipend."

I thought for a moment. "I admit, having Emma right away hadn't been part of our plan, but we were fine. Don't forget, I had a job, too." When I thought back, I remembered those years as being happy. Challenging, but happy. To say we'd been poor was an understatement. Diapers and baby food had taken such a massive chunk from our budget that Dan and I had lived on ramen noodles and popcorn. It never occurred to me that my parents might have been concerned.

Fiona was watching me like she could read my mind. "You'll always be my daughter," she said. "After everything that's happened, don't you think it's time to stop with your investigations?"

"I can't," I said. "Don't you see? As long as the killer is out there, I'm in danger."

A long sigh escaped Fiona's lips. "That may be true, but I fear things might not end well this time."

* * *

After leaving my mother at the inn, I drove back to my house, where Darcy greeted me with his tail wagging. My mom had never had a dog, or she would have known Darcy wasn't about to let me off the hook. It was late, but I couldn't turn away from his hopeful eyes.

"Okay, boy, but only a short one tonight." I pointed a warning finger.

He pulled his leash off the hook and wagged his tail even harder, knowing he'd won.

Mist settled over the village, shrouding the street lights in a glow that would typically make me reach for my camera. The diffusion of light against a dark background was a photographer's dream. It was all so very London-esque, making me think of serial killers and cloaked men hiding in shadows. Behind every tree and every lamppost, I imagined the killer lurking.

My mother's words joined the chorus of warnings. I quickened my pace. As much as I wanted to push aside thoughts of recent threats, I couldn't. Wherever the killer was, they wouldn't stop until they were caught. Despite my determination to move forward, one thing was clear.

Someone wanted to kill me, too.

Chapter Thirty

The next morning, the fog lifted, and the sun was shining brightly. Even after my panic-filled jog home the night before, I'd slept well. It wasn't until I stepped out of the shower that I realized I'd slept so soundly, I hadn't heard Emma come in. Her bedroom door was closed, and I considered giving it a tap as I came out of the bathroom. I thought better of it, knowing she'd been out late and probably needed to catch up on her sleep before her drive home. Our paths would cross before she left.

I went straight to my room and dressed, winding my wet hair into a bun and loosely wrapping it with a scarf. After my minimal makeup routine, I lifted my phone from the dresser to check my calendar. No appointments until late afternoon. Perfect. I'd spend a quiet morning in the studio, editing photos and catching up on proposals.

Eager to get started, I left my bedroom and walked into the hallway, only to find Emma, shoes in hand, tiptoeing up the stairs. Startled, we both froze. With effort, I closed my mouth, trying to compose my expression into something…less surprised. The defiant lift of Emma's chin said I'd failed miserably.

"OMG. Tell me you weren't waiting for me." The bored tone in her voice sounded forced.

"No. I'm heading out to my studio."

Her lips curled, and it was clear she didn't believe me. It struck me that our entire weekend had involved a delicate balancing act. I thought I'd done an admirable job of biting my tongue. I liked Connor and would be thrilled if he and Emma ended up together someday. Just…not quite yet. It had only been a few months since Emma's breakup with a man she'd hoped to marry.

Emma walked past me to her bedroom door. With her hand on the doorknob, she turned to face me. "Look, Mom. I'm well aware you think I'm rushing into things." She sounded tired. "But you're wrong, and I don't have time for one of your interrogations right now. I need to get packed so I can pick up Gran and drive her to the airport."

I'd almost forgotten my mom was leaving. Since Emma was headed back to Boston, it made sense that she'd drive her. My mom's flight wasn't until later in the evening, though. She didn't need to leave right away. "How about a quick cup of coffee before you go?"

Emma paused, as though thinking about it. Then, shaking her head, she said, "I'm kind of in a hurry. Besides, I'm not up for a talk. I'll grab a cup on my way out."

"All right." If there was one thing I knew about Emma, it was that once her mind was made up, there was no budging her. "Drive safely, and tell Gran I hope she comes back soon." I stepped forward to hug her, and felt encouraged when she hugged me back.

I headed downstairs, grabbed my backpack, and strode toward the kitchen door. Darcy sprawled on his back, and I stooped to rub his belly. I felt like Emma was pushing me away—something she'd been doing more frequently since Dan died. I shared some of the blame. I was holding her too tightly, afraid to let her go. The thought of losing her, too, was unbearable.

I tucked the thought away and headed to my studio. Someday we'd get back to how we used to be. We *would*.

"Good morning," I called as I opened my studio door, coming to an abrupt halt as soon as I entered.

"Morning, Mrs. B," Penny said without looking up from her computer monitor. Next to her, all ridiculously handsome as always, stood Ciarán. *Great.* He looked at me, the corners of his mouth lifting into the barely-there smile I found so mesmerizing. I mumbled a greeting, doing my best to mask my surprise. He was leaning forward, his palms resting on Penny's desk. The sleeves of his striped Oxford shirt were rolled just below his elbows, revealing muscular forearms. My heart skipped a beat.

Forearms, Bobbie? Seriously? When did you start caring about forearms? But I had to admit, his were oh-so nice.

From the corner of my eye, I caught Penny's glance. She seemed to be assessing the situation before refocusing on her screen. "Mr. D thinks he knows what's wrong with our website."

"Oh…" This wasn't what I'd planned for the morning, and aggravation crept in. Finding my voice, I said, "I'm pretty sure I made it clear I wasn't ready to deal with an overhaul of our website."

Penny's head shot up. "If not for our website, you wouldn't have been alone, waiting for a no-show customer with the door unlocked. Excuse me for worrying about our safety." She huffed. "Besides, we can't put it off forever."

Ciarán straightened, looking uncomfortable. "I should probably…" He stepped toward the door.

Pinning my assistant with a stern look, which I suspected wasn't nearly as intimidating as I intended, I sighed. As much as I valued her help in the studio, her professionalism needed work. I took partial responsibility for that. I tended to treat employees more like colleagues, failing to draw a clear line between our roles. This wasn't the time or place for a reprimand, so I forced a smile and met Ciarán's gaze. *Heaven help me.*

"I'll walk out with you." It seemed like the polite thing to do, and I could at least manage that much.

Once outside, I closed the studio door and stopped, turning to face him. "I'm sorry if Penny wasted your time." I blew my bangs from my face. "She shows a lot of initiative, but she should have checked with me first."

"Not a problem," Ciarán said. "We ran into each other at Rose's, and she asked if I could walk over and take a look. I didn't mind. If I'm not mistaken, there's a latte waiting for you inside."

I couldn't help letting out an exasperated groan. "So much for reprimanding her. I do appreciate the way she takes charge of the administrative tasks. To be honest, I'm not sure where I'd be without her."

"I should be so lucky." Ciarán's expression relaxed, the corners of his eyes crinkling. "From what little I saw, the problem with your website looks like an easy fix. And Penny is right about you being safer if there weren't random intruders in your studio."

"Good point." I shuddered at the memory of being alone when I heard the crash.

"Did you find out anything about what happened yesterday?"

"Not yet. It seems unlikely it was my late client." I studied him, remembering the way Muffy had clung to him the night before. Since I'd moved her up on my suspect list, I had to ask, "What can you tell me about Muffy?"

"Muffy? Okay, wow." His ears reddened. "I don't know her very well. Recently widowed with a young child. It's tragic."

"True," I said, even as I wondered about her rush to move on. My thoughts were mean, and I'd never, ever give voice to them. There was no recipe for grief. How she truly felt was something I had no way of knowing.

"She seems eager to make friends in Stonebridge," Ciarán said.

"I've noticed," I mumbled, leaving it at that. *Friends?* Was he being evasive, or was it possible he was as clueless as Nate was? "Although she seems to have it in for Mackenzie."

"Oh? I wouldn't know about that." He paused, clearing his throat. "I think your website is adding appointments to your calendar before the client confirms. The good news is that you have potential customers visiting your site."

Smooth. He'd steered the conversation back to safe ground. So, he didn't want to talk about Muffy. "I guess that's good news, then," I said, allowing the shift.

"I have a web developer friend in East Dorset. He's quite good. If you'd be more comfortable working with someone else, that is."

"Oh." I was tongue-tied. Feeling the sting of my fingernails on my palm, I unclenched my fist. "It's not that. I mean, when I'm ready to have the work done—" What was it about him that thoroughly unhinged me? Acting like this... It wasn't me.

"Look, I—" Ciarán sounded tentative. "I apologize if I offended you. I certainly never meant to."

The man was much nicer than I deserved. "If anyone should be apologizing, it's me. I was rude the other day, and I didn't mean to be."

"Nate told me you're grieving. I'm sorry for your loss. I was too forward." He paused. "I would like to meet with you to discuss business, though."

The sound of a car door drew my attention. I looked toward my driveway as Emma moved around her car from the trunk. She opened her driver's side door, our eyes meeting. I was acutely aware of Ciarán watching us as I lifted my hand. Emma nodded back before lowering herself into her car. Within seconds, her engine started, and she backed out of my driveway.

Ciarán seemed to study my expression. To his credit, he remained silent.

"It's been a rough morning." I let out a weak laugh, feigning indifference.

"Having daughters can be challenging." Ciarán offered his hint of a smile. "I always assumed that sort of thing would have happened less if my wife had been around more. Forgive me for feeling somewhat relieved to see that's not necessarily the case."

This time I laughed. "You have a daughter?"

"Two," he said. "And a son. My oldest daughter is twenty-nine, going on fifty. My youngest is in her final year at university but seems to want to delay graduating for another two or three years."

I was intrigued. Twenty-nine. I'd heard Nate say Ciarán was fifty, like Alicia. He would've been a young dad. And why hadn't his wife been around? I reminded myself—firmly—it didn't matter. I was not interested in him. *Not. At. All.*

I squared my shoulders. "You said you wanted to talk business?"

"Our businesses complement each other. I've been hoping to connect with you on ways we can leverage that."

I looked down at my feet, sure my cheeks were crimson with embarrassment. When he asked me out for a cup of coffee, had he only wanted to discuss business? I'd shot him down, assuming he meant it to be a date.

"I have clients who need quality photography for their websites," Ciarán continued. "I think we can help each other out. Would you be interested in talking about it?"

I raised my head, a mixture of excitement and mortification warring within me. "Yes," I said. "Definitely. I'd like that very much. I'm sorry, and more than a little embarrassed if I misunderstood your invitation."

"You didn't," he said. "But no worries about that. I got your message. Loud and clear." His lips lifted slightly, softening his words.

"Oh, right."

"If you ever change your mind, I think you'll find I can be pretty good at the friendship thing."

I had no doubt he was extremely good at *the friendship thing*, but I was less sure that I could be friends with a man who made my heart race.

"I'll keep that in mind." My gaze landed on his forearms. What was it with me and forearms all of a sudden? When I looked up, Ciarán wore an expectant expression. "Sorry," I said. I needed to end this discussion before I completely humiliated myself, assuming that ship hadn't already sailed.

"When you're ready, have Penny give me a bell. I'll set up a meeting with her and leave the location up to you." He took a step back, preparing to leave. "We'll keep it all business."

"Thanks," I said, a mixture of relief and disappointment battling it out. The thought that keeping it all business wasn't what I really wanted nagged me. But, of course, I did. I *did*. Still, I couldn't shake the feeling I'd treated him badly.

"I know it's a cliché," I said, "but the way I feel, it's not about you." When Ciarán's gaze met mine, I cringed inwardly. *Seriously, Bobbie? The whole* It's not you, it's me *thing?* Why couldn't I ever leave well enough alone?

But then he chuckled, his green eyes shining with his sudden smile. "I think we'll work together just fine. I'll look forward to Penny's call." He turned and walked back toward the street.

I stayed in place, watching his broad back as he walked away. His stride was relaxed, maybe even a little jaunty. As I reached for the end of my scarf, I chewed my lip. I could do this. I could figure out how to have a business relationship with him. I'd be a fool not to. Already, I'd been foolish to ignore the no-show appointments. While walking back toward the studio, I rolled my shoulders. When Penny called to schedule a business meeting, I'd also have her set up a consultation for our website. As Ciarán had said, it was strictly business. And I wasn't one to shy away from that.

Chapter Thirty-One

When I reentered the studio, Penny sat with her eyes glued to her monitor, seemingly engrossed in her work. Without a word, she lifted a to-go cup of coffee in a silent offering. Not over my annoyance with her for bringing Ciarán to the studio, I accepted the cup, thanked her, and turned to climb the stairs to my loft. I wasn't prepared to confront her, and I needed time to think about the best way to approach the topic. Did she deserve a reprimand for overstepping? Gratitude for her initiative? Something in between the two?

I sat at my desk and turned on my computer, surveying the list of projects I hadn't finished the afternoon before. The more creative tasks—sorting and editing photos—called to me. Ignoring the proposals, I opened a file for an engagement shoot from the weekend before the festival. I took a sip of my coffee while reviewing my notes, and my tension eased. They were such a cute couple. Young—reminding me of Dan and me at that age. So naïve, so certain things would never change. To be fair, through all the ups and downs of graduate school, raising Emma, and keeping up with a mound of bills we couldn't afford to pay, our love had never wavered. The financial strain had lessened once Dan finished school and signed on at one of Boston's top universities. He'd been successful as a medical researcher, and we'd been happy.

I clicked the mouse and worked to the background hum of Penny answering phone calls and typing on her keyboard. After watching the photos fill my screen, I sorted them, flagging the best ones for editing. I preferred to keep my photos natural, but they still needed some tweaking.

My first steps always included adjusting the white balance and exposure. Then, I could move on to the fun part—finding the perfect crop, playing with shadows, adding a slight blur to soften the skin, and fine-tuning the saturation and luminosity of colors. I loved editing photos almost as much as I loved taking them.

When I finished, my mind drifted to my suspect chart. I opened it and added notes about Muffy's research. Then there was Jackson. Anger over Mackenzie's interference wasn't a strong motive. But picking up and delivering her tea gave him a mega opportunity.

That left Harmony and her housemates. They were all linked to both victims, but the only motives I could come up with were for killing Iris, not Mackenzie. I hovered my cursor over their names, thinking about deleting them, but I didn't. Our new theory could be flawed.

Sunshine poured through the skylight above me. I'd lost track of time. I closed the file and shut down my computer. The dregs in my cup had long gone cold. I stood up, discarded the cup, and peeked over the railing. It was time for a talk with my assistant.

Penny looked up, her eyes narrowing as I walked down the stairs. The soft *tap, tap* of her tongue ring filled the otherwise quiet studio. When I reached Penny's desk, I said in a calm voice, "I'm not angry."

"Could have fooled me." She raised her chin.

I'd never been much of a disciplinarian, but this was a discussion we needed to have. I took in Penny's defiance and reminded myself of how far we'd come. The truth was, I relied on her. Softening my words with a smile, I said, "Decisions that have to do with this studio, particularly ones that will cost me money, need to be discussed with me first. I can't have you making these decisions on your own."

Penny was quiet as she seemed to compose herself. "I didn't," she said. "What happened last night, it scared me. You could have been hurt."

"Even so." I softened even more.

"It's not like I hired Mr. D to fix the website. I know I need your permission for that." She tapped her tongue ring against her teeth. "I ran into him at the coffee shop, you know? He'd already heard about what happened with the intruder. And I…" Penny swallowed. "I guess I asked him if he had a minute to check it out. He seemed happy to do it and all."

"Ciarán and I talked outside," I told her about the potential work for some of his clients and my decision to go forward with fixing our website. "I told him you'd give him a call. I want two separate meetings, and include yourself in the one to discuss the problems with our website."

Penny's mouth stretched into a wide smile. "You mean it? That would be so awesome!" She glanced at her computer screen. "I'm on it, Mrs. B." Her fingers tapped the keyboard. "The end of the week is wide open."

I stifled a laugh. "I need to get some lunch. Can I bring something back for you?"

"Nah. Mackenzie packed me one." Penny held up a brown bag.

"Speaking of Mackenzie," I said. "I want to talk to her again." I knew Vermont statute wouldn't allow her to tell me about Muffy's book borrowing, but if I worded my questions right, I might pick up something in her mannerisms.

"That's perfect, then," Penny said. "She should talk to you, too."

"What about?"

"It's about River." Penny started to unpack her lunch. "This morning I heard her talking to someone on the phone, and she sounded kind of upset. When I asked her about it, she said River was demanding more money. She said he's been bugging her for the past couple of weeks."

"Money?" I asked. "Why?"

"He claims Harmony didn't charge her enough. It wasn't the dollars Mackenzie was upset about. She wanted to talk to Harmony first, but River kept bugging her." Penny took a bite of her sandwich. "She's at the library. Toddler story time should be wrapping up. I don't think she has anything else scheduled for today."

My hunger forgotten, I was eager to get to the library. "Perfect. I'll go there first and then stop at the Rosebud for a snack. I'll be back in a bit."

* * *

The thing I loved most about living in the center of the village was my proximity to almost everything. After giving Mr. Miller an automatic wave, I cut across the church's lawn and rounded the corner onto Bridge Street. Housed in Stonebridge's first one-room schoolhouse, the library sat near the village-side entrance to the covered bridge. Although tiny, our town was lucky to have its own library, and even luckier to have a librarian like Mackenzie who was knowledgeable, enthusiastic, and dedicated to our community. As I approached, Saskia bounded out the door, trailed by Tallulah.

"I got new books," Saskia greeted me.

Tallulah carried a lumpy tote bag that looked heavy. "Hi, Bobbie." She gave me a tentative smile that reminded me of Gino's assessment. Vanilla. But then, I liked vanilla.

"Are you coming out of the toddler story hour?" I asked.

"Little Miss Sassyfrass loves it." Her use of River's affectionate nickname for Saskia caught me by surprise.

Saskia twirled in circles on the library's lawn. "I got books about u'corns."

"Unicorns!" I laughed. I'd never outgrown my love for the mythical creature. "Those are the best books ever!"

"I know." Saskia giggled. "Come on, Lula, I want to go home and read my new books."

"Lunch first," Tallulah said with a sigh that didn't sound the least bit exasperated.

"I'll let you get to it," I said as I watched Saskia. "We can't let unicorn stories wait."

After saying our goodbyes, I took the remaining steps to the library's entrance. I opened the door to the musty smell of books and dusty floors, which still carried the faintest hint of chalk embedded in their cracks. It wasn't difficult to imagine the sounds of children's laughter echoing from years past, their timid voices reciting numbers, letters, and snippets of poetry.

"I'll be right with you," Mackenzie's voice called from beneath the desk by the entrance.

"No hurry." I took the moment to look around the large room, which was packed with book-laden shelves. Wheeled carts served as end caps, displaying what appeared to be the newer releases. As I took a step toward a book with an intriguing cover, a flash of fuchsia appeared from under the desk. Mackenzie stood, brushing the knees of her faded jeans, and smiled. With her arm, she brushed her choppy bangs from her face, making them stick out at an odd angle.

"The electricity in this building could use an upgrade." She wiped her palms on her thighs before tousling her hair back into place. "I found this great lamp at the flea market a couple of weeks ago, and I knew it belonged on my desk." She flicked the lamp on, illuminating the dried flowers embedded in its shade.

"You bought it at a flea market?" I admired the craftsmanship. "Lucky find."

"For sure." Mackenzie beamed. "Anyway, what can I help you find?"

"Nothing this time," I said. "I was hoping you had a minute to chat."

"I made a pot of coffee. Can I tempt you with a cup?"

"Always."

"Great. Have a seat." She pointed at a chair near her desk before turning to a nearby bookshelf, where she poured coffee into mismatched mugs. "Cream or sugar?"

"Both," I answered before adding, "Please. Light and sweet. I just ran into Tallulah and Saskia leaving with a colossal bag of books."

Mackenzie nodded and stirred my coffee before handing it to me. "Saskia loves books. If I didn't know better, I'd say she takes after Tallulah. She was a bookworm as a child, too. When I'd walk past her house in the summertime, she'd be on her front porch reading instead of playing with the other kids." Mackenzie chuckled. "Of course, in our neighborhood, that was probably just as well."

I sipped the coffee, which was amazingly good. "Your neighborhood was dangerous?"

"I'm not sure I'd go that far," Mackenzie said with a scoff. "But yeah, it was troubled. Don't get me wrong. Brattleboro is a great town. Our little neighborhood—not so much. When Tallulah and I figured out we were from the same place, it wasn't as much of a joyful reunion as a congratulations for getting out."

I remembered Harmony telling me Mackenzie and Tallulah had grown up in the same area. "It's so funny you didn't recognize each other."

"Well, besides the twenty or so years that have passed, not to mention our five-year age difference, back then, I was kind of goth." Before Mackenzie finished her sentence, the door opened, and Harmony floated into the library as if carried on the breeze.

"You were goth?" Harmony asked. "Oops, sorry. I didn't mean to eavesdrop. It's kind of hard to picture."

Mackenzie laughed. "It's true. I wore my hair in long braids, à la Wednesday Addams. Add to that lots of black eyeliner, deep purple lipstick, and I went by my first name, Ashley. Mackenzie is my middle name. Tallulah was just a kid, around nine or ten. And she went by Lula." Mackenzie took a sip from her mug and looked at Harmony. "Would you like a cup?"

"No thanks," Harmony said. "I just came in to see if you have any new romantasy books."

"I ordered the latest Rebecca Yarros novel. It should be here next week."

Harmony's eyes lit up. "Sign me up for that one."

"Done," Mackenzie said.

Harmony leaned against the edge of Mackenzie's desk. "You were talking about your wayward youth?"

"That's one way of putting it," Mackenzie said. "I was telling Bobbie about the neighborhood where Tallulah and I grew up."

Harmony nodded. "Tallulah told me about that. I got the impression she had an unhappy childhood. Something about her mother not being well."

"To put it mildly," Mackenzie said. "The way I remember it, her mom was making her stepsister sick. I'm afraid I didn't pay much attention at the time. I had my own mom to deal with."

"Do you mean Munchausen by proxy syndrome?" I'd read about it at one time. The caregiver, most often the mother, sought attention by making a person in their care sick.

"That sounds familiar," Mackenzie said. "As I said, I was dealing with issues of my own. Coming home from school to find my drug addict of a mom passed out didn't leave me much time for getting involved in local gossip. She died of a drug overdose at the ripe old age of thirty-five."

"I'm so sorry," I said.

"I have Vickie Sue to thank for my relatively stable teen years." Mackenzie let out a soft chuckle. "Taking in a rebellious teen must have been tough for her. She'd never married and had no experience with kids, let alone a smart aleck like me. I'm her brother's daughter, and considering my dad took off when I was a toddler, Vickie Sue and I hardly knew each other."

Harmony shifted to sit on the corner of Mackenzie's desk. "That must have been hard."

"It wasn't ideal." Mackenzie waved her hand as if waving the past away. "Enough about that. Tallulah and I both made our escape, and all is well."

I regarded the young woman sitting next to me. She'd certainly matured past her rebellious goth phase. So much so that I credited her with much of Penny's recent growth. Even with our occasional issues, the change in Penny over the last few months seemed miraculous.

"Everyone at the masquerade party thought I was either drunk or on drugs."

"We were only concerned." I hoped we hadn't seemed judgmental.

"Yeah. No worries. But the thing is, after watching what my mom went through, I don't touch the stuff. Not even alcohol. My cider was plain. Travis knows this. Penny told me about the photo of him. He never would have done anything to my drink."

"We're just trying to figure things out," I said. "Someone saw you and Travis arguing."

Mackenzie sat back and laughed. "That's Travis for you. We have so many rivalries going on. He was making fun of my *Harry Potter*-themed costume. He's more of a *Lord of the Rings* fan." Mackenzie paused. "Was that why you came here? To talk about Travis and Tallulah?"

"Not exactly," I said. "There are two things I'm looking for info on. Penny told me about River."

Harmony straightened. "What about River?"

"Right. I asked her not to do that." Mackenzie's glance skipped between Harmony and me. She took a sip from her mug, appearing hesitant to say more.

I understood her discomfort, but if River was hounding Mackenzie for money without Harmony's say-so, Harmony needed to know about it. "Penny said River was asking you for more money."

"What for?" Harmony blinked, a range of emotions playing across her face. "I don't understand why he'd do that."

Mackenzie still hadn't spoken, so I asked Harmony, "How closely do you watch your household accounts?"

"Not very," Harmony said. "River has taken care of our bills for years."

"It's not a big deal." Mackenzie looked at Harmony. "You were more than generous when I stayed with you. Now that I'm on my feet, I'm willing to make it up to all of you. I was planning to discuss it with you first."

Harmony turned her attention to me. "And you assume this relates to Mackenzie being poisoned?" She looked like she was trying to hide her exasperation, but doing a poor job of it. "Honestly, you seem determined to pin this on one of my housemates. What do you think he's done?"

"I'm trying to find the killer," I said. "If they happen to be one of your housemates, so be it. I haven't had a chance to process this yet, but it's worth looking into." I paused, remembering how Rose and I overheard River and Saskia while hiding beneath Iris's desk. "I overheard him telling Saskia to keep a secret from you and Tallulah. A surprise, he called it."

Harmony's eyes narrowed. "If he called it a surprise, it was a surprise." She deflated. "I'll ask him about it."

I felt more confused than ever. "I haven't reached any conclusions. We don't even know the source of the poison. It could have been a mushroom, as Mackenzie originally thought. But that doesn't exactly help River since he showed her which ones to pick." As I said this, I saw Mackenzie shaking her head. Ignoring her, I continued. "Another possibility is Mackenzie's tea being tampered with."

"So basically, you're focused on River."

I ignored the heat in Harmony's stare and explained about Jackson and the odd entry in Iris's ledger.

Harmony slumped. "I don't know what to say. I vaguely remember Jackson being at our house that day. He was looking for Iris, but she was out making deliveries. She might've left Mackenzie's tea behind and asked him to pick it up for her. It could all be perfectly innocent." She straightened again. "As for River and the mushrooms. He would never."

It wasn't worth arguing about. I didn't have all the facts yet, and River's motive didn't make sense to me. Killing Mackenzie wouldn't get him the funds he wanted.

Mackenzie broke our silence. "You said there were two things you wanted to ask about. What's the second?"

"Muffy," I said. "I heard something interesting about her last night."

Harmony stood. "I'll leave both of you to it. I'm teaching yoga this afternoon and need to run."

"What about Muffy?" Mackenzie asked as soon as Harmony left. "I really don't think her crusade over children's books is personal."

"Maybe not," I said. "But what I heard had to do with researching herbal medications shortly before her husband died."

Mackenzie's fingers fidgeted in her lap. "That sounds interesting."

"Does the library have many books on the topic?" I asked.

"We have a few, if you're interested." Her voice was casual, unlike her gaze, which bore into me with an intensity that didn't seem like her. "What we don't have, I know I can get through our library network."

Although Mackenzie couldn't legally give me a direct answer, her awareness of what was available through the network, along with the sharpness of her stare, seemed to hint that she'd helped Muffy.

"I'll let you know," I said, satisfied. Muffy had been studying herbal medicine. Now I needed to find out why.

Chapter Thirty-Two

When I left the library, my mind was whirling. I hadn't eaten lunch and was famished. Rose always had something tasty to eat.

I waved to Mr. Miller for a second time as I walked past his house. When he responded to my greeting with a harrumph, I smiled. The normalcy was exactly what I needed at that moment.

Next, I passed my house and peeked down my driveway. I couldn't help feeling deflated when I saw Emma's car was still missing. I knew she had time to come back before taking my mom to the airport, but she hadn't. Pushing my disappointment aside, I mounted the steps to the coffee shop and almost collided with Muffy, who was on her way out. Her surprised expression transformed into a broad smile, one that didn't quite reach her eyes. It was a shame, really. Beneath her thick fringe of bangs, Muffy had the biggest, roundest, dark brown eyes I'd ever seen. How beautiful they'd be if they weren't so calculating.

"Bobbie, how nice to see you again." Her words held all the warmth of a Vermont ice storm.

"Likewise."

I'd barely gotten the word out before she spoke again. "I saw Ciarán leaving your house this morning."

My studio, not my house. Not that it was any of her business. Her tone put me on edge. "You were outside my house?"

"You live on Main Street," she huffed. "The parking spots near the library were full, so I parked in a spot across the street from your house."

I should have felt relieved, but I found myself thinking she had more to dish out. I forced a smile. "Story time was this morning. Did you take your daughter?"

"Oof! You can't possibly think…" Muffy crossed her arms over her chest. "I guess you aren't aware of the kind of children's books they have there."

"It's been a while since I read children's books, but Mackenzie is awesome." Without thinking, I added, "It makes me wonder why I saw you hanging around outside her house yesterday."

Muffy's eyes widened. "The librarian? Why would I hang around her house?" Her forehead creased. "Wait. Does she live on River Street?"

I stared at Muffy, baffled by how her cheeks turned bright pink. I couldn't help it, but a part of me was enjoying her discomfort.

"How would I know that?" Muffy pinned me with a hard glare. "It's a good place to walk. The road is quiet, and the river is pretty."

I often walked on River Street for those very reasons. But I didn't for one second believe her explanation. Before I was able to form a coherent follow-up, Muffy dropped her pretense along with her fake smile.

"You didn't tell me why Ciarán was at your house so early in the morning."

While I admired Muffy's tenacity, I was losing my grip on politeness. "And you didn't tell me why you cared."

She rolled her eyes. "I need to know he's not some kind of player, okay?" She must have noticed the incredulity in my raised brow, because she added, "We're going on our first date tonight. I'm hoping it's the beginning of more."

I did all I could to keep my expression neutral. Ciarán and Muffy were dating? Huh. It was no secret she had him in her sights. But hadn't he just told me he was interested in—I let out a slow breath—being friends. *Fine.* Ciarán's love life didn't concern me.

At all.

I held Muffy's gaze. Who was I kidding? Of course, Ciarán would be interested in her. With a smile that made my face ache, I said, "No problem then. This morning was all business."

Muffy let out a relieved sigh, and her expression beamed. "I should have known. I mean, *really.*" She visually assessed me before gleaming with triumph. Presumably satisfied I posed no threat, she bounded down the Rosebud's porch steps.

I froze as I watched her cross Main Street to her car. She'd as good as called me unattractive. I mean… I wasn't a fashion model or anything, but I'd always thought of myself as reasonably cute—in that girl-next-door kind of way. I was so stunned, I'd forgotten I was standing in the Rosebud's doorway. It wasn't until a couple pushed their way through the exit, flicking me with a surreptitious glance, that I snapped out of my daze.

Fine. Just fine. Muffy's opinion didn't matter. I was fine, *totally fine.* I shook my head and entered the coffee shop with a quick thought flashing through my mind: *Muffy is not a nice person.* She was a woman who would stop at nothing to get what she wanted. I made a mental note to move her up on my list of suspects.

* * *

"Hey, girl," Rose called from behind the counter. Raising her arm, she gestured for me to come over. "I've got something to show you." After my talk with Mackenzie, I hoped that whatever she had would shed some light in the murky cave I seemed to be crawling through.

Rose pulled her phone from her pocket and poked at the screen. She plunked the phone on the counter in front of me. "Selfies from the masquerade party. There are three of special interest. Take a gander while I make you a latte. Oh yeah, and I have the most scrumptious apple crumb muffins."

"Yes, please." Apples made for a healthy lunch. Satisfied, I peered at the first image on Rose's phone. It was a selfie of Rose and William. Super adorable. "Cute," I called to her.

"Look closer." The hissing of the espresso machine nearly drowned out her words.

I lifted the phone and reviewed the image, recalling how excited Rose had been in her Daisy Buchanan costume. She'd pulled it off so well. Her fondness for reliving her hours as Daisy notwithstanding, I was certain her costume wasn't what she wanted me to look at. With my photographer's eye, I looked beyond the obvious subjects to examine the easily ignored background elements.

Rose had been watching me and met my gaze. "Keep scrolling."

In the corner of the first photo, blurred just slightly, Jackson and Iris appeared to be arguing with Mackenzie. But I already knew about that. In the next photo, Iris was no longer facing him. Her angle made it difficult to discern her expression, but Jackson's cheeks were red, his lips pinched together, and he looked…livid. I wasn't sure how to interpret the last photo. Iris was no longer in the frame, presumably having left the marquee, but Jackson was glaring at Mackenzie from over his shoulder. He appeared to be leaving the tent.

I looked up. "How did you get these?"

"I took them right before William and I left to get my camera." She placed a steaming mug of milky coffee on the counter and pointed at the picture. "Remember? I forgot it."

"I remember," I said. The angle of the photos explained why I hadn't seen Rose. We'd have been on opposite sides of the tent. "I saw a small part of this argument. It was shortly after the party started. But I could only see Iris's and Mackenzie's capes. Were you able to hear what they were arguing about?"

"No. If I had to guess…" Rose paused. "In light of what we've learned, I'm wondering if maybe, just maybe, Iris changed her mind about going to France?"

"And then Jackson, enraged, followed her?" I checked the timestamp. "This photo was taken shortly before Iris was killed." My mind raced with the implications. Either Jackson had lied to me, or we were wrong. Even so, I was confused. Who'd been the intended victim? Iris? Mackenzie? Or both?

"I feel horrible," Rose said. "If I'd only known what was going on, I might have seen something when we ran back for my camera."

"You couldn't have known," I said. "Besides, you were heading the other way. I wish I'd seen these before I talked to Mackenzie."

"Can you text her?"

"I don't think I have her number." I pulled out my phone and scrolled through my contacts. "I'm heading back to the studio after this. I'll ask Penny.

A boisterous voice followed the jingle of the doorbell. "Ah, there you are. Penny thought you might be here." Jackson dropped onto the stool next to mine.

"What's up, Jackson?" Rose snatched her phone from the counter and stashed it in her pocket.

"I came to tell you that I'm leaving for France earlier than planned."

Words stuck in my throat.

Rose didn't seem to be having the same issue. "How much earlier?"

"I booked a flight for tomorrow," Jackson said.

I jerked my head to study him. I couldn't believe he was planning to leave so soon. We still didn't know who Iris's killer was.

Rose's brow furrowed. "Are you allowed to leave in the middle of an investigation like that?"

"Of course," Jackson said. "I'm not under arrest."

Yet. But I knew he was right. Detective Cram had Jackson's contact information, but he'd need to arrest him if he wanted to detain him. "Aren't you being a little hasty?"

Jackson smoothed his hand along the side of his head. "There's no reason for me to stay."

"Not even for Iris's funeral? Or to learn what happened to her?" I was stunned. Jackson's attitude seemed cavalier.

"Iris's funeral won't bring her back." Jackson slouched as if he were collapsing inward. "Besides, I didn't know her family. Being there would be weird. I'll keep following the investigation, but I feel like I need to get away from it all."

He sounded sincere. I knew from experience how grief played on other emotions. Even as I thought this, a small part of me wondered whether his rush to leave Stonebridge gave meaning to Rose's selfies. It would only be a matter of time before the police found out about his argument with Mackenzie. His expression in the photos was akin to rage.

"Don't worry, this isn't goodbye," he said. "I have a few things to wrap up before I come around to say my official *au revoirs* later."

As Jackson left, my head flooded with thoughts and images that needed somewhere to go. I didn't know what to make of his planned departure. Sorrow showed itself in so many ways. But what if that wasn't what I was seeing? The car chase and the crashing photo booth. Could Jackson be responsible for both? It was nearly impossible to accept. Had I been staring the killer in the face all along? I shuddered even as the idea solidified in my mind. He'd been close to the investigation, inserting himself at every step.

Chapter Thirty-Three

I stuffed the last bite of my muffin into my mouth and rested my head in my hands. Everything was a jumbled mess, but the pieces were all there. I was sure of it.

"What are you thinking?" Rose asked.

"Did you know Ciarán and Muffy are dating?" Yikes. That was not what I'd meant to say.

"Get out!" Rose's already round eyes grew even rounder. "No way. I don't believe it for a second."

I told her about my encounter outside the café. "Forget I said anything. I shouldn't have brought it up."

"You like him." It wasn't a question.

"No… Possibly…" Who was I kidding? "I really don't want to."

Rose reached across the table to squeeze my hand. "Oh, sweetie, Dan would want you to be happy."

Words caught in my throat. "I know."

"Then, what's the problem?"

I felt comfortable talking to Rose. She wasn't pushing me the way Alicia was. "I'm afraid if I let myself fall for someone, I'll forget Dan. I can't do that. Not ever."

Rose squeezed my hand again, her blue eyes sparkling. "That won't happen. You made so many memories together. No way you'll forget them."

I bit my lip and nodded.

"Well, one thing's for sure," Rose said. "Ciarán has *not* fallen for Muffy. Come on, let's be real, he hardly paid any attention to her last night, and that was with her hanging all over him. He spent most of the evening talking to your mom."

"Let's drop it, okay?"

"Consider it dropped," Rose said. "But on a similar note, I'm pretty sure I know why Muffy was hanging around outside Mackenzie's house."

That perked me up. "Out with it."

"Guess who moved into the house next door to Penny and Mackenzie?" Rose bounced with eagerness to share her news.

"No way..." I said. "Ciarán? You're sure?"

"Way!" Rose squealed with excitement. "Maybe Muffy wasn't stalking Mackenzie after all."

"That's a relief." I was glad to have a puzzle piece fall into place, but I was less enthusiastic to learn that Ciarán lived on the road where I walked almost every day. I'd think about different routes later. "What do you make of Jackson's change of plans?"

"Bizarre, right?" Rose had no trouble with the sudden topic change. "I mean, what's his rush? He doesn't want to hang around and find out what happened to Iris?"

"I hate even to imply this, but what if he already knows?" I grabbed the last muffin from the plate. Having devoured one already, I wasn't hungry, but I was a nervous nibbler.

"It's a terrible thought," Rose said. "Do you seriously think he was the one chasing you in the truck?"

"Or trying to crush me in the photo booth? I can't fathom it. It's much easier to picture River doing it."

"If Jackson was at Iris's and she texted him to pick up Mackenzie's tea, he could have slipped something poisonous in."

"We both saw her jars. I think most people know that both digitalis and nightshade are poisonous." I continued her train of thought. "It could have been an impulsive act." It seemed possible. Jackson's actions often gave me whiplash.

I told Rose what I'd learned about River secretly asking Mackenzie for money.

"That's interesting for sure," Rose said. "Extortion. Murder is always about love or money."

I laughed. "Extortion seems a little strong. But, yeah. Mackenzie said he got upset when she suggested talking to Harmony about it." I bit into my muffin, chewed, and swallowed before continuing. "It doesn't make sense to me. It's not like Mackenzie can pay him if she's dead."

"True." Rose tapped a finger to her chin. "Oh, I know." She stared at me with excitement. "River didn't want Mackenzie talking to Harmony. He was totally cooking the books."

"He was more worried about Harmony finding out than he was about getting the money." I smiled. "You're a genius."

"I don't hear that very often." Rose laughed. "It totally could have been River. He could easily get into Iris's apothecary."

"Good point," I said. "I wonder why he needed money without Harmony knowing."

The door swung open, and a group of tourists entered the café. Rose greeted them with a warm smile.

"I'll be right with you," she said.

"I'd better head back to my studio. Can you text your selfies to both Penny and me? I want to look at them on my monitor."

Rose fiddled with her phone. "All set," she said. "See you later?"

"Wine and whine on my patio tonight? The weather will be perfect for sitting around the fire pit. Maybe if we let loose a bit, we'll figure it all out."

* * *

Only the top of Penny's head was visible behind her computer monitor when I entered the studio. She lifted her chin in greeting and handed me three slips of pink paper. "I talked to Mr. D. We set up two appointments."

"That was fast." I read the messages. Two appointments with Ciarán, and a photography consultation with a potential client later in the afternoon. Only two days to prepare for discussing my website. I had a little more than a week to prepare for the other one, a lunch meeting.

"The website meeting will be here," Penny said as she kept typing. "He said to choose a location for the other one and suggested the Mill House."

Lunch at the inn. Public but quiet. And Gino would be there. It was as good a choice as any I could think of. I told Penny to go ahead and set it up.

"No probs," she said. With a final tap on her keyboard, she rested her hands on the desk and looked up. "How did it go with Mackenzie?"

I gave her a quick recap.

Penny scoffed. "So basically, Muffy used herbs to kill her husband, and River showed Mackenzie where to pick poisonous mushrooms."

"Interesting interpretation," I said. "I'm not quite ready to go there. But Rose found some interesting selfies on her phone."

"I saw them. I even synced them to our software. I figured you'd want a closer look." Penny pointed to her monitor. "It looks like Jackson and Mackenzie were having a big blowout."

"Mackenzie didn't tell you about it?" I asked.

"She mentioned Jackson being angry, but we didn't get into it. I can ask her when I get home."

"Please do." I inspected the photos more closely. There was no question that Jackson was livid. "He stopped by the coffee shop to tell us he's leaving for France tomorrow. He said that staying here won't bring Iris back."

"For real? That seems strange, and by strange, I mean shady."

"I don't disagree. But it's like he said, sticking around won't help Iris. Part of me doesn't blame him. He's going through a tough time."

"If something happened to Mackenzie, I'd want to see justice done." Penny stood. "He's been off since Iris was killed. Just saying."

"Grief is tricky." It was all I could think to say.

"I'll take your word for it." Penny gathered her things. "I gotta go. I left Hope with a babysitter and promised to be home early. You saw the note for this afternoon's consultation. This one's the real deal. The client made the appointment over the phone. Douglas, or something like that. His name is on the slip I gave you. He's looking for business headshots."

"I've got it covered," I said.

"I'll text you when I find out what the argument was about." When Penny left, I took over her place behind the reception desk. After the incident with the intruder, I wasn't comfortable retreating to my loft while the studio was unlocked. At least from Penny's desk, I could watch the door.

On the large monitor, Jackson's red face stared at me. Penny's insistence that his behavior was suspicious made me wonder if I was being too blasé about his plans to leave. Wanting to get away didn't seem unreasonable. Like Penny, though, I'd want closure first. I'd known Jackson since moving to Vermont, but that didn't mean I knew him well. Being a member of the camera club didn't make him innocent, either.

I stared at the image until it became blurry. That's when I noticed a shadow in the background—more like shadowy figures. I blinked to clear my vision before returning my focus to the screen. Through squinted eyes, I concentrated on the out-of-focus blobs. Sure enough, two figures appeared at the edge of the frame. One looked tall and lanky, the other was small, like a child. River and Saskia? I already knew they'd been on the green that night, but something was unsettling about seeing them in the photo.

After staring for too long, I pushed the thought aside and opened my bookkeeping software on the second monitor. With a website consultation only a few days away, I needed to ensure I had the necessary funds. I found the proposal Ciarán had forwarded. It seemed reasonable enough—not that I was familiar with the pricing structure of web design. Both Harmony and Nate sang his praises, which convinced me his pricing was fair. I was rearranging numbers in my spreadsheet, preoccupied, when I received a text message from Penny.

Iris was waffling about leaving.

Jackson lied? My phone pinged with a second message.

Jackson was furi—

I hadn't finished reading the second text before the door opened.

I looked up and froze.

"Don't act so surprised." Jackson strode toward me. "I promised to stop by. But consider this an *au plaisir* rather than a goodbye.

"*Au plaisir?*" All knowledge of the French language vanished as my heart jumped to my throat.

"Until we meet again," Jackson said.

"Right." His words sounded friendly enough. So why was my body frozen to my chair? I gave the clock a glance. Only a few minutes had passed since I last checked. My appointment wasn't due for a couple more hours. I was alone.

No, not alone. I was shut in my studio with a potential killer.

Chapter Thirty-Four

"A re you all right?" Jackson cocked his head, and a smug grin lifted the corners of his mouth. "Don't worry, *mon ami.*"

"W-worry?" I clamped my mouth shut.

Jackson's grin widened. "About me coming back. I'll be back before you know it."

Although his arrogance was irritating, my annoyance did little to ease my apprehension. With all the courage I could muster, I pulled myself out of the chair. "I hope you have a wonderful trip." I wondered how he'd explain Rose's photos, but playing dumb seemed safer. Then I remembered… *Oh no. Do I still have the picture on my monitor?*

"What? No hug?" Jackson stepped forward, and I reached behind me, my fingers searching for the mouse. As I glanced at the screen, fumbling to close the image, he moved next to the desk and pulled me into a hug. I felt his chin lift over my shoulder, and the embrace went from tight to suffocating. In that moment, I knew my efforts to close Rose's photo hadn't been successful. His attention was on my monitor.

He gripped my shoulders and stepped backward. I looked down, afraid of what I might see in his expression.

"What's this?" His voice sounded full of disbelief.

I turned to face the screen. "One of Rose's selfies from the masquer—"

"Unbelievable. It's not what it looks like. I loved Iris. You must know that." His thumb dug into the tender spot just below my shoulder as he reached for the mouse with his other hand. He clicked to the next image.

As he leaned in for a closer look, he pinned me against the desk while clicking the mouse. I could only assume he was trying to delete the photos, but he must have known that wouldn't get rid of them. With each click, his grip tightened. His frenzied energy felt terrifyingly familiar as my mind traveled back to another time with a different killer. It was an experience I'd vowed never to repeat. And yet, I'd somehow ignored all the warnings.

With my mind spinning, I held my breath and counted. By the time I reached five, the studio door creaked open and in walked Tallulah, with River and Saskia behind her.

Jackson's attention snapped toward the doorway, and he stepped backward. The air I'd been holding in my lungs came out in a whoosh. Never had a client's entrance been more fortunate. Freed from Jackson's grip, I smiled and greeted my saviors.

"I hope we're not interrupting something." The inflection in Tallulah's voice made her statement sound like a question.

"Not at all. Please come in."

Jackson ran a hand along his head and lumbered toward the door. "*Au revoir*, Bobbie. Take care of yourself."

The shift from *au plaisir* to *au revoir* wasn't lost on me. This time, he was saying goodbye. With a slight tip of my chin, I watched him go. When the door shut behind him, my body relaxed with relief, but there was something else, too. Something inside me felt immeasurably sad. My relationship with Jackson had often been tenuous, but he'd been more than just a club member. I was losing a friend.

I shifted my attention to Tallulah and River and gestured toward the seating area. "Have a seat. I'll be with you in a moment." As they took their seats, Saskia skipped to the corner where a stash of toys sat on a shelf.

Although my heart had slowed, my fingers trembled as I sent a message to Rose. I may have let Jackson leave my studio, but I couldn't let him escape. Detective Cram needed Rose's photos right away. Then, the investigation would be in his hands, and I would be free, lucky to have escaped danger.

I didn't wait for Rose's reply, knowing she checked her phone sporadically while working. Tucking mine into my pocket, I turned to my new customers. "What can I do for you?"

Tallulah stood, but it was the sound of Saskia's precious little voice that drew my attention. The stuffed animals appeared to be having an animated conversation. From what I could gather, the pink mother bear was explaining something about lavender fields to the little yellow bunny. It was endearing and utterly heart-wrenching. An image of my daughter's emotionless departure filled my mind. I loved the woman Emma had become, but a tiny part of me couldn't help wishing she were four again. I hadn't known back then, but life had been so much simpler. "They're so sweet at that age."

"That's why we're here," Tallulah said. "Time is fleeting, and we want to capture it."

"You'd like to set up a photo session for Saskia?" The idea excited me. Saskia was an adorable child.

"More than that. We want it to be a family photo shoot," Tallulah said, her cheeks turning red. She lowered her voice. "You know what I mean."

I did. She wasn't related to River, Saskia, or Harmony, but found family was family, too.

"It was Iris's death that made me think of it," Tallulah continued. "River and Harmony agree."

Along with engagement shoots, family photos were my favorite sessions to book, despite their challenges. Trying to get everyone posed and smiling together while snapping photos was a bit like herding cats. The results were incredibly rewarding.

"No one ever regrets family photos," I said. I walked to the coffee table and pulled some albums from the pile. I handed one to Tallulah and another to River. "You'll find examples of my work in these. Take your time browsing for ideas and let me know what interests you. If you decide to book a shoot, knowing what you have in mind will help me plan the locations.

Tallulah took the album from River's hands. "Why don't you take Saskia for a creemee? I'll look through these and set everything up."

Seemingly happy with the prospect of escape, River perked up. He stood and took Saskia by the hand.

"Bye, Miss Bobbie." Saskia flapped her little hand as River ushered her toward the door.

"Bye, Miss Saskia. I'll see you soon." I waggled my fingers and couldn't stop smiling at the sound of her giggling response.

On the sofa, Tallulah was already perusing my albums.

"While you do that, can I offer you a cup of coffee or tea?"

"Coffee sounds nice," Tallulah said without looking up. "I drink it black."

I left her engrossed in my photo albums and went into my kitchenette. I pulled a mug from the shelf and reached for a coffee pod. To photograph Saskia would be a joy. She had an innocent and sunny personality. I already imagined her white-blonde hair braided on the sides. Wildflowers—definitely. I spun the carousel of coffee pods and paused when I glimpsed the Wild Meadow Herbs logo peeking out from behind. That couldn't be right. I kept a canister of tea bags in the studio. Iris's herbal tea, I kept in my kitchen for bedtime. I reached for the bag, pulling it from the shelf, bewildered.

I studied the bag labeled with Iris's familiar handwriting. Sereni-Tea, my favorite. It was the same tea blend Iris delivered to me the afternoon she was murdered. Thinking back to when I met Iris and Saskia on the street, I specifically remembered taking the bag she gave me into my house. Hadn't I? I was sure I didn't return to my studio. Closing my eyes, I could see the familiar bag sitting in my kitchen cupboard. I'd tucked it behind the one I had yet to finish. My neck prickled, and the hair on my arms raised.

This was wrong—all wrong.

Chapter Thirty-Five

I turned the bag in my hand, stunned. Then, it struck me. The intruder. They must have knocked the mug to the floor while stashing the tea on my shelf. But why would anyone do that? Mackenzie's unexpected delivery from Jackson crossed my mind. I hadn't asked him about it. Harmony had assumed Iris asked him to deliver it, but I hadn't followed up. Maybe he did it on his own—delivering deadly tea to Mackenzie, then doing the same for me.

I pulled my phone out of my pocket and started typing. After several shaky attempts and numerous corrections, I opted for a direct question and hit send.

Why did you deliver Mackenzie's tea?

To my relief, three dots wavered on my screen.

Tallulah gave it to me

My heart pounded as I watched the three dots reappear.

She said Iris wanted it delivered right away

I jolted, nearly dropping my phone. *Tallulah.* Tallulah had given the tea to Jackson. Tallulah had marked the ledger with a red X. Tallulah—I gulped—had poisoned Mackenzie's tea. Hadn't Harmony told me Tallulah was helping Iris with her herbs? I'd completely missed it.

My thoughts jumped back to Rose's selfie, the shadows in the background. River and Saskia. No Tallulah. Tallulah was supposed to be with them. But she wasn't because—

The sound of shuffling footsteps brought me back to the present. I looked up. Tallulah lurked in the doorway, blocking my exit.

"I was wondering when you'd find my gift." Her voice had an evenness that sounded wrong. Gone was her soft, girlish voice, her benign demeanor.

"You poisoned Mackenzie?"

With a defiant lift of her chin, Tallulah scoffed. "I failed, obviously. In my haste, I made an error in my formulation. I meant to add belladonna, but I fear I must have added foxglove instead—and not nearly enough of it."

"Belladonna?" My voice was a hoarse whisper.

"Deadly nightshade."

Oh. Keeping my eyes trained on the large woman in the doorway, I said, "And this bag?" I held it up. "Does it have deadly nightshade in it?"

"*That* formula I got right." She took a step forward. "It's a learning process."

"What if I'd served it to a client?" I shivered, the stifling closeness of the room doing nothing to keep me warm. The idea of killing a client, even accidentally, chilled me to my core.

"It was a risk I had to take," she said. I watched as her mask fell away, revealing steely eyes and a stiff jaw. Her placid expression was nothing but a memory.

I struggled to find my voice. "But why? Why would you want to harm Mackenzie? Why harm me?"

"I heard Harmony mention it to you," Tallulah threw her hands in the air, exasperated. "Mackenzie remembered me from our old neighborhood. It was only a matter of time before she remembered the rest of the story."

I couldn't think straight. "The story about your mom? What does that have to do with me?

"It has nothing to do with you, except that you're nosy. You would have goaded Mackenzie until she remembered."

"There's more to the story?" Mackenzie hadn't made it sound that way. I needed to concentrate. Nothing added up.

Tallulah's voice was full of disdain when she spoke. "My mom would never have poisoned my precious little stepsister."

Oh...OH!!

My mind raced with her implication. "You were the one making your stepsister sick?"

Tallulah took another step. She was close enough that I could smell her soapy scent. It was plain and clean, befitting her bland persona. Her formerly bland persona.

"I was a kid, okay?" She spat out her words. "And I wasn't trying to *kill* cute little Beatrice. I just thought if she were sick all the time, my mom would get tired of taking care of her."

"Instead, your mom cared about her," I said. "More than you expected her to."

"That's not it!" Tallulah clenched and unclenched her fists. Her whole body went rigid. "Instead, I got sent away. Six months in a mental facility. Can you imagine spending six months of your childhood in a mental facility?"

I couldn't. It was too horrible to imagine. But heaven help me, I thought she probably belonged there. She needed help.

"That must have been hard," I said. I had little sympathy for the homicidal maniac standing before me. But for the young girl who was crying for her mother's attention, my heart ached.

"As you can guess, I couldn't have Iris or River hearing *that* part of my story."

"I'm so sorry. I can't imagine how awful it must have been."

"Ancient history. Harmony and River can never know. Never." She glared at me and took another step forward.

With a gasp, I tried to sidestep, but I'd only cornered myself. When I sent Jackson away with nothing more than a curt goodbye, I thought I was safe. Instead, I placed him in the police's crosshairs while trapping myself with a crazed murderer. I could try to keep her talking, but for how long? I gave my watch a glance. Time had officially come to a standstill. My upcoming appointment would be too late to save me.

I needed to think, to gather my wits. I was going to die, but there was a lot I wanted to understand. "How did Iris die?"

Tallulah blew out her breath, plainly frustrated by my ignorance. Her eyes shimmered with an odd gleam. "You know the answer. Harmony told me the club worked it out. Yet one more reason to get rid of you. You're a lot smarter than you look."

Seriously? If there were a quota for the number of insults a person should endure in a day, I thought I'd hit it.

"When Harmony first brought you to our house, I figured you'd be no problem. I didn't get her confidence in you. It pains me to admit how wrong I was." Tallulah shifted. "I didn't mean to kill Iris."

"Please tell me you didn't do it in front of Saskia."

"What do you take me for?" Tallulah sounded incredulous. "I stayed in the market after River and Saskia left with their creemees. They took the sidewalk around the village green. When I finished paying, I cut across the green by the fountain. I saw Mackenzie when we passed by the party the first time. Seeing her made me so angry." Tallulah's face turned red.

"You thought she should be dead." I'd found the missing puzzle piece a few moments too late.

She dipped her chin. "So, when I approached the fountain and saw the long cape, I thought it was her. Oops."

Tallulah's apathy shocked me. She'd killed a young woman—an exceedingly kind and generous one—and she was making light of it? Frantically, I looked around as she moved closer. I had nowhere to go. The kitchenette had no windows, and Tallulah blocked the only exit. I was trapped.

"All in all, I'm pleased with how things worked out. I was happy about Iris going to France, of course. But now she's gone for good. River and I get to keep Saskia."

"But you're a killer," I said. Poor Saskia. Not only had she lost her mother, but a murderer was trying to take her place.

"I told you. That was a mistake!" She took another slow, lumbering step forward. "My first attempt at Mackenzie failed. I made a mistake with Iris. But you... I'm going to get you right."

With no escape, I scanned the room for a weapon. I still held the bag of tea and my phone. The tea was lethal, but only if I brewed a pot and poured it down Tallulah's throat. That was not a plan. I needed something else. No sooner did I spy the box cutter on the table than Tallulah lunged for it, grabbing it before I'd even moved. For a woman of her size, she was quick. *Good to know.*

With a flick of the release, she opened the box cutter and lunged toward me. "Time for your accident."

Chapter Thirty-Six

I jumped to avoid Tallulah's jab, dropping my phone to the floor. Instinctively, I stooped to reach for it.

"Leave it!" Tallulah shrieked.

I straightened, holding my palms to face her. "I'm going to have an accident?" I gulped.

"Don't play dumb," she said. "You knew this was coming. And it has to look like an accidental fall."

"B-b-but," I stammered.

"No buts. This is your own fault, and you know it." Tallulah waved the box cutter in front of my face. "For the first time in my life, I found a family where I belonged. You just had to ruin it for me. You and Mackenzie. I'll take care of her later."

"But Jackson knows you're here." I squeaked out the words.

"That's why it has to be an accident." She rolled her eyes. "The stairs to your loft. You're going to trip and take a little tumble to the bottom. Now get moving." She thrust the blade toward me. With little room to move, dodging the graze of the sharp blade was almost impossible. Her message was obvious. I was to walk past her so she could follow me up the stairs.

"You don't need to do this." But I knew she did. I'd discovered her secrets—secrets that would send her to jail.

"Don't be ridiculous," Tallulah said. "Get moving."

I edged past her, walking as slowly as I dared. Tallulah hadn't meant to kill Iris, but she was still a killer. After my accident, she would go home and pretend nothing happened. Saskia trusted her, was comfortable with her, and over time, River would come to depend on her, too. He may never love her the way she hoped, but I suspected the illusion of a happy family would be enough for her.

A sharp point pricked my back, bringing my thoughts to the present. Time was up. When I reached the staircase, I looked up. This was one of her better murder plans. I could picture it playing out. After working in my loft, I'd stumble clumsily down the stairs, probably breaking my neck when I landed. If that didn't happen, Tallulah would be there to finish it. Then, assuming Jackson hadn't already left for France and he told Detective Cram about Tallulah's visit, when questioned, Tallulah would tell him that I was alive when she left. No one would be able to prove otherwise.

There was no way out. I plodded up the stairs. If I didn't come up with a plan before I reached the top, I was as good as dead. My only solace was the prospect of seeing Dan. He'd be waiting for me. I was sure of it. Then, an image of Emma flashed in my mind, and I knew I wasn't ready. What would it be like for her, losing both parents so suddenly? We needed a proper goodbye.

I took the last step into the loft and turned. It was a long way down. The staircase was steep. Each tread of hard, rustic wood had the potential to strike the fatal blow. Tallulah jabbed the box cutter at my face and grabbed my arm with her other hand.

"Don't even think about trying to move."

A loud creak came from the studio door, and Emma's voice called out. "Mom? Gran and I made it as far as the state line when she—" Emma appeared at the bottom of the stairs and came to a sudden halt. "What's going on?"

"Well, this is inconvenient." Tallulah turned to face Emma, letting go of my arm. "No one move, I need to think."

Taking advantage of Tallulah's distraction, I tipped my head toward the door. It was enough to know that Emma had come back. I would never let a deranged killer harm my daughter. Silently, I mouthed the words, *I love you* and cast Emma with a stare I hoped she'd interpret as, *Run for your life.*

Emma mimicked my stare with one of her own, as if to say, *Are you for real right now? I'm not leaving you.*

Tallulah's voice interrupted our attempts at telepathy. "Two accidents it will have to be." With her arm extended, she pointed the box cutter at my throat and twisted to shout at Emma. "You! Get up here."

I gave my head a quick shake.

"I said, get up here." Tallulah's shrill voice made Emma jump, but when she swung the box cutter, she aimed it right at my throat.

"I'm coming." The sound of Emma's voice surprised me. It sounded more resigned than scared.

Tallulah looked at me, beaming with triumph. "See, it's best to do as I say." She turned to watch Emma, who stepped onto the first tread.

With Tallulah watching Emma's progress, this would be my only chance. Offering a quick prayer for forgiveness, I knew what I needed to do. As I lifted my foot, I gestured to Emma with a jerk of my head. She placed her foot on the second tread, as if following Tallulah's orders, but not before pressing a finger to her chin the way I'd always done with Dan. *Message received.*

Gathering strength from my daughter's calm presence, I aimed my foot at Tallulah's backside. If I did it right, Tallulah would only lose her footing for a moment, just long enough for me to rush past her, grab Emma, and run out the door.

I didn't do it right.

Chapter Thirty-Seven

My stomach clenched as I watched Tallulah's body tumble down, down, down. I winced with each thud on the hard treads. Emma jumped back while reaching forward with her hands as if she could soften Tallulah's landing. The descent seemed endless. With a final *whomp*, Tallulah landed in a crumpled heap at the bottom.

"Oh no, oh no, what have I done?" I rushed down the stairs to where Emma was already caring for Tallulah.

Her hands were gentle as they moved over the woman's prone body. "She's alive."

I offered another quick prayer. This one was for Tallulah's life.

"This is all my fault," Emma said. "I recognize this lady. She was on the village green that night. I should have remembered."

"How would you have known?" I squeezed Emma's arm before patting my pocket and remembering my phone on the kitchenette floor. I ran to grab it and punched 9-1-1. No sooner had I returned to the entryway than the door opened, and Darcy bounded into the studio. Next to Emma, he bent his broad head over Tallulah, and a stiff ridge appeared on the back of his neck.

I handed my phone to Emma so she could talk to the emergency dispatch, and wrapped my arms around Darcy's neck, burrowing my face in his thick fur. "How did you get here?"

My mom stepped inside. "I was sitting in the car and heard him barking from inside the kitchen." I wasn't sure how much she'd heard, but she seemed to have made a quick assessment of the situation.

"You were waiting in the car?" I asked, remembering Emma was supposed to drive her to the airport in Boston.

"Until a couple of minutes ago. I wanted to give you and Emma some time to yourselves." Her voice sounded huskier than usual. "Something felt off. I had no idea."

As I murmured my agreement, Jackson appeared, a bead of sweat trickling down his forehead. Rose, her cheeks a deep shade of crimson, followed behind.

"*Mon Dieu!*" Jackson gulped air while taking in the scene at the base of my staircase. "I should have gotten here sooner. When you texted about the tea delivery, something didn't seem right. It took me a few minutes to figure it out. I'd just left the coffee shop and was about to drive home to finish packing."

"He ran into the café looking all kinds of frazzled." Rose's hand flew to her chest. "Jeezum crow! The expression on his face scared me half to death. He kept saying you were in danger. We got here as fast as we could." Rose stepped forward, her arms held wide.

Her embrace was warm and sturdy. It felt like home. Until then, I hadn't realized my whole body was trembling. The sound of Emma's voice hummed in the background as she relayed the incident to dispatch—unconscious, breathing, possible concussion... Rose and I disentangled our limbs.

"Good thing I followed Jackson." She leaned closer to whisper. "To be honest, I was still a little nervous about him."

"You didn't...?" I held up my phone and gestured toward Jackson. I was hoping Rose hadn't sent her photos to the police.

"I wasn't able to," she whispered. "But I did send out a group text."

Tallulah groaned, lifted her head, and blinked. Emma looked up. "That's a good sign," she said before turning back to her patient and speaking in a voice that was both gentle and professional. "Can you move your foot for me?"

"What happened?" Tallulah's lids fluttered open, and her eyes darted between us, filling with panic.

"An ambulance is on the way." Emma's voice was calm. My pride swelled, watching my daughter kindly patting the arm of the woman who'd, only moments before, threatened her.

"Noooo," Tallulah groaned.

"Bobbie?" Harmony stood in the doorway. She gaped as she surveyed the scene. "Tallulah? What happened?" She lowered herself to kneel on the floor next to Emma.

"It would seem we found our killer." Jackson's voice was matter-of-fact, but I read genuine concern in his expression.

I surprised myself—and Jackson—by throwing my arms around him in a tight embrace. "I'm so sorry I suspected you. I didn't even bother to wish you luck on your trip."

As we separated, Jackson blushed. He ran his hand along the side of his head, appearing to gather his composure.

Harmony's head jerked up. "What are you saying? Tallulah killed Iris?" Disbelief shook in her voice as she whispered to her housemate, "How could you? Iris was our friend. We trusted you."

With my hand resting on Darcy's head, I glanced at my mother. It was all starting to get to me. My mom's gaze was gentle as she stepped toward me and wrapped an arm around my shoulder. I leaned into her, comforted by her familiar scent—warm and spicy, with a hint of vanilla. Her arm felt like a safe harbor, shielding me from the chaos. The sound of sirens broke through the din of voices in my studio, and I was comforted by that, too.

It wasn't long before Greg Lacey from the rescue squad entered, followed by the same two paramedics who had taken care of Mackenzie during the masquerade party. Last, but certainly not least, Detective Cram and his young police officer wedged into my studio. The acoustics made the din unbearable.

Like a hawk, Cram scanned the studio while issuing instructions to his officer. He raised his fingers to his lips, and a shrill whistle pierced the pandemonium. "Okay, everyone except for the paramedics, Miss, and Mrs. Brooks, outside. Officer Brown will accompany you."

The detective wore an unmistakable grimace when he looked at me. "It appears you never learn."

I had no fight left in me. Besides, he wasn't entirely wrong. I smiled in a way that was meant to look deferential. While I wanted to think my wits had saved me, luck and timing had played a role, too. I wasn't really cut out to be a detective.

In the background, I heard Emma talking to the paramedics. Detective Cram peppered me with questions. The basics, for the most part—who, what, where, when… I answered him with as much respect as I could muster. It seemed to appease him. Even he must have been able to tell how shaken I was. By the time we finished, the paramedics were loading Tallulah onto a stretcher.

"So if I'm hearing this correctly, you pushed Miss Leblanc down the steps." Detective Cram peered at me.

Emma jumped to her feet. "It was self-defense. Tallulah forced my mom to the top of the stairs. She was planning to kill her."

"She was planning to kill both of us," I said

Detective Cram scratched something in his notebook, then he snapped it shut. "I'm sure we'll be talking again."

"No doubt," I said as I followed him outside.

Darcy stayed close beside me, seeming hesitant to let me out of his sight. I scratched behind his ears and told him what a good boy he was. I don't know how he knew something was wrong, but he did.

We both turned to see Alicia rushing down the driveway. "First, Rose's text, then the sirens rushed past my store." She gulped in a breath. "When they pulled into your driveway, I thought I might have a heart attack. There's quite a crowd in front of your house." She pulled me into a hug so tight I could barely breathe. "What am I going to do with you?"

I laughed as we each took a step back. "You're crying!"

"No, I'm not." She swiped a tear from her cheek.

"Yeah, okay."

"So…Tallulah. Frankly, I didn't have her on my bingo card."

I let out a puff of air. "I did. I guess I wasn't paying attention when her name was called. Turns out her bland expression and soft voice were fake. That was one mask that was scary to see come off."

I explained Tallulah's plan and how Emma had interrupted her.

Penny emerged through the ruckus and edged her way toward me. "Rose texted," she said. "I should have been here with you."

"No." This wasn't Penny's fault. It wasn't anyone's fault. Not even mine. Tallulah was the killer. She was singularly responsible for everything that happened. "We had no way of knowing how unbalanced she was. She masked it well."

"Jackson said Tallulah showed up with River and Saskia? Were they here for a consultation? They weren't on our calendar."

With a wry chuckle, I said, "We've got appointments for customers who don't show, and customers without appointments who do."

"Good thing the wheels are in motion to get that all straightened out. I already called and rescheduled today's appointment."

"Thanks," I said. "He completely slipped my mind. I wouldn't want a customer here right now."

As the paramedics carried Tallulah to the ambulance, we cleared a path and watched. From her stretcher, Tallulah searched the gathering before landing her gaze on me. Her expression was laced with loathing. If looks could kill, she might have been more successful.

I overheard one paramedic say she was stable. A couple of cracked ribs, most likely a concussion, and possibly a broken ankle. For that, I was immensely grateful. When I pushed her down the steps, I hadn't wanted to kill her. But Mama Bear had kicked in. My actions would be called self-defense—which they were—but it was Emma I wanted to protect.

Detective Cram took his leave, but not before telling me he would need a formal statement. I knew the drill. The hush that fell over us dissipated as my friends circled me, everyone talking at once.

Chapter Thirty-Eight

aces—and voices—surrounded me as I stood on my driveway, overwhelmed with emotion. Everything that had just happened in my studio hit me with a force that took my breath away. But I was safe, and Emma was, too. She'd come back to talk. I wasn't sure how much my mom had influenced her decision, but I wasn't about to quibble with the results.

The chatter stopped when Harmony stepped forward. "Bobbie, I'm so sorry. When I asked for your help, I was so sure no one in my house could do such a thing."

"No one ever wants to suspect their friends, do they?" Then I remembered Harmony had arrived before the sirens. "What made you come here?"

"Other than Rose's urgent text?" Harmony's eyes looked glazed. "After talking to you and Mackenzie, I was all out of sorts. I have to admit, I was more than a little miffed with you." Her faint smile felt like an apology. "I stopped by Ciarán's office for a chat. Talking to him always seems to help me. He has a lovely aura—shades of indigo…" She paused. "Anyway, he helped me see how unfair I was being, and I wanted to make it right."

I made a mental note to look up what an indigo aura meant—not that it mattered. I mean, I didn't believe in that stuff.

"When did you figure out it was Tallulah?" Harmony's question drew the attention of everyone milling about my driveway.

"Not soon enough," I said. I explained how I found the bag of tea and texted Jackson. "It was Jackson's reply that snapped the last clue into place. Until then, I thought *he* was the killer."

Jackson's eyes bulged. "I hate to say this, but your sleuthing skills need work."

"I can't argue with you, there," I said. "But in my defense, Rose's photos looked pretty incriminating. Why were you arguing with Iris and Mackenzie at the masquerade?"

"Mackenzie was siding with River, and Iris was defending her. Then, Iris told me she wanted to postpone our trip to France until after the holidays. I refused to listen to her." His face crumpled, and I wondered if that had been their last conversation.

"Did you follow her to the fountain?" Rose asked.

Jackson shook his head. "I started to. But then, well, I figured she just needed time to come to her senses."

It was all so incredibly sad. He had his trip to France ahead of him, but it wasn't the future he'd planned. I knew what that was like.

Alicia spoke up. "So the truck chasing you and the falling photo booth. Those were both Tallulah?"

"Wait," Harmony said. "What truck chased you?"

I looked at Harmony, surprised. "You didn't know?"

Harmony shook her head, and I thought back to the wine and cheese party. She hadn't been there when we talked about it. It seemed odd I hadn't mentioned it to her later, but I couldn't remember doing so. Her expression clouded when I filled her in.

"That's why I was late to the party," Harmony said. "My car wouldn't start, and I had to wait for Tallulah to come home with the truck. She left our house shortly after you did."

It was all making sense. Tallulah had heard me tell Harmony I was planning to visit Mackenzie at the hospital. All she had to do was wait in the parking lot. And then, the photo booth. I remembered how she'd been one of the first on the scene, feigning concern. She would have been tall enough to push the booth from the top.

Rose put an arm around my waist and said, "I'd better get back to the coffee shop. I left Ethan in charge, and heaven only knows how he's holding up. You're okay, right?"

"It's over. It's really over." I gave her a quick hug, relief washing over me. The killer had been caught, and no, I wasn't okay, but I would be. "You'd better go relieve Ethan."

She raised her voice. "We should probably leave you now. I'm sure you want to spend time with Emma and your mom." Rose had the uncanny ability to read me. I was so lucky she was my friend.

With a tired smile, I nodded my thanks.

In no time, my friends took Rose's hint and mumbled about needing to pack or get back to their shops. Jackson, Harmony, Penny, and Alicia hugged me before leaving, with promises to catch up after I had a chance to decompress. A wave of tiredness washed over me as they walked away. I looked from Emma to my mom, and realizing Fiona should be on a plane, my mouth dropped open.

"You're missing your flight," I said to her.

Fiona's husky voice held a hint of humor when she spoke. "Let's focus on what's important, darling. I'll make us all a cup of tea, assuming you have store-bought tea bags."

I couldn't help laughing as I nodded. "Lady Grey," I said. We walked to my kitchen, Darcy at my side.

"It's okay, boy." I took his head in my hands and planted a kiss on top of his head.

He followed Emma and me into the living room, settling next to me after I dropped onto the couch. Emma sat at the other end with tears pooling in her eyes. We were silent for a moment, too choked with emotion to speak.

Emma swiped the corner of her eye before a soft smile appeared. "That was some kick. When did you take up karate?"

I appreciated her attempt at levity, but the memory of Tallulah's tumbling body made me shudder. "Thank goodness I didn't kill her."

"It would have been justified. When I drove back to Stonebridge, that was not the scene I expected to find."

Tears welled. I tried to blink them back. "I had no idea you knew Dad's and my signal. You saved my life."

"After all the parties I attended with you? Of course, I knew the signal.

You saved yourself. And me." Emma studied me for a moment. "I'm so sorry I left in such a tizzy this morning. It reminded me of our last fight, and I'd told myself I would never do that again. I expect you to treat me like an adult, even when I'm acting like a moody teenager."

I wiped the tears from my cheeks and nodded. The whole thing was my fault. She'd acted like a teenager because that's the way I'd treated her. And that needed to stop. Emma was an adult with a life of her own. Her decisions were hers to make.

My mom entered the room carrying a tray with a steaming teapot and mugs. She set it on the coffee table and poured each of us a cup. Thankful for the warmth between my fingers, I inhaled the scent of black tea with a touch of citrus.

"Don't mind me," my mother said. "Emma wanted to come back so you could talk. So talk."

When I'd asked about her flight, she hadn't answered me, so I asked her again.

"It's all settled," she said. "I extended my stay at the inn and will rebook my flight for another day." Decisive, as always, my mother left no room for argument. I'd always envied, and sometimes resented, her self-assurance. This time, I found it reassuring.

I blew over the top of my scalding tea and turned to Emma. "I'm sorry I gave you a hard time. I stuck my nose where it didn't belong."

Emma set her mug down. "It's not that. I want your nose in my life." As if to illustrate, she crinkled her own. "But I'm not a kid anymore. What Connor and I decide about our relationship is our choice. Besides, you jumped to conclusions. When I told you we're keeping things friendly, I meant it. I hope it'll be more someday, and I think Connor does too. We're not ready yet."

"Oh…" It was all I could say. She was right. When she'd crept up the stairs, I'd made assumptions. I couldn't avoid feeling concerned that she and Connor were rushing into things. So many big things had happened in her life all at once. First, she lost her dad—a dad she was extremely close to; then she transitioned from college to her new career, and I was sure she was missing her friends who'd moved away. Then, I'd moved away, too; and to top it off, she'd broken up with her longtime boyfriend. It was a lot of change, along with the complications of a new, long-distance relationship.

"You're doing it again. I can literally see the gears turning in your head." Emma turned to Fiona. "Gran, is this the way you were with Mom?"

Fiona chuckled. "I may have given her my two cents' worth now and again. But when your mother was your age, she and your dad were already newlyweds."

"Were you against it?" Emma asked.

"Not at all. I loved your father. Your mother was a little bit wild, and he seemed to tame her."

"Mom?" Emma peered at me.

Heat rushed to my cheeks, and I knew they were bright red. I hadn't been *that* wild. My mother's laugh saved me from having to answer.

"Your parents were in love. Although they were rather young for marriage, I trusted their commitment. I knew they'd find their way, just as your grandfather and I did."

I looked at my mom. She seemed relaxed, holding her mug, a serene smile softening her face. Maybe we weren't so dissimilar, after all. Throughout my childhood, my parents' love for each other had been obvious to me. They'd set an example for marriage that both Alicia and I had followed. I hoped Emma would, too.

"I'm sorry I jumped to conclusions," I said to Emma. "I'm well aware I need to let you make your own decisions, and really, I trust you to do that."

"I must have looked pretty sus when I came in this morning, hoping you wouldn't hear me."

"That, you did." I laughed.

"It wasn't what you were thinking. Connor and I were watching Harry Potter last night, and it turned into a movie marathon. I fell asleep on his couch."

I reached across Darcy's sleeping body to squeeze my daughter's hand. I was thankful she'd told me—not because I needed to know, but because knowing she trusted me with her private life meant the world to me.

"You don't need to worry about us jumping into something we aren't ready for. Ryan and I weren't meant to be together. I'd only been hanging on because having a boyfriend was comfortable. He wanted to get back together with me over the summer, but I didn't even consider it." Emma lifted her mug to her mouth and took a slow sip before setting it back on the coffee table. She pursed her lips together and studied my face. "Sometimes I wonder if your concern about me moving too fast has more to do with you than me."

Heat crept up my neck. From across the room, I could feel my mother's gaze. Words churned in my mind, but no reply came to me.

"I know things have been hard since Dad died." Emma's voice was soft. "And I get it if you want to move on. It must feel scary for you. If I'm being honest, I selfishly dread thinking about you with someone else. But, you must know Dad would want you to be happy." She swiped a tear that trickled down her cheek. "That goes for me, too."

Chapter Thirty-Nine

Two weeks later…

The remaining weeks of October lazily drifted toward November. Stick season—that's what we flatlanders thought this time of year was called. In his patient way, Nate corrected me. It was deer season. Someday, I'd learn all the Vermontisms. No matter what it was called, the colorful leaves had fallen to the ground in giant mounds, leaving the trees bare. This was one of the quieter seasons in Vermont—the period between busloads of leaf-peepers and the onslaught of skiers. Mom-and-pop businesses closed, giving their owners some much-needed downtime and the rare chance to get away.

But first—

"What do you say?" Connor laughed as he greeted a young group of dinosaurs, fairies, and butterflies.

"Trick-or-treat!" they chorused.

"You look so pretty," Emma said to a shy little princess as she held out a cauldron of miniature candy bars. Emma had driven to Vermont earlier in the day, claiming she was picking up my mom to drive her back to Boston for her much-postponed flight. I knew that wasn't the only reason, but I admitted to myself that she and Connor were an adorable couple.

Wrapped up like mummies, their smiles revealed how much they enjoyed their roles of treating the young children and terrorizing the older ones. Next to them, Darcy seemed content to sit in the grass, looking regal in his tuxedo. He'd given me his hangdog look when I put it on him, but he was basking in the admiration of almost everyone who passed by.

In rural Stonebridge, where homes were spread apart and dirt roads were too dark for trick-or-treating, Main Street and the area surrounding the village green was the place to be on Halloween night. Two days before, Alicia had informed me that with my in-town location and front porch, I was obligated to host a Halloween party. She didn't need to tell me twice. Rose's fortieth birthday fell on the same day, giving us double the reason to celebrate.

With Rose and Alicia's help, I transformed my home using strings of pumpkin lights, hanging ghosts, lanterns, spider webs, and a rather frightening scarecrow who held his pumpkin head in straw hands. Along with filling buckets with candy, I bought a killer charcuterie board from the super-sweet woman who owned the Vermont Cheeseboarder, and made an adult-only vampire punch that looked a little too much like blood, but was delicious anyway. Thanks to additional contributions from both Rose and my ever-resourceful sister, the spread was party-worthy.

All along Main Street, houses were decorated, front porches were lit, and music played—including next door, where my mother sat with my cranky neighbor. The sound of Mr. Miller's low rumble, followed by my mother's throaty laugh, drifted across our yards on the cool evening breeze.

If I'd thought the Harvest Festival was a big deal, it was only because I'd never experienced Halloween in Stonebridge. The entire village, it seemed, adults and children alike, strolled from house to house, greeting neighbors and gathering treats. Children carried bags and buckets, teenagers cruised Main Street on ATVs, and adults sipped from tumblers filled with a variety of unknown beverages.

On this unseasonably warm Halloween night, I'd donned a ragged, patchwork dress and drawn stitches on my neck and the sides of my mouth, in a decent imitation of Sally Ragdoll. After pushing the bright red strands of my wig from my face, I sipped punch from my mug and swayed on my porch swing, taking it all in. The colors on the trees may have faded, but Rose more than made up for it in her tie-dye jeans jacket and pleather leggings. Atop her red curls, teased high like Sandy's at the end of *Grease*, perched a sparkling tiara with a bedazzled *40*. But nothing glowed more than her broad grin when Alicia and Nate appeared in the doorway with a candle-laden cake.

"Make a wish," Alicia said. "It's not every day you get to turn forty."

Rose leaned forward, the flames lighting her face. "Don't remind me."

Next to her, William kissed her cheek. "You'd better blow those things out before they burn the porch down."

"All right, all right," Rose said, giggling. "Here goes nothing." She sucked in air and puffed her cheeks. And when the candles extinguished, it felt like we'd all let out a collective breath, blowing our shared stress away.

"What's going on here?" Gino's brash voice came from the sidewalk below.

"My birthday. Come join us." Rose beamed. "I can't remember the last time I had so much fun on my birthday."

"And tomorrow, we fly off to Mexico for a bit of R & R." William took Rose's hand in his.

"More than a bit of R & R. Sandy beaches, warm sunshine, and fruity cocktails, here I come!" Rose squealed.

"Sounds fantastic," Gino said, joining me on the porch swing. "I'm taking a couple of weeks off, myself. I'll be heading back to Brooklyn for some good old-fashioned family time."

As if on cue, the opening chords of "Happy" played from my speakers, causing Rose to squeal again. Although I'd set up a playlist of spooky Halloween music, Rose had switched it out, declaring her fortieth birthday party required dancing. She grabbed William's hand, coaxing him to the other side of my porch, which she'd designated as the dance floor.

It wasn't long before Nate, Alicia, Emma, and Connor jumped in.

"Let's show them how it's done, Baby Doll." Gino offered his hand, grinning his big, brash grin.

"Let's." I winked.

Gino danced the same way he did most everything—with unapologetic exuberance. Matching him move for move, dancing fed my need to let go. After the stress of Iris's murder and Mackenzie's poisoning, I thought things would quiet down. And they had, in a way. At least the murder investigation had come to a close. Tallulah had been charged and was awaiting trial from the security of a jail cell. I'd been busy with fall photo shoots, as well as my mother's extended stay in Stonebridge. She seemed happy to stick around, but like all snowbirds, as the weather turned cold, she itched to get back to the Florida sunshine.

As Gino twirled me around our makeshift dance floor, I caught sight of my mother, laughing at something Mr. Miller must have said. She'd spent a week at the inn, then another, presumably to help me through this emotional time. I enjoyed our time together in a way I never would've expected. We took day trips to Saratoga Springs, the state capital in Montpelier, and several small art galleries. I discovered my mother was more than just a formidable presence. She was warm and funny. As I watched her talk to my crotchety next-door neighbor, I marveled at their growing friendship. Never had I seen a more unlikely pair.

Gino grabbed my hand and twirled me, my gaze landing on the sidewalk where Ciarán and Harmony had stopped to pat Darcy.

"Don't look now," Gino said, leading me into a twirl.

"I'm way ahead of you," I answered.

Nate must have noticed the pair at the same time we did. "Come join us," he called.

Harmony headed up the stairs, but Ciarán looked hesitant, his gaze landing on me as though seeking permission. I smiled in answer without missing a step. It was a party, after all. The more, the merrier.

"I wonder why he didn't bring Muffy," I said as Gino pulled me back.

Gino's eyebrows lifted. "Come on. You know better than that." He twirled me again before drawing me close. "Besides, Muffy went back to Connecticut."

"She left?" I asked, my heart quickening to the beat of the song.

"Where have you been? We've got loads and loads of catching up to do," Gino said. "And believe me, I can tell you a thing or two."

The song ended, and gasping for breath, we returned to the porch swing. Next up on Rose's playlist was a slower, country tune, and I relaxed with a fresh cup of punch, scanning the happy faces surrounding me. Nate leaned against the porch railing with Alicia in front of him, his arms circling her waist. He said something in her ear that made her smile.

Emma and Connor went back to harassing the thinning groups of trick-or-treaters. I caught my daughter's eye, and she paused, smiling as she returned my gaze. Her facial expressions were always full of meaning, a bit like reading a story. This one felt reassuring. As she resumed her conversation with Connor, I realized I could learn a lot from her and her willingness to keep moving forward.

Also on the sidewalk, Jackson joked with Connor. His change of plans surprised me. He claimed his rushed departure had been more about escaping the stress of the investigation than about getting to France. After Tallulah's apprehension, and the atmosphere in Stonebridge calmed, he'd decided to stay until December, taking more time to clean out inventory and evaluate his future.

Next to Harmony, Ciarán sat in a rocking chair, appearing content, as I was, to be enveloped in friendship. He glanced at me and nodded. I lifted my glass in salutation. The only missing camera club member was Penny. She and Mackenzie had brought Hope by earlier. Too young to enjoy Halloween, Hope had an early bedtime, and Penny seemed relieved for the excuse to go home.

As promised, Ciarán and I met for lunch at the inn. The meeting had been strictly professional. I wish I could say my heart had gotten the memo, but that would be a lie. Even so, one of his clients hired me, and another asked Ciarán to take the initiative, which meant I'd be working closely with him to design an aesthetic for his client's website. I was optimistic I could do it without too much heart pounding.

Harmony, River, and Saskia had moved forward with Tallulah's plans for a family photo shoot—sans Tallulah. I ached for the little girl, but she seemed amazingly resilient. I took it as a sign she was being raised in a loving home. Any fleeting worries I had about River's secret dissipated when laughing, Harmony told me how he often bought his daughter candy behind Iris's back. Everyone at the commune was aware of it, but they played along. When I mentioned it to her at the library, she'd been so upset over learning about River pressuring Mackenzie that it slipped her mind. Already, another young woman had moved into the rambling farmhouse, someone Harmony had met at the community center.

Muffy, it seemed, had moved back to her home in Connecticut. Sometimes I wondered what happened between her and Ciarán, but it didn't really matter. Not because I didn't care. No matter what I told myself, I did. But I'd pushed him away and couldn't pretend I'd been wronged.

I still wasn't one hundred percent sure about Muffy's research. I thought she was the type to seek youth from a jar of La Mer rather than a DIY herbal remedy. But when I mentioned it to Alicia, she confirmed Muffy had not only bought coconut oil, turmeric, and some essential oils, she'd also asked where she could get her hands on shea butter and calendula. Her purchases seemed to prove me wrong. One thing I knew for sure, she hadn't poisoned Mackenzie.

The opening chords of "Sweet Pea" sliced through the fog in my mind, and I found myself swaying to the slow rhythm. In my younger days, I'd been a dancer, and the urge to move to the beat was hard to resist. As couples headed across the porch, I glanced at Ciarán and had a surprising thought. I wanted him to ask me to dance. He wouldn't, of course, and I couldn't blame him.

"Go on, then," Gino whispered. "You know what you need to do. Go ask him to dance."

"After the way I've behaved toward him, there's no way he'll want to dance with me."

Gino shook his head and chuckled. "Oh, Baby Doll. For someone who fancies herself as a modern-day Miss Marple, you sure do miss a lot of clues."

"Oh really," I deadpanned.

"He's waiting for you." Gino gave me a gentle nudge. "It's up to you. Go get him."

I couldn't, could I? But why not? Gino's words rang true. After rejecting Ciarán multiple times, it was my turn to risk humiliation. I swallowed, collecting my nerves. I wasn't ready to date—not yet. But sometimes, on days when I was being brutally honest with myself, I wondered if I used my grief as a mask. If I hid behind it, I didn't have to put myself out there. I didn't have to figure out who I was meant to be without Dan by my side. I could forever remain the melancholy widow, the one everyone pitied. But I didn't want that. As annoying as she'd been, Alicia was spot-on when she claimed it was unlike me to shy away from making new friends.

Ciarán and Harmony were chatting, and I hoped they wouldn't mind my interruption. I gathered every ounce of courage I could muster. Yes, I could do this. It was only one dance—a baby step. Setting my glass on the railing next to me, I stood and walked over to Ciarán. He rose from his chair and scanned my costume with an amused grin. I returned his grin with a flip of my bright red tresses.

Doing all I could to rein in my racing heart, I looked at Ciarán and was once again mesmerized by his lower lip. My plan hadn't included staring dumbly, so I lifted my gaze to meet his and managed a weak smile.

My thoughts flashed back to our first clumsy encounter—the way I'd nearly fallen over after stepping on his shoe. I laughed nervously and said, "I think maybe I'd feel more comfortable if you stepped on my toe...or something."

Ciarán's green eyes twinkled with a combination of recognition and humor. He chuckled while placing the toe of his shoe on my boot.

Relief at his willingness to play along swept over me, and I said, "Hi, I'm Bobbie. I was wondering if you'd like to dance." I placed my hand on his arm. "With me."

He let out a deep laugh. It was a good laugh—friendly, relaxed, and genuine.

I smiled back. "It's always a man's prerogative to decline an invitation to dance, of course." I'd barely finished my sentence before I, too, was laughing.

"Oh, no," he said. "I'll not be declining your invitation." His fingers brushed the small of my back, sending a tingle up my spine as he led me across the porch.

We joined our family and friends, picking up the beat together. Ciarán was clearly comfortable dancing, and that dangerous feeling I always had when I was around him started to fade. As we swayed to the music, I took in the scene around me, moving my gaze from those closest to me to the villagers meandering down the street, and my mind wandered.

There was something about wearing a costume that was freeing, hiding behind another persona. But I also wondered how many people hid behind masks of their own making. Tallulah had used a mask of calm, plainness to hide her darker side. Over the past few weeks, I'd gotten a clearer view of my mom. Her strength and confidence weren't a mask per se, but throughout my childhood, they'd hidden much of her softer side—her warmth and humor. She'd been a trailblazer for younger women, and I was surprised I'd never understood how hard that must have been.

Most of all, I had to admit I'd been hiding. As Alicia pointed out, I'd been shielding myself from making tough decisions. Thinking about my future was something I needed to do, even if I didn't feel ready. It was going to be a long, difficult internal conversation. I met Ciarán's gaze and smiled. No, we wouldn't be going out on dates anytime soon, but I thought I might be willing to try the friendship thing. In the meantime, taking my mask off and opening myself to possibilities was a big step forward.

A Note from the Author

Acknowledgments

Once again, I find myself overwhelmed by the incredible amount of support I received while writing this book. It's almost impossible to know where to begin.

Thank you to the team at Level Best Books for getting my book out into the world, especially my editor and publisher, Shawn Reilly Simmons. I'm proud to be an LBB author.

A heartfelt thank you to my beta readers, Trish Esden and Lori Roberts Herbst. I genuinely appreciate your friendship and encouragement. Your feedback is invaluable, and I can't begin to thank you enough!

Big hugs to my critique partners: Paula Charles, Leah Dobrinska, Christina Romeril, Annie McEwen, Adrian Andover, and Iris March. You read the messiest bits of my writing and came back for more. You're all amazing friends and writers. Your encouragement means the world to me!

To my readers. I'm so honored you're here. I hope you enjoy your time in Stonebridge, Vermont, half as much as I do.

To the wonderful residents of Jamaica, Vermont. Your enthusiasm and encouragement for my books overwhelm me in the best possible way.

To my family. Once again, thank you for your love, patience, and support. I couldn't do this without you.

About the Author

Kara Lacey is the author of the Camera Club Mysteries. Along with her husband, she lives in a tiny village nestled in the beautiful Green Mountains of Vermont—the inspiration for her novels. Kara is a photography enthusiast who also enjoys hiking, skiing, and getting cozy with a good book. When she's not at her laptop creating havoc for her characters, you can find her rambling through the forest with her husband and spirited Labrador retriever, camera in hand.

Kara is a member of Sisters in Crime and Sisters in Crime-New England.

AUTHOR WEBSITE:

https://karalaceyauthor.com

SOCIAL MEDIA HANDLES:

https://www.instagram.com/karalaceyauthor/
https://www.facebook.com/karalaceyauthor/
https://karalacey.substack.com/

Also by Kara Lacey

Caught on Camera: A Camera Club Mystery

www.ingramcontent.com/pod-product-compliance
Lightning Source LLC
Chambersburg PA
CBHW020751310726
48969CB00002B/481